CW00529961

Requiem for a Hard Man

Requiem for a Hard Man

Published by The Conrad Press in the United Kingdom 2021

Tel: +44(0)1227 472 874
www.theconradpress.com
info@theconradpress.com

ISBN 978-1-913567-67-5

Copyright © S.C. Bradbury, 2021

The moral right of S.C. Bradbury to be identified as author of this work has been asserted in accordance with the Copyright, Designs and Patents Act 1988.

All rights reserved.

Typesetting and Cover Design by: Charlotte Mouncey, www.bookstyle.co.uk using photography by Mark McNestry on Flickr, Michel Stockman and Viktor Keri on Unsplash.com under CC BY-SA 4.0
The Conrad Press logo was designed by Maria Priestley.

Printed and bound in Great Britain by Clays Ltd, Elcograf S.p.A.

Requiem for a Hard Man

S. C. Bradbury

'And the Angel shewed me a pure river of the water of life, clear as crystal, that flowed out of the throne of God and of the lamb.'

Book of Revelations

November 29, 1977

The lad's finished his story; and waits for a reaction.

The man studies him. He's struck by how young he looks; standing there with that gun, the weight of it pulling his arm like a scarecrow's without its stuffing. Ridiculous. Then he remembers how young *he* was the first time he touched a gun; let it loose on some doe-eyed boy - just like this one.

And he feels sorry for him, despite everything. Never seen him this raw, this broken. Matted hair falls over desperate eyes and through the greasy clump there is the flicker of tears. One even rolls down his cheek, catching the light from the bar... The lad confessed, bared his soul. Who is he not to forgive him?

A couple of steps and he's touching his shoulders. And he could grab the weapon, he knows he could, yank it from his grip and be out of here in seconds. Or turn the gun on the boy... and finish it.

But he can't do either. And he can't stop what's about to happen.

He cups his neck like a dad would. He knows it's what the lad needs. Then his thumbs creep to the front... and start to squeeze. Eyes widen, the disbelief, the hurt and then the rage. But the man presses harder, bending the lad's face as he gasps for air.

He hears the gun go off as if it's coming from somewhere else; echoing in the closed space, the reverb taking him back to when a gunshot was as common as a birdcall.

Then he feels it in his stomach - the burning pain, unfurling deep and hollow. Three more shots he's falling onto him and they're stumbling, collapsing against the bar. The boy pulls away and the man struggles to hold himself up, his eyes closing. He hears the gun thud to the floor. Then sobbing as the boy scrambles away, up the stairwell, his shoes scraping on the concrete steps.

The man blacks out – seconds maybe. He comes to and someone is by him as he withers. It's a familiar voice, an older feller.

'Get up. You can hack this, you bastard.'

'Where am I?' He glances up. He's on his back looking up at the ceiling - the cloistered ceiling of his basement club. His blood... he can feel it... spreading warm onto the dance floor...

So, this is it, it's happening. He's thought about it a million times. And no surprises here, no, it's just as bad as he imagined. He's seen it too many times not to know. He's heard the screams and the death rattles. He's rolled it over, looted and buried it. And here he is. *He* is now the dying man.

'You've got it sorted. You've got this, you.' The familiar voice again. 'I'll call someone.'

'Don't go.'

'You'll die if I don't.'

No medals for that one. The man on the floor tries to make out the blurred face above him. He knows him now, the owner of this voice. He hears him again.

'Look at the state of yous. What has happened here… what?'

'I've made a pig's ear… is what.'

The dying man coughs and tastes blood, senses it on his chin. Then some vomit. He feels a firm grip on his shaking hand. Then the voice again:

'Say a prayer, man. Do what you have to do.'

Ah, prayer…

'Do it.'

Even now, lying in this state, the man dithers. The day on that frozen German field, the riverbank with the weeping willow that drooped into the ice that held it fast, the decades since, and the three tormented days before now, do they all lead to this?

'We saved the world,' he finally says, '… from Hitler… didn't we?'

'Go away with you. Say your prayers, man. There's no priest here, so say them.'

'Saved the bloody world -'

'For God's sake, man.'

The dying man hears voices and wonders… are they here to save him? Or are they coming from the other side?

'Say your prayers.'

His throat is filling with blood. He doesn't have a lot of time.

'We did that…'

'Do it…'

9

'Saved it…'

'Say them…'

'From Hitler…'

ONE

November 25, 1977

I thought I'd give it five more rings just to be sure. Did that for a bit, thinking he'll pick up any minute. But he didn't. I put the phone down.

I looked outside. The sky was getting darker by the minute. About half an hour of light left, give or take. Hanging cloud. Below it a distant strip of white stressed the rooftops. The chimneys stuck up like sore fingers against this band of light; a last effort, a brave sod off before all was dark.

I had a nip of my Johnny Walker Red and the burn was nice. Lit a cig and inhaled.

The window was misting up, so I wiped it. It was a grim landscape, but it was mine. The row was missing a house or two and the row beyond that. These gaps were care of the Luftwaffe on a bugger of a night in 1940. Thirty-seven years ago the bombs had carved a nice, little path through the neighborhood. They'd finished in an area now a croft, across the way from my boozer, The John Bull.

I threw on my overcoat. I picked up the Luger 08 and unwrapped the hanky, catching the smell. Oil. It always took me back and my heart did a mad jig. I handled it for a minute, enjoying the weight. I dropped the clip and checked it. Full. I slid it back in. I took another drag.

I looked outside again. The scene was comforting, crippled as it was. The derelict buildings were familiar as toast. And there was pride there, no mistake. They were like the battered teeth of a worn out prizefighter. Something left of a time when England was at its best; when folk in them refused to roll over for Hitler or *any* of those Nazi bastards.

I finished the whisky, wrapped up the Luger and put it back in the drawer. It would do when the time was right, but not right now. I grabbed my Trilby and locked the door to my office. I went downstairs to the pub.

Some old fellers sat fixed on dominoes and younger scallies conspired in the corner. Danny Simms was organizing the night's festivities. Old Timer was behind the bar drying glasses. Soul music drifted out from the Wurlitzer jukebox, a fifties vintage bought from a yank back in the day. The music mingled with the band setting up on the small stage, the mic check, the drum bangs and the low chatter. What was playing now? 'What's Happening, Brother?' Marvin Gaye.

One of my son's favourites.

'Big night, guv,' said one of the kids.

'That's right,' I said.

'I feel funny coming tonight, guv, not having served like,

and it being the Legion an all.'

'Don't be mithered with that,' said Danny. 'It's to raise money. Come one, come all. Spend some dosh. It's for a good cause.'

'Right then, I'll do that.'

I knew he wouldn't. Lippy was a mouthy kid with red hair and a missing front tooth. He didn't think we needed an army anymore, since we had no empire; or what we'd got wasn't worth a two-penny squabble over. I had to admire his bottle but I gave him a thick ear over that one.

Danny saw me looking at the worn scrim at the back of the stage.

'Can't think of everything,' he said. He took a puff of his inhaler then sparked up an Ultra Light cig.

I looked at the Union Jack on the other wall. 'Forgot about that too?' I said, pointing to the tatty, smoke stained flag. Even from a distance it looked a disgrace. We approached it and I pointed to a Guinness stain on the lower right-hand corner, the remains of a wild piss-up months before. I could've thumped him and he knew it.

'I'm not making excuses,' he said. 'But you do know, guv, the minute we throw that in the wash it's done. It'll fall to bits.'

'It's older than the statue of Marlborough, that thing,' said Old Timer.

'Just like you, eh?' said Lippy.

'You're barred you cheeky, little get.' Old Timer went back to his pint pots, muttering to himself.

I went behind the bar. I helped myself to some peanuts and a mickey bottle, and stuffed them into my overcoat pocket.

'I'll see you at half past seven,' I said. 'I'm home for me tea,' I lied. I got some Senior Service and started to unpeel the packet.

Danny nodded. 'Righto, guv.' He sucked on his cig through sausage fingers then shouted to the pub. 'Right you lot, home to your wives. We've a do tonight in case you'd forgotten.'

Groans all round.

'How many charity events do you have for that bleeding Legion, anyway?' said Lippy.

'It's not a bleeding Legion to you,' Danny said. 'It's a *British* Legion for vets who've fought for their country. Not idle gits who sit around cribbing about the music selection.'

'When are we getting you on the dance floor, Danny, you big bugger?'

'When I look at you I think National Service. That's what's missing with this country, kiddo. National bloody Service.'

'I'm not arsed, me.'

'You'd be useless anyway. Get home to you tea, you lippy little get. Look sharp.' Danny called to the mic fella. 'How are we doing here?'

'You'll be able to hear her at least.'

'That sounds promising.'

'Testing, testing, one two.'

I was on my way out of the door.

✳

It was perishing cold so I walked sharpish to the car. The kids guarding it ran up, pushing and shoving and standing on my Oxfords. I could smell the street on them. I handed them some tanners and shoved them off. Then they were gone, tear-arsing to the newsagent for liquorice sherbets and cigarettes.

I got into my 1975 Ford Cortina. I turned the ignition and

the 8- track lurched into action spilling out Sarah Vaughn, 'My Tormented Heart.'

Looking to the croft opposite, the three-storied mill was suddenly there. It flashed brilliant like a light bulb in a darkened room. I was back to that night in December 1940, when it'd been blown to buggery, when me, Bill Shaw and Corey Blaine were on the roof watching the flares and incendiaries at Salford docks two miles away. I could, even now, taste the sickliness of the Players Navy Cut fags we'd nicked and the smell of cordite from the docks. Then the splatter of bombs, closer and closer, just time to dash to the second floor before… And pulled from the rubble a day later with nothing but cuts and a fear of closed spaces that plagued me to this day.

I wondered if my son had seen such things he might've been stronger.

I lit a Senior Service and strained my eyes. The land was now flat and empty but for old mattresses, sideboards and such. As usual the old tramp stood by the oil-drum fire, feeding the flames with one hand and rocking his pram with the other. The poor, old sod was a million miles from the tough air-raid warden of all those years ago.

I ejected the tape. The compilation of '50s and '60s artists had been a fiftieth birthday present from Neil. Right now I was in no mood. I pulled the car out and instead of heading to Broughton I started southwest towards Stretford. It was the long way round but I was in no hurry. I tried to kid myself he'd just forgotten the appointment with his mam and the counselor. He'd be sifting through rare soul records on Oldham Street or shooting pool in Rusholme. But really I knew.

The last sliver of light was disappearing over Trafford Park and it started to rain. On went the wipers. The passenger wiper was down to the metal and made a row, so I threw in another tape. More compilations. It was the lesser of two evils. As I drove round Moss Side I went through 'It's All in the Game', Tommy Edwards and 'Going Out of My Head', Little Anthony and the Imperials. I still wasn't in the mood. I turned off the 8-track but the squeak was worse. On went the tape again. Picking up speed on Barlow Moor Road, The Royalettes hit me with 'It's Gonna Take a Miracle.'

It was a relief to pull up to the Victorian mansion, now a cluster of flats. Miserably dark, the only light came from the upstairs units. Neil's ground floor was pitch black. I got out and went to the gate, broken, hanging off its hinges. The lawn was littered with rubbish, and the coloured glass effort surrounding the doorway was missing more squares. I put the first key in and the door opened, turning on the hall light. There were two doors, one to Neil's flat, one for someone else. A staircase led up to the other units. I fumbled for the second key and went to the door.

I put the key in. I stayed still for a minute. I was there again. The suffocation of that night in the mill, trapped upside down unable to move, Corey screaming and Bill laughing as if we'd fallen off a bloody playground roundabout. So, I shook it off then opened it, the door – to Neil's flat.

The light from the hall spilled in. The musty carpet smell was never so welcome. No sour, putrid reek - thank Christ. I turned on the light and called the lad's name. Nothing. I went through the living room and kitchen doing likewise. Then I rounded the corner into the bedroom. I stopped when I saw a light peeping through the crack of the door to the bathroom.

That's where we found him the last time.

I walked to the door and flung it open. He wasn't there. I sat on the bath and lit up. For a minute I questioned getting all aeriated. Missing an appointment was hardly the end of the world. But looking around I knew. The place looked like a bomb had hit it; overflowing rubbish bins, a ruin of unwashed pots, laundry where it fell. I'd seen this before, the telltale signs, self-neglect and the rest of it. But I needed to be sure. So I got up and started looking for evidence.

Fifteen minutes later I sat on the bed and there it was, right under my nose. On the side table was a syringe, tin foil and spoon. I wrapped the paraphernalia in a handkerchief, stuffed it in my pocket. I wandered into the living room. I found myself on the settee staring at the coffee table, stained with tea and coffee rings. I picked up the phone and called the pub. Danny answered.

'It's me,' I said. 'I'm at Neil's. He's gone AWOL again.'

'What? When did you -?'

'It doesn't matter. Listen, make a few phone calls, see what's what.'

'I'll get some fellers together. They can get out and have a proper mooch. You're not at home, then?'

'I'm at his flat.'

'I don't get it. '

'Brenda called earlier.'

Pause. 'Why didn't you say?'

'Wanted to be sure.'

'I'm sorry, guv. Don't worry we'll find him.'

'I'll be in around eight.'

'You sure?'

'Don't be daft. I'm not having him mess tonight up. Talk later.'

I put the phone down. They all knew the drill, all the haunts where Neil could be. They'd cover the North End of Manchester, Pendleton, Crumpsall, Ancoats. For the south I'd talk to Mary Brown. Then I called Brenda.

'It's me, I'm at the flat. He's not here.'

'Is there -?'

'No, I haven't found any of that.' I felt the drug paraphernalia in my pocket. 'I've got folk out looking. We'll find him.' Silence. 'You still there?'

'Are you coming home for tea?'

'I can't, love. I'll keep looking then I'm at the pub. I can't miss the Legion do. Besides, there's not much else we can do at this point. He'll show up somewhere when he wants to… Look… I'm sorry I lost me rag. Alright?' I heard nothing. 'Brenda.'

'Just find him.' She hung up.

I was still mad at her. She'd waited until four o' clock to tell me he was a no-show. He was supposed to have dinner with her then go to the counselor for an appointment at two; but I knew my wife. She'd have told herself he was on a Blackpool piss-up, or got waylaid at a record bar in Stoke-on-Trent. So, she'd spent the day baking like a mad woman, making pies of every kind and knocking back Harvey's Bristol Cream. Then full of Dutch courage she'd finally called Amanda, Neil's old girlfriend, and she said he was using again. Then *I* got the phone call.

I picked up the phone and called Mary Brown. No answer. Strange. I knew she had to be home at this time. I called again. Nothing.

I sat there smoking in that cold, empty flat thinking of him. I inhaled aggressively to calm down. It didn't work, so I looked at the mantelpiece where there was a framed photograph of me, Brenda and Neil as a baby. In the middle was a picture of me as a corporal just before being demobilized in '47. Above that hung a display case with my service medals, The Germany Star, The Defense Medal, War Medal and the General Service Medal.

I remember him being mad about the war, and the questions had come fast and furious. But what can you tell folk in all honesty, what can you, let alone your own kid? So, I'd dodged and weaved until he stopped asking, or when teenage interests got him; when the music and dancing had stolen him away to crumbling dance halls and musty basement clubs. But even then he'd come back at me. So, I found common ground, 'cause it was the black US servicemen that started the scene here. It was their music that I played in my coffee house on Oxford Road in the fifties and later in the clubs. So, I'd regaled him with adventure stories of Manchester after the war; the gambling, strip joints, the cabarets and jazz clubs; the Mecca of the North, as it was known. And he'd been mesmerized and mollified. Somewhat.

I looked above my service medals where there was a nicer display case. It held my Military Medal. There was a picture of George VI on the silver medallion with the red, white and blue ribbon and a single bar. Below that on the mount was inscribed, 'For Bravery in the Field.'

✴

I was at the other door. I'd talked to the tenants upstairs, asked if they'd seen him. None even knew him. I now knocked on this last door, a drab looking effort across the way from his. I heard the faint thump of a Northern Soul song behind it. I knocked again. I heard movement on the other side and knew they were at the peephole. Thinking I was a Peeler.

'Listen,' I said. 'I'm just looking for Neil Dunne. I'm his dad... You hear me?'

The door crept open still on the chain, and a skinny lad peered through the gap. Music spilled out. His mouth chewed ten to the dozen and I could smell Juicy Fruit gum. A speed freak, already ripped and it wasn't six yet.

'You Mr. Dunne, Jackie Dunne?' he said.

'That's me,' I said. 'And you?'

'I saw him.'

'When?'

'Last night outside your club.'

'Was he with anyone?'

The kid's eyes shifted.

'Was he with Mac Collier. Macker?'

More shifting.

'Look, just tell me. I'm his dad. No one's going to say owt.'

'Yeah. They were having a natter down the side, like.'

'Did they go inside?'

'No, just stayed in the alley.'

'What time was this?'

'About half past nine.'

Pause. 'Right. Thanks.' I started to go.

'Can I get in free next time, Mr. Dunne?'

'Not if you're taking that shit.'

'What do you mean?'

'You know what I mean.'

20

'At least it's not smack!' He snapped his door to.

Neil being seen was something, but it was no comfort; particularly knowing Macker was with him. I sat in the car fuming about this bastard who was once part of my crew. The time I'd put into him didn't bear thinking about, and how did he pay me back? By dealing smack to Neil right under my nose. And the hiding we gave him would've sent any other scally running for the hills, but not this one. He'd not only stayed, but challenged me at every turn. Then he went to Bill Shaw cap in hand. And Bill, the idiot, had taken him on.

✳

The rain had stopped but it was dark, blustery, visibility bad. I drove slowly, leaving the happy hedgerows of Didsbury. I was soon pulling into the car park of The John Nash Crescent, the miserable concrete of Hulme.

A half-inflated ball flopped in front of me. I pulled up sharp when two kids entered my beam. I honked the horn and one of them gave me two fingers. The other kid nudged him and the offender, when realizing who I was, legged it like an animal, elbows kicking wildly out. I parked the Cortina and got out. Leaning against a burned-out car, smoking a joint, were two Jamaican fellers.

'We'll look after it, man. No charge for you, Jackie.'

I pointed to the ruined vehicle. 'That doesn't inspire confidence.'

'CID,' one of them said, grinning.

I indulged them with a smile, locked the doors, and gave them a couple of quid anyway. I headed for the alley that led to the courtyard.

I battled the usual gust of wind as I entered the crescent. The silhouette of the massive structure was soon all round me. It arced and loomed like a giant's dentures. Many folk were now home, and the dotted-lights became gold fillings on a miserable grin. I heard the growl of a feral dog as I climbed the stairwell to the deck access and Mary Brown's flat.

I wasn't feeling well disposed to Mary right now. She'd been on at the club last night and would've heard about Macker and Neil. The woman missed nothing, but she'd said sod all to me. If she'd told me I could've been on it. Immediately. As it was I'd lost valuable time.

I fucked and blinded as I nearly tripped. The lights on the walls were blown or smashed, and the alcoves cast shadows at every turn. I kept my hand off the handrails. They were caked in dog dirt for the Peelers. Nice.

I was getting rattier and rattier as I climbed. I tried to remind myself how long I'd known the woman; at least since '56 when she stepped off the boat from Jamaica. I had a coffee lounge on Oxford Road, and the black yanks from the base in Warrington spent a lot of dosh there. So I gave her a job, thinking they'd feel at home being served by someone like them. It worked and she met her husband there in '57, a yank scally from Detroit. They had market stalls, loan-sharked the black clubs, divvied all the smoke in town, and rented out villas in Spain. In short, they were quid's in and I got a piece of it all. I recalled this, but as I huffed and puffed up the dark steps I was still fuming.

I reached the third level panting like a miner with black lung. I walked along the deck, reached a door and rang the buzzer three times. I was now well irked from schlepping all the way here. The long time before Mary answered didn't help. She was thrown by seeing me, I could tell. I walked by her talking.

'Doesn't anyone answer their phones in this town?'

'Am I going to like this?'

I went to the kitchen-dining area. A demi-john was upside down in the sink. The smell of jerk chicken battled with the whiff of cannabis. Theodore lay on the front room couch with eyes closed and earphones on. Sam Cooke was probably on the turntable. I paced and turned to Mary.

'I've been calling you. What's going on?'

'Some of us do have lives, you know.'

The years had whittled away her Jamaican sound. She now had a Salford clip and the irony to go with it.

'What is it?' she said, going to the demi-john. 'It must be big to bring you down here.'

She knew too bloody well. That's why she hadn't answered the phone; that was my theory anyway.

I hadn't seen her in a few months and she'd lost weight. I put it down to her son Jez doing time in Strangeways. Other than that nothing had altered. The apron was still strung round the flowered dress, the Afro had grown a bit, and her stocking-less feet were still stuffed into worn slippers. Apart from the gold tooth, she still looked like someone's auntie.

'What do you think it is?' It was my shorthand reply for trouble with Neil.

She turned to Theo on the settee. She whistled and his eyes popped open. He fumbled like a zombie hauling itself from the grave. Then he caught his foot in the headphone wire and nearly pulled the turntable off the side.

'If I got penny every time he did that I'd be a rich woman.'

'Hey man, what's up brother?'

There it was, a Detroit twang split with thirty years of Salford.

'I need a crew. Our Neil's gone AWOL again.'

'Are you sure?' he said, scratching the back of his neck.

I figured Mary hadn't told him anything. He was a lousy liar and the less he knew the better was her tack with him. I pulled out the handkerchief, splaying it in my hand. The needle glinted under the light above the table.

'I've just been to the flat.'

Mary ignored a look from her husband. I clocked it though.

'Jesus tonight, man,' she said, grabbing a paper towel and giving it me. 'Wrap that up before you get a disease.'

I did as I was told. She had that effect.

'I'm sorry, pal,' said Theo.

'I thought he was doing alright,' Mary said, getting out her cigs. 'Wasn't he doing something with Brenda? Meetings or some 'at?'

'Well, it means nowt now, does it?'

It put years on me to keep a civil tone. Mary clocked my mood. She offered me a Woodbine. I took it and lit us up.

'I'll put Adolphus on it,' Theo said. 'They'll find him in a couple of hours if he's anywhere in South Manchester. You've got Danny doing the north?'

I nodded. 'And all this on top of a Legion do.'

'How's Brenda bearing up?' Mary said.

'Better than me.'

'I guess you want me at the club again.'

'If you could.'

'I'll keep an eye out. But we'll need someone on the door. It'll be busy tonight.' She picked up the demi-john, wanting

24

to wrap up our confab.

'I'll send Danny over later on,' I said.

'Can't you spare anyone else? He's neither use nor ornament. Spends half his time chatting up skirt, that one.'

She walked into the living room. I followed her; getting aeriated she was fobbing me off. Theo was behind me.

'I was told Neil was outside the club last night,' I said. That brought everything to a halt.

She turned. 'That's the first I've heard and that's gospel that is.' She walked to a curtain, pulled it back, and walked through the jackhammered hole leading to the next-door flat, their shebeen. We followed. It was a familiar room kitted out with a bar, jukebox, wicker couches, comfy chairs and side tables with tasseled lampshades. The walls had tropical-scene wallpaper. Mary crouched by a huge still. I sat in a comfy chair while Theo hovered.

'Who told you anyway?' she said, keeping with her task.

'Some kid I grilled… said he was with Macker.'

She turned. 'It won't be Macker flogging to him, love, I'll tell you that for nowt.'

'Then who?'

'I have no idea, but *no one* who knows Neil and you is daft enough to sell smack to him.' She spelled it out like I was four years old.

'I agree, man,' said Theo. 'It has to be a nobody; some dumb-ass, just starting out.'

I could sense Theo covering for Mary because he'd clocked she was lying. I understood why she didn't want agro between Macker and me. The kid was now with Bill Shaw. If I went to town on him she'd be implicated, after all she's with me. Her

25

kid was still locked up and she couldn't risk anyone getting to him. So, I understood her dilemma but it didn't help me with mine.

'Get him a drink, love. He'll be needing it,' said Mary.

Theo grabbed some of their sugar-cane homemade brandy. He handed it to me.

'Chateau Mucho Collapso... Well, what do you think?'

'I could run me car on it.'

'When did you get so fussy?' said Mary, without turning.

A few seconds slumped by. Theo filled me up again.

'Well, let's keep the Cadillac going,' he said, being Theo.

I was getting cheesed off, so I said. 'You'd tell me, wouldn't you, Mary... if you thought it was Macker.'

She turned to me. 'Why are you giving me this attitude, you?'

'Now, now,' said Theo.

'Shut up. Who's grafting down there in that club when Neil's not up to it? Eh? Mistress Muggins here.'

'Mary -' said Theo.

'Zip it. Bloody walking in here getting all Bolshie. I don't have eyes in the back of me head, man.'

She did. But I said nothing. I drank. I watched Mary place the demi-john under the condenser nozzle. She turned it on and liquid emptied into the vessel. It swished and made a gurgling sound.

I had to go. Mary was well put out by my visit and the hint of her negligence hadn't helped. So she was narked and I was narked – for different reasons. And Theo, bless him, had to juggle the atmosphere with forced pleasantries, all of which were just winding me up. But I just sat there. I felt like I was melting into the chair.

'I have to get back to 'The Bull,' it's all bloody go,' I said, struggling up. I turned to Theo. 'Are you coming to the Legion do?'

'I can't if she's at the club. We'll be busy here.'

I asked how their Jez was doing and Theo told me. He was coming up for parole. I made sure Mary heard my concerns about her son; not that I wasn't invested, we all went back years. I headed back through the flat, Theo following. I handed him some notes.

'We'll find him,' Theo said, taking the money.

I heard Mary turn off the valve. Then a clang, as it sent a jolt through the still.

✳

I headed back to the car. I knew they'd be talking about me; about it all, Neil, the ructions it was causing, the bloody lot. I sat for a few seconds, the wind whistling through a small gap in the window. I wound it up. I took a bit of whisky.

I'd accomplished a few things at least. Theo was on with finding Neil. I knew he'd have Adolphus rooting through every rat's nest in South Manchester. I'd got Mary on for tonight at the club. And I was almost sure it was Macker who was flogging to Neil. I'd known Mary too long not to know when she was fibbing.

Coming out of the crescents I stopped the Cortina and called Brenda. If Neil were to call anyone it would be her. If only to let her know he was alive.

'Any news?' I said.

'No. Where are you?'

'About. I've got folk looking.'

'Eat something, you'll be boozing tonight.'

'I might be late… if he's not found by midnight. I won't sleep if I don't know he's even…'

There was a silence on the other end, but she was thinking. I could hear her thinking. Then:

'I've long known… that I might lose that boy; it's the only way I can keep vertical. It's you I now worry about, Jackie…'

I said nothing. More thinking on the other end.

'Father O' Connell's coming over,' she said. 'I just want you to know, so I'm telling you and that's that.'

'You do what you need to do, Brenda.'

'I need this, Jackie.'

'I said fine, didn't I? I'll be doing something concrete.'

She sighed. 'Corey Blaine called again. What's going on with him…?'

I said nothing.

'Jackie?'

'He's home for his mam. She's got cancer.'

'I'm sorry to hear that, but this is the fourth time he's called.'

'I'll deal with it.'

'Cos this is getting daft, this.'

'I said I'd sort it!' I breathed. 'I'll deal with Corey Blaine. I'd better get going, I'll see you later.'

I hung up and went back to the car.

I remembered the day she started praying again. It was after Neil's first hospital do. Two years ago now. A barbiturate overdose that first time, long before the smack. O' Connell had suddenly showed up on the ward. I'd ignored him and left. I hadn't been to confession since September of '44 just before being carted off to Belgium, so I wasn't going back now. He could whistle. As for Corey, my old army mate, he was another born-again Catholic I couldn't be doing with. And it wouldn't do an ounce of good to tell Brenda why he was really pestering me.

✳

I drove in silence. The wind had picked up and wild gusts blew across the Mancunian Way, hauling clouds of dead leaves with them. I came off the parkway and went through the lights under the Piccadilly railway bridge and curved round onto Great Ancoats Street. I took a right on Old Mill Street. I went by the warehouse I owned that held Neil's record inventory; thousands of records we'd shipped from Detroit when we were both there, not six months since. They were supposed to be in a record shop I'd planned for him on Tib Street. But they weren't.

As I got deeper into Ancoats, memories of Bill's and mine adventures swept over me like a tidal wave. We'd been drunk for two years straight after Germany, brawling all over town for no good reason than to feel something - to feel alive. Corey had hid at his mother's drinking alone, while Bill and me were the toast of the town. The three of us had hauled one another through nine months of bitter fighting in Europe. We'd been through a lot. Now we were all at odds. It was bloody heartbreaking.

I pulled into the curb opposite The Shamrock. Bill's Mercedes looked well out of place on the run-down street. Macker's red Capri was nowhere in sight. I took a bit of the whisky. I didn't have time to wait, so I got out of the car, walked to the pub and went inside. I had a few seconds to take the place in before all eyes clocked me.

Smoke hung in a line across the room. It smelled of men, smoke and feet. The carpet was shiny near the bar, and there was the sickly-sweet reek of stale beer. It was easy to see why Bill had brought in Macker and the trade that came with him. If appearances were anything to go by, he was struggling. Or he was spending his gelt elsewhere.

The jukebox in the corner was like mine, bought from me in happier days. 'Love and Happiness' by Al Green was playing. Standing just inside the door I was noticed. I went to the bar.

'A large whisky when you're ready.'

Wally, the barman, was all a dither. He looked to the boozer for advice. I followed his gaze locking eyes with as many as I could. I recognized Bill's two main lads, Ray and Didds, two fellas in their late thirties I'd known for years. They began to put out their cigs in the ashtrays, never a good sign.

I leaned against the bar and scanned the room again. The Irish tricolour was draped in the corner. It always got me when folk who came over with the potato famine, like Bill's people, still beat the Republican drum. England had done all right for him, but apparently nostalgia for Ireland was more important. I got back to Wally and noticed he hadn't made a move.

'Is some 'at wrong?' I asked.

No reply. Al was still crooning away. I was about to pull Wally across the bar when I heard a voice by the door.

'Put it on me tab, Wally, I'll have the same.'

I turned and there was Macker all grins and glitter. He sauntered in. He leaned on the bar.

'What are you doing here, Jackie?'

I stepped in. 'I don't suppose you've seen our Neil in the last while?'

'I haven't seen him one bit, mate,' he said, his face a picture of innocence. 'You laid the law down, that's good enough for me.' He pulled out his cigs. 'Why is he in trouble? Drugs again, is it?'

'You tell me.'

'I am telling you. I respect all of your demands. I don't want to cause ructions, do I? I'd be daft to.'

He inhaled and puffed out a couple of smoke rings. For a second I saw the Lower Broughton street kid who'd swept my offices, kept the yards clean, fed the guard dogs; the young teenager I'd encouraged to go straight.

'What is the matter with you, Macker?' I said. 'You could've kept working with me, made a decent screw but no, you choose to work for Bill Shaw... two stinking, bloody drug dealers together.'

There was a shuffle from the population. Ray and Didds got up from their seats. The drinks arrived. Macker knocked his back, wiped his mouth and said:

'We've all got to make a few bob, haven't we? It's all right for you lot, the old guard; you've got it all sorted. What about scallies like me, just starting out? What's left for us?'

'And what's Bill Shaw's excuse?'

Ray and Didds started a slow prowl in our direction. Macker sensed it and barely lifted a hand to stop it. I clocked it, the lad's authority. This kid was unusual; there was no denying it. I let him go on.

'We don't like smack any more than you do, but that's the future, isn't it. Bill Shaw is the best thing that ever happened to me. It's a pity you two don't get on anymore. He is an old mate, after all.'

'We grew up in Cheetham Hill together. End of.'

'You went through the war though, didn't you. That must count for some 'at.'

I saw mischief in the lad's eye. I was positive Bill wouldn't share our war secrets with civvies. But then again, I was sure he'd never sell hard drugs.

'What would you know about that?' I said.

'Just that. Nowt else,' the boy piped. 'I'm not mithered, it's none of my business. It's just a bit tragic you can't be mates, that's all.'

'Well, when he stops peddling smack in this city maybe then we can chat about old times. Now where is my son?'

'We'll find that lad of yours before tea time.'

I turned and there was, Liam Shaw, standing at the bottom of the stairs. I hadn't seen him in a while and he'd aged. He was still dying his hair but his sideboards were going grey. He wore a paisley shirt that struggled with his belly. The snakeskin belt looked like it was about to snap and launch - wiggling about the room. His arms were still big, giving the shirt a run for its money, and his bulging flares tapered down to Cuban-heel boots. If this was a man marrying twenty years his junior, you could keep it.

He still wore the Death's Head ring on his pinky. He'd never removed it since lifting it from the dead Waffen SS soldier thirty-two years ago. His finger had grown round it like a tree bulging around a fence. All in all, though, he was still Bill.

'Simmer down fellers,' said Bill. 'We all know Jackie and me go way back. We have a dust up now and then, that's all. Don't we, mate?'

I turned to the pub, pulled out a roll and held it up. 'I'm

offering two hundred quid to anyone who can tell me the whereabouts of Neil Dunne.'

I knew this offer was like taking a slash right in the middle of Bill's carpet. I wanted chaos, brawling, anything was better than this.

'We'll put the call out and do it for nowt,' Bill said. 'Wally, a bottle upstairs.'

He mounted a couple of steps and turned. Then with a familiarity that took the clock back thirty years, he said:

'Are we finding that lad of yours or not?' He looked to Ray and Didds. 'You two, upstairs. Macker stay put.'

The kid was put out. This was promising. I could have another go at Bill. Time with him was scarce nowadays. Threats on the phone were all that passed between us. Maybe the ructions the drug had started had given him pause. We would see.

✳

Bill's office was as I remembered it. The desk and swivel chair occupied most of the room. A set of weights lived against one wall keeping company with a filing cabinet, and a ratty mirror hung lonesome like. The SS dagger was still stuck into his desk like a mad Excalibur, and he had his Walther 38 out in pieces on the desk. Next to the gun bits were oil, a rag and a pistol barrel cleaner. I noticed a framed picture of June, Bill's young wife, smashed and on the floor.

'What can I say,' he said. 'She's driving me mad.'

Wally appeared with a bottle of Jameson's, plunked it on Bill's desk and left. Bill sat and brought out a couple of glasses. Ray and Didds hovered in the doorway like the henchmen of

Al Capone. Funny, it was. I stayed standing.

It was impossible to ignore the wall piece. There it was, as it always had been. Mounted and framed, was a collection of German medals and stuff, all looted thirty-two years ago. Iron Cross First Class, a Wound Badge in Silver, a Close Combat Clasp in Gold, soldier identity tags, and two German soldier's pay books were all behind glass on the wall. The one pay book belonged to the Waffen SS soldier who'd earned the medals. The other one was a Luftwaffe cadet's, given to Bill by Corey Blaine.

Bill poured. 'A reminder, mate; of what a hard bastard really is. 'Those krauts were soldiers. We'll never see an army like that again, and I say it to anyone who asks, 'cause the kids in this town don't have a clue. If I had blokes around me like that, I'd be invincible. By the way, has Corey Blaine been calling you?'

'No.'

'He's been calling me.' He turned to the case and pointed at the cadet's pay book. 'He wants that back, can you believe. I told him straight no bloody way, man. But he won't give up. Making my life purgatory.' He lit a Park Drive. 'Fancy wanting it back after all these years. The man's not right in the head… short a few bob, that one.' He smoked. 'No, but the Fritz's… what soldiers.'

I remembered Macker's insinuation downstairs. 'And what do you tell them, if folk ask?'

'Don't worry everyone gets the flannel, the history book flannel. I'm well away on that.' He inhaled. 'Mind you, I've told these lads what a field day it was for us scallies. A thug's paradise it was, that war. After the fighting, mind. I mean, when and where else could you shag a man's wife *and* his daughter, nick all the silver, send it home to your mam *and* shoot the bugger if he creates. God bless Unconditional Surrender.' He turned to Ray and Didds who grinned and snorted in the doorway. 'But honestly, the Fritz's… they hardly had a fecking army left. Nowt but scratch units… Luftwaffe, Wehrmacht and Waffen SS. Fought their bleeding hearts out, they did. Made us look a right shower of cunts most of the time. Wiped the bloody floor with us.' Smoke funneled down through his nostrils. 'But this cunt, here,' he pushed the drink towards me, 'Military Medal, this cunt. Took out a bleeding machine gun nest. Saved the whole platoon. He'd have gotten the bleeding VC is he was owt but a private.' Bill sipped from his glass. 'All they did was lift him to corporal. Twats.'

'We always knew you were hard, Jackie,' Ray chirped.

'Aye,' Bill went on. 'Ambushed by an MG42 we were. Thought we was dead. There was me and Corey with the Bren gun - Jackie with the bleeding tripod way over there. Not that we could get a shot in.'

I started to blush. Too much had been said in front of the civvies already. Bill made it worse by telling the story of what happened, eyeing me all the way through. Then he raised his glass.

'Anyway. To brave buggers everywhere.'

'Here, here,' said Ray and Didds.

I was tempted not to drink. I knew Bill was laying it on to soften me, but I didn't want to blow the meeting. So, I necked it and put the glass on the desk, upside down. We were here to talk proper, no pleasantries. The move was well noted by Bill.

'I hope you have all your tin on display, Jackie, and not stuffed away in some bloody shoebox somewhere in the loft.

Folk need to know the sacrifices, mate. We all made sacrifices. So, where is the thing? The Military Medal?'

'Neil's got it on his wall in his flat,' I said, lighting up. I only mentioned this to bring the conversation back to Neil.

'What a good lad, that's good that is….' He flicked his ash.

'Macker isn't selling to him. He knows I'd cut his balls off.'

'Somebody is.'

He sighed. 'I am bending over backwards for you and your boy. Keeping my lads out of your gaffs, what the fuck else do you want from me?'

'You know what I want.'

Bill shook his head and poured another drink for himself.

'You could stop this right now,' I said, leaning forward on the desk. 'You know you could. All the riff-raff and dead-legs, they look to blokes like us. And you wouldn't be on your own, you wouldn't. There's dozens in this town, proper blokes, what feel as I do. You stop it, it dries up - like that.' I snapped my fingers.

'What am I, a bleeding charity? And by the way, they'll all be at it when they see the gelt that can be made.'

Bill puffed on his Park Drive. I watched the blue smoke billow from his mouth. He looked like he was thirteen again.

'My God, your mother,' I said. 'She's rolling in her grave right now. Three overdoses in the last two months and one dead. I hope you're fucking proud of yourself.'

He cocked his head to one side. 'Look at you, waltzing in here like this. You're not right in the head you, man.'

'*I'm* not right in the head?'

'Nobbling every geezer in town you think might be dealing. My wife's a pisshead, but I'm not going round to all the pubs in Salford telling them they can't serve rum and black. They'd have me shot, and well they should. No, I get her to a clinic, the best in Cheshire, and keep her home of a night.' He pulled out a card from his desk drawer and put it on the table in front of me. 'Altrincham Detox Centre. Give them a call. Please.'

I came off the desk. 'You think you're untouchable, do you?'

'Neil's a drug addict, folk sympathize, everyone respects that; and believe you me, it's the only reason some bugger's not had a go at you.'

'You called it off, did you?'

'I wouldn't tell you if I did, you might think I like you.'

I looked at his grinning face and wanted to dent it, drag him across the table and pummel it. Instead I said:

'Do you know the sentences for dealing smack?' I leaned in again. 'A London villain just got fourteen years. Are you willing to risk that?'

'I hope that's not a threat.'

'Take it as you want. But with kids popping their clogs left, right and centre, how long do you think the council, the plod, or anyone half decent will tolerate this shit?'

He sniffed. 'By the time the Peelers wise up it'll be tall, fat drinks and beach crumpet for me.' He grinned like a Cheshire cat. 'You know the drill.'

'Fourteen years, Billy Shaw. You're not getting any younger.' I put my cig out in his ashtray.

He looked at me, breathed out and pushed his chair back. 'All right fellas, escort Jackie Dunne off the premises. He's just been barred.'

I felt the heavies moving in. I looked at the SS dagger sticking up from the desk. Bill saw this and reached out, flicking up the clinic card on the desk, holding it high.

'Here, a private clinic. Get that lad sorted once and for all. None of us need this bollocks.'

He stood up, leaned over the desk, stuffed the card into my jacket pocket. I straightened up, trying not to lose my rag. Pollute a kid's body then offer to clean it up. The man had no rhyme or reason. It was time to go.

'And you be careful, Dunne,' he said, pointing at me. 'Time in jail is better than no time at all.'

A threat, a bloody threat as well. My mind was whirling.

'Let's go, soldier.' Ray grabbed my collar. Didds was on the other side and gripped my bicep, ushering me forward. The manhandling, the disrespect and the threats, it got to me and I suddenly pulled up. They both froze and came in close, tightening their grip expecting me to have a go. I thought better of it. I'd lost the advantage anyway. Ten years ago I could've flattened the pair of them. They'd have been on the deck puking in seconds. But then what? They'd have gotten the better of me in the end, then as well as now, then it would be the back room for me. I put my forearms up and they relaxed.

'Steady, man, steady,' Bill said. 'We're not kids any more, Jackie. Know your limits, man, know your limits.' He looked to Ray. 'Give him some slack, lads.'

They let me go at the top of the stairs, a useless, silly mark of respect. As I walked down all eyes of the boozer were on me. They started chanting the Manchester United song:

'U-N-I-T-E-D United are the team for me
With a knick-knack, paddy-wack, give a dog a bone,
Why don't City fuck off home.'

I ignored them as I walked by and it got louder. It followed me out into the street and I could still hear it as I got to the Cortina. I was about to unlock the door when I heard a voice behind me.

'We don't want you to come to any harm, Jackie. But your Neil… he's turning us all into enemies… you know…'

I turned and stared him down. Then Macker faltered, turned and slunk back inside. I got in the car. I put in the keys and sat for a moment. I took a blast from the mickey. I started her up and pulled away.

✳

I was soon in the warehouse alleyways that made Gaythorn. I made my way down the side street to the club, my dance venue, the present I'd given to Neil for his twentieth. Even at nine o' clock there was a line up. The kids were huddled, shifting slowly through the large, oak door. Smoke peeled up from the queue and sailed away. Feet stomped in the cold. I drove by slowly and could hear the music; dance soul curling out and echoing round the street.

Mary would be down there in her club clobber; khaki's and Docs, earplugs in and sitting at the bar reading The Evening News.

I continued on round the corner to the back alley behind the club. I stopped the car and got out. Looking down on the shiny damp cobbles, I squinted. As my eyes adjusted to the dark I saw the fag ends, beer cans, and the odd needle from the previous night. There was an empty baggy and some tin foil. They had been here, Neil and *someone*. I grabbed a Tesco bag from an overflowing rubbish skip. I wrapped the paraphernalia in my handkerchief, threw it in the bag and stuffed it into my overcoat pocket.

I lit up and waited, looking up and down the alley. I could see the faint lights flashing through the blacked-out basement windows, and there was the thump of the bass and drum; the rock beat of the rhythm guitar and then the horns, the jazz cords. What was it? 'Seven Days Too Long' Chuck Wood. Jesus; I knew more than most of the kids.

I got it. I got it all. Everything he was mad about with this Northern Soul stuff, I understood. He'd got his love of music through me, after all. I'd always had the vinyl going. It was a constant in the house and he heard it all, forties jive to fifties croon.

I listened to the music for a bit. I thought of the sprung dance floor he'd pestered me for. How we'd schlepped all the way to some spot in Oldham that was for the wrecking ball. How we'd humped the horsehair floor back in pieces, reassembled it after jackhammering a foot down into the concrete to make the wood true to the floor. Such efforts we made for him. Then there was the Detroit trip to buy the thousands of records, him and me. It all had such promise.

I thought of him out there somewhere in the city. If he hadn't had a hit in a while he'd be hunched up in pain, sodden, clammy. Or be unconscious in what he thought was bliss. Or worse.

✳

Ten minutes later I was at the canal basin in Castlefield. I'd parked the car on Deansgate. Under the viaduct, surrounded by old supermarket trollies and burned-out cars, I made my way. Shafts of light shone down from the street lamps above, cutting through the dark.

I wandered for five minutes, finding nothing but empty beer cans that scrunched under me as I walked. The air was rank with rotting rubbish, stale alcohol and old, damp masonry. Eventually, I saw a figure lurking by a mossy wall. I went up to him.

'Have you got any gear, mate?' I said.

'Are you a copper?'

'Like I'd tell you if I was, you berk. Do you have any?'

Pause. 'I got barbs and chalkies.'

'No, no. Smack - I need smack.'

'Him over there.'

I turned, following his nod. There was a small figure leaning against a railing. Next to him the canal was treacle black. I went up to him.

'You got any smack, mate?' I said.

'Piss off. I'm waiting for a friend'.

'I'm not a Peeler. Give me some smack while you're waiting.'

'Are you fucking simple?'

'Is that a yes?'

'I'll carve you, you cunt, if you don't leave me be.'

'I guess that's a no.'

He started to go. I grabbed him and he swung around with a blade. I blocked, twisted his arm and hit his elbow, snapping it like a cream cracker. He squealed, a boiled child falling to his knees, and the Stanly knife scattering off onto the cobbles. I went through his pockets and pulled out some baggies. I kicked them into the canal and he cursed blue bloody murder. I grabbed the scruff of his neck and yanked him up where he wiggled like a puppet, clutching his arm and crying bitterly with the pain.

'Is this Bill Shaw's game? Macker?' I slapped him. 'Shall I keep going? Is this Mac Collier?'

'Yeah, Macker. Don't – don't. Me arm, me fucking arm.'

'Have you seen Neil Dunne down here?'

'What? Who?'

Slap. Shake.

'Kinell, don't.' Cry, cry. 'I won't flog to him. He's Jackie Dunne's kid.' Sob, sob. 'No one flogs to him - too dangerous.'

I turned his head to the light to get a proper gander for future reference. He saw me as well.

'Oh, 'kinell... Jackie Dunne -? Please, please.'

I slapped again and shook him. 'I catch you again flogging this shit to *anyone* – it will be the last thing you do. You understand?'

'Yeah, please!'

I dragged him to the steps leading to the viaduct and hauled him up. He wept and screamed all the way. I got to the top still holding him.

'So, you've not seen Neil Dunne tonight? Don't lie.'

'I haven't... that's God's honest, that is!'

I looked into his eyes and figured he wasn't joshing me.

'Flag a taxi from here,' I said. 'Get to the infirmary - you'll need that plastering.'

I threw him away and he slunk off whimpering into the night.

I went back to the top of the steps and looked out. I could see the train bridge further off. Light from the street cast shadows, bending the arches of the railway line into fairy-tale sizes.

I came here as a lad, I remembered. Bill and me would nick cars, joy ride them, then launch them burning over the top. It was like a gift, a sacrifice to the giants I imagined living there. So, we'd feed the man-eating monsters living in the cave that held the ogre, the two-headed creature that might rip us to bits. But would be merciful - if we fed them a Ford.

A couple of tramps huddled round a flickering fire in the gloom of an arch. I shouted.

'I'll give a hundred quid to anyone who can tell me where Neil Dunne is.'

My voice echoed through the hollowed-out brickwork. I immediately felt like a desperate idiot.

'Shut your bleeding gob. Folk are trying to sleep here.'

Silence. I lit up and walked back to the car leaving the two lost souls to their fire.

Bill wasn't lying when he said Macker wasn't flogging to Neil, I could tell. It made sense that he wouldn't tolerate it. We went too far back. And he knew Neil as a kid when we were all closer. So, I figured Macker was giving him a song and dance. The bigger question was why Macker was risking his life doing this – selling to my kid.

❋

The John Bull was lit up. The smoky windows showed mobile shadows; folk nattering, moving to the sound of the music. Parked cars lined the road, and the odd taxi brought in stragglers anxious to get into the warmth of my boozer. It looked like a good night. As I left the car I looked for the warden, the old tramp. It was pure habit. But he was nowhere to be seen.

I recalled the bollocking me, Corey and Bill got for being on the roof of the mill. And the warden had been right, of course. But it was a few nights later, while the three of us were recovering in a Cheshire sanatorium, that the man's entire family was killed. They'd been hiding in the official shelters, the ginnels at the back of houses, and taken a direct hit. He'd come across the scene himself and never recovered. So now… he still pushed the pram his baby daughter once used.

But we did plan revenge against the Third Reich, me, Bill and Corey Blaine, we did indeed. And we got it. Four years later in 1944 we bloody well got it.

Inside were members of the local British Legion and their wives. The pub was dressed as before but a banner was added above the bar:

'British Legion Late Autumn Fund Raiser.'

On stage was an aging beauty. Peroxide hairdo, evening dress, the lot. Her red gown set off matching gloves, and behind her, the worn scrim popped her out like a clown in a beige tent. She'd just finished a song and was starting into some dirty jokes.

I made my way to the bar shaking hands with all who offered. It took some time and folk were polite, ignoring my lateness. I could see Danny in a tuxedo fretting at the bar. He waved and I squeezed my way over.

'Where the bleeding hell have you been?' he said. 'I'm sick with worry here.'

'Any messages?'

'No. Anything with you?'

I shook my head. A whisky was at my elbow. I took it up.

'So what's the plan?' he said.

'Have to wait and see. If Adolphus can't find him then I'll

44

be out tonight, I suppose.' I knocked the drink back. 'He's somewhere out there. We'll talk about it later.' I looked about. 'Good crowd. Sold some raffle tickets?'

'Right to the end of the roll, me.'

'Look at you,' I said, eyeing his tux. He smelled of Lifebuoy soap and Hai Karate aftershave.

'Lewis's sale. I thought why the hell not.'

'You'll be wanting a raise next.'

'Too bloody true.'

We turned to the stage. The peroxide bird was working the crowd. She saw a tall feller coming from the toilet.

'Look at the size of him,' she said. 'What happened love, you fall asleep in a greenhouse? Bloody hell. Is it true what they say about men with big hands? They've got big feet.' The crowd laughed. 'Eh, have you heard this one? There's a priest and a rabbi who are great friends, see. One's called Patrick, the other Jacob. One day the two are having a drink and Patrick says to Jacob, "Hey, Jacob... I know you lot aren't allowed to eat pork, right?" "Yes, that's true, Patrick. Jews can't eat pork." "But there must've been a time," says Patrick, "when, as a young man, a trainee rabbi, that you tried a nice bacon butty." Jacob looked at him then said: "Well, it is true," says Jacob, "that when I was a young man I did have a bacon sandwich, I admit it." "Ah, it all comes out now," says Patrick. "And didn't it taste absolutely marvelous, all that lovely fat dripping down onto your chin, eh?" "Yes," says Jacob, I admit it… it was absolutely marvelous." "Ah, I knew it," says Patrick. And they drink. Then Jacob says to Patrick. "Patrick, I know as a priest that you're not allowed to enjoy a woman." "Yes, that's true," says Patrick. "I have to take the vow of celibacy." "Eh, but," says Jacob, "there must've been a time, when you were a young man, that you had a go, partook in the pleasures of the flesh?" "Well, if truth be known," says Patrick, "there was this one time when I was a silly young man just before going into the seminary that I did… I laid with a lady." "Ah," says Jacob. *It's a helluva lot better than pork, isn't it?"*

The audience erupted. Danny nearly choked on his pint. I cracked a smile.

'She's a rough one,' I said. 'What's her name?'

'Betty Wainwright. She was cheap.'

I shook my head. 'I wanted a class act, not a scrubber. If she starts stripping I'm closing us down,'

'Nah.' He grinned, took a blast from his inhaler and sparked up an Ultra Light. With his crew cut and handlebar moustache he looked more like a Cossack than a Manc doorman. But he looked a tough nut and that was all that mattered. The row of sleepers from his lobe to the top of his ear added to it all. He smoked his cig through fingers that bore the tattoo *Love*. *Hate* was on the other hand, of course.

'Let's have another song, eh?' said Betty. Then she launched into 'It's Not Unusual.'

We drank for a second then I told him to go over to the club. I wanted him over there, since Mary wasn't exactly forthcoming when it came to Neil. I didn't tell him this.

'Okay,' he said. 'There'll be no bother here. Except Corey Blaine's shown up… all the way from Canada.'

'What state's he in?'

'What do you think?' he pointed to a corner.

Corey was comatose. He'd aged in the six months since I'd seen him. His curly salt-and-pepper hair was thinner, greyer

- his eyes more sunken. There was a stack of pint pots in front of him and a full whisky glass.

'Looks a bit worse for wear, I know,' Danny said. 'But what can you do, I had to let him in. You know what he's like. Oh, and he's asking for you. Do you want me to turf him out before I go?'

'No. No, I'll deal with him later,' I said. 'You get off as soon as you can. Keep me posted. I'll be here 'till twelve.'

Danny nodded and made his way to the door. I looked to Corey, knowing it was just a matter of time before he jerked awake and clocked me. I was relieved when Betty started singing 'Paloma Blanca' and the dance floor became busy with folk jiving. I made my way to the stairs.

I unlocked my office and refreshed my glass and mickey from the Johnny Walker bottle. I looked out at the blackness and thought of the warden shivering somewhere. Then I caught a movement below the window. There he was, shuffling along with the pram. I got out a pound note and scrunched it into a ball. I opened the window and tossed it out. The old man picked it up and looked up to me. He then sniffed, pocketed the money, and went on his way.

I heard a sound behind me. I turned and there was Corey hovering in the doorway. He looked pale and sweaty.

'How's your mam?' I said.

'She liked the flowers,' he said, leaning against the frame. It seemed to be holding him up.

I looked outside and nodded at the warden as he ambled across the croft.

'He gave us a right bollocking, didn't he,' I said. 'When they pulled us out.'

'When we came back from the hospital -' slurred Corey, 'you had plans to tell him about your Ma and Da... sitting in this cellar... during raids.'

'Aye. Wouldn't give up their ale... not for Hitler, Goring or any of the bastards. That was my dad.'

He nodded and wiped his forehead. 'That's the spirit,' you said. 'The spirit of England... that I want to copy.' He blinked trying to focus. 'You were going to tell him that.'

'You have a memory.'

'Then his family....' He shook his head and blew out through his mouth. It made him burp.

'Unpredictable, life,' I said

'Not really.'

I could sense it coming, the kind of verbal that only the Catholic can spout. I knew it would be useless to talk about the warden's kids, what *they* had done to offend God to deserve being blown to bits. I knew I'd never win that game with Corey Blaine. Instead I said:

'Stuff happens... and my folks romp the war, no harm at all... 'cept liver damage.' I turned to him. 'You've got to stop calling the house. Brenda's getting funny.'

'Then give me the thing.'

'I told you, I don't even know where it is,'

'It's the pay book, the pay book -'

'No, *Bill* has the pay book, Bill,' I said. 'You gave me the dog tag, the *dog tag*, right? And I have no idea where it is.'

My patience was running thin. To be pestered now after thirty-two years for a kraut's identity disc, a dog tag Corey had given me *himself* was beyond it. And I knew he'd never get the pay book back from Bill.

Corey came off the doorframe. For a second it looked like he might leave.

'Does Bill still have all that shit on his wall?' he said. 'Sick bastard.'

'Why can't you just have a good time? It's a charity event, Corey.'

'Those RAF twats, sat in the corner… fucking nest of murderers.'

'Alright, mate,' I said. 'It's home time.'

I ushered him to the landing. There was no resistance, but it was a right performance getting him down the stairs. Each step was an eternity. The last thing we wanted was a scene. Once at the bottom I started to lead him to the door. Betty was in full throttle.

'Guantanamera, guajira guantanamera,'

'Just one more drink, Jackie, eh?' Corey droned. 'And I'm gone.'

I looked about the room. The atmosphere softened me.

'One more then a taxi home,' I said. 'Alright?'

Corey nodded and I went to the bar. I quickly ordered a single whisky and a ginger ale. Betty was chortling away.

'Guantanamera, guajira, guantanamera,'

I was just getting Corey's drink when I heard his voice on the microphone. I turned. He'd snatched the mic from Betty and was bellowing into it keeping the tune of the song, but bending the lyrics.

'One Bomber Harris, there's only one
Bomber Harris, One Bomber Harris,
There's only one Bomber Harris.'

The band had stopped. I started to the stage but hit a wall of punters, all giving Corey a wide birth. I had to squeeze slowly and politely through. Meanwhile, Corey turned to the RAF contingent in the room.

'For all the heroes in the corner... women and children, Jesus. No match for you lot. Benzene gel, high explosives... from twenty thousand feet - that's fucking fair, eh? Easier than looking at the mess, right lads?'

'One Bomber Harris, there's only one Bomber Harris -'

I got to the stage and wrenched the mic away. Before he could protest I frog-marched him towards the door. The band started to improvise. Once outside I let him go and he tottered to the wall where he was sick. Old Timer, his forehead shiny with sweat, was suddenly there.

'I've called a taxi,' he said.

Corey steadied himself against the wall and wretched again. We looked on. Old Timer handed Corey the bar towel and turned to me.

'I thought we'd got rid of him... bloody nutter.'

'I'll take him home,' I said.

'You're better than most, you.'

I opened my car and we piled Corey into the back. Old Timer closed the door.

'Was he really like this all through Germany?'

I said nothing.

'If he was the Boche he'd have been shot as a traitor.'

I took out a fiver. 'Give this to the taxi for his trouble.'

'Keep it. It won't be wasted. Our bombardiers won't be staying after that little performance.'

He disappeared inside.

✳

Corey snored like a dragoon as I drove into Broughton. His mouth hung open like a man about to die. The car smelled of sick. An ambulance was suddenly behind me, sirens screaming away. I pulled into the curb and it flew past. I considered just leaving him by the side of the road; he deserved nothing less. I cursed him. Fifty thousand of our lads died in that bombing campaign and you go on like that.

I sat for five minutes listening to him snore. I had to take him home, I owed him that much. He was tied to me like a lame dog, a wounded animal that I no right to lose. The war had done its bit on him. We'd seen every kind of slaughter, but within all that... I'd added to his misery. I knew that without decisions made by me, he wouldn't be such a mess.

I pulled up at the row house. It was shabby and dark. There was a clumsy scene at the front of the house, then a battle with the living room door. I ended up heaving him onto a settee. It had a worn, floral pattern and looked like it was from the twenties. I straightened up and caught my breath. The room was a suffocating size. Ugly, tasseled side lamps sat stubbornly on end tables. It smelled of old people.

I made sure he was settled and a lamp was on. A crucifix hung on the mantelpiece wall. I turned away from it to see Corey pale as the dead. I felt pity and disgust at the same time. Then I caught a pleasant scent. Over in the corner were the Lilac flowers I'd sent to Shauna Blaine, Corey's ailing mam.

I'd only fleeting memories of this house. As kids I spent most of my time with Bill. Corey wasn't anywhere near the tearaway we were. We looked after him because he was a soft but loyal kid. He was like our mascot. After the war when Bill and me were ransacking the city, Corey lay in his own filth; a wounded bird unable to move. He stirred.

'My boy... my boy...'

'Go to sleep, you feck,' I said. I didn't need Corey wailing over his dead son.

He shifted and I went to leave. I caught his eye in the lamplight.

'That dog tag... find it for me, Jackie.'

'I told you I don't know where it is.'

It was true. All the souvenirs from the war I'd hidden years ago, stashed in my mother's loft. I wouldn't have been able to find them for love nor money.

'How's Neil?'

'Neil's fine.' I reached the door.

'My God, you poor man.' He looked up at me with pitying, watery eyes. 'You poor, poor man... *The Sins of the Father...*'

I left him. As I was walking down the hall I heard him.

'The Sins of the Father...'

I moved quickly to the front of the house. The light from the street snuck through a tiny window by the door and landed on a hall mirror. It reflected another crucifix hanging sullenly on the opposite wall. The house suddenly throbbed with suffering. I fumbled with the door, swung it open and went out. I heard a faint voice from upstairs, Corey's mam calling him.

The cold air singed my nostrils as I stole down the path like a thief. I was lightheaded when I got to the Cortina. I leaned against the body, ferreting for the keys. Once in I started the engine and screeched away, almost taking the corner on two wheels.

The Sins of the Father? How bloody dare you, Corey Blaine. I am a hero, mate. I saved your Irish arse and the rest of the bleeding unit. I am a hero, sunshine - a fucking hero; and don't you forget it.'

✳

I drove aimlessly for about an hour. I finally decided that I couldn't avoid the pub any longer. Luckily, I arrived just as folk were leaving. The cars were thinning out, and I was suddenly aware of the isolation of the building. There was a blackness wanting to swallow the pub. I was literally surrounded by crofts and derelict houses, all slated for demolition.

I pulled in feeling exhausted. I knew I'd be out all night looking for the lad, so I opened the glove box and necked a couple of Black Bombers. I needed the amphetamine. As I swished them down with the whisky, Mary's Jeep screeched to a halt ahead of me. She jumped out and ran up to my window. I rolled it down.

'I've got Neil,' she said, looking harried and breathless. 'He's at the club. He came down.'

'How is he?'

'Well enough to fight like the devil. Danny had to restrain him. We've locked him in the stock room. You need that bleeding phone at the club fixing - driving in this town of a Saturday. Come and get him, he looks shocking.'

'I'll follow you in the Cortina. Half a mo.'

I breathed a sigh of relief and I went back in the pub. I was pleased to see the warden sitting in the corner with a hot toddy. Betty Wainwright was putting on her coat and managing to sup a rum and black at the same time. A cig hung from her mouth.

'Well, that was a turn up for the books,' she said, frowning at me. 'For Christ's sake who was that bloody lunatic?'

'Sorry about that,' I said, helping her with her coat. 'It's sorted now.'

'A bit late for me, love.' She turned to me. 'Oh, you are a gent. How rare.' She smoked. 'But honestly, that kyboshed the evening for me, it did and then some. I never got them back after that. I'll have to think twice about coming back here, love.'

'Have you been paid?'

'He's just give it me. The old feller, yon.'

'Here's an extra twenty.'

I took some notes and handed them to her. She cocked her head to one side and smiled. She had large crooked teeth.

'Oh that's nice. You're all right, you.' She looked me up and down. 'It's nice to see a well-dressed man. That's a fitted suit that, I can tell; English wool, no doubt; and the cut, vintage 1940s, that. I know because me dad dressed similar.' She inhaled. 'I love it - the waistcoat, fob watch, the Trilby, overcoat. You're like Trevor Howard in *Brief Encounter.* She exhaled, funneling the smoke high into the air. She looked at my forehead and cheek. 'That's a war wound, isn't it, that scar. I can tell. You didn't get that at a Saturday night brawl in Smedley, did you? Sorry to be nosy, love, but it's nice to be in the company of a war hero. Fancy taking me for a drink? I know a nice spot.'

'I can't, love. Family emergency.'

She had another drag and blew out smoke from a wide mouth. 'Pity,' she said, sticking the notes down her cleavage. 'Maybe next time.' She downed her drink, dabbing the side of her mouth with her gloves. 'Anyway, I'll be off then. Cheerio, lovey.' She tickled the air with her fingers and swayed to the door. I heard the door go as I went to Old Timer at the bar.

'We've found Neil,' I said. 'Can you do the cash?'

'I'll sort it, ' he said. He indicated the warden. 'I'll take him home and lock up, don't worry.'

✳

The rain was on again. I put some Sinatra on to cloud out the din from the wiper. The crowds were spilling out from the pubs and gangs of kids and revelers were staggering all over. It was the usual mayhem. Sometimes they'd be gallivanting across the road with no warning. Horns were going left, right and centre and the odd cop car went flashing by on its way to some mischief.

As I drove I started grinding my teeth. I was sweating like mad and my heart danced like a Dervish in my chest. I now regretted necking the speed, and I was sorry I hadn't called his mother from the pub. She had the patience with him. We didn't need me losing my rag and making things worse. Then I had an idea. I'd get Danny to leg it up to the phone box on Oxford Road and call Brenda. Yes, that's what I'd do. Then I relaxed a bit and enjoyed Frank.

We arrived at the club and pulled in. We got out of our cars and walked to the door. The rain had stopped and all was quiet. Mary had obviously kicked the kids out and it was eerily quiet; the kind you get after a deluge; or before a storm. Even the sounds of carousing up on Oxford Street seemed a thousand miles away.

Almost together we noticed the front of Macker's Capri, parked on the corner. We looked at one another and went over.

There it was, unmistakable. We both looked around. I tried the door. Locked.

'I'll get Danny to come up and keep an eye out,' Mary said. 'He can't be far.'

Mary was ahead of me as we went down the steps of the club. I could hear Bob Marley's 'Natural Mystic' playing on the sound system. Danny would do this after a night on the doors. He liked his Pernod, peanuts and reggae, the peace and quiet of an empty club.

As I descended the steps the smell of sweat, talcum powder and Brut Faberge got stronger. Even a couple of hours of dancing were enough to leave the room pungent, heavy. At the bottom Mary pulled up sharp, rooted to the spot. She looked back at me, paused then moved off. I came down and looked into the alcove where her attention had been.

There, sitting at a table opposite Danny, was Macker. He was smoking madly and chewing ten to the dozen. When the kid saw me his chewing slowed, then his jaw dropped like Marley's ghost. I came further in. Mary sighed and moved to the bar, rubbing her forehead. She didn't want this.

'Not two minutes after Mary left,' said Danny, 'I was having a fag at the door. And who shows up but this cunt. Looking for Neil, no doubt... so I yanked him in.'

He beamed like a cat dropping a mouse at its owner's feet.

'It's all bollocks, Jackie,' said Macker, 'I was waiting for me bird. We were going to a concert at The Factory. That's God's honest, that is.'

Danny smiled and shook his head. They'd been through this.

'Who's playing?' I said. 'At The Factory?'

'I'm not arsed, me. I just do as I'm told, you know what it's

56

like.'

'Lying little get.' Danny kicked him under the table. Macker flinched.

'This is what he's like. Look at the state of me.' He pointed to a swelling lip and eye. 'Dragged in here like this, given a leathering, jacket ripped to buggery. Seventy quid, *seventy bleeding quid* down the Swanee.'

The room was warm and thick. I was thankful for the waft of cold air that had followed me down the steps. I took my mickey out and went to the bar. Mary had wandered to the far end.

'Mary, love,' I said, 'can you get me a glass?' She went behind the bar and put a glass on the top for me. I could feel her giving me a look but I ignored it and poured the drink.

'Las Vegas down here, isn't it,' Macker said. 'Closed early, eh? They'd have all gone tearing over to Smarties or Pips in sunny Shude Hill. Crap disco sounds is better than no sounds at all, especially of a Saturday night. Eh? Eh?'

'Shut your trap, you,' Danny said.

Bob Marley finished on the sound system. Danny got up to put on another album.

'Can we change the music, mate?' Macker said. 'It's doing my head in that.'

Danny leaned in close. 'You want more agro, you?'

'You know what I mean, Jackie? It's been purgatory here, listening to that. The whole bleeding album he's put me through. I'm ready to shoot myself right now. How long we going to be here, mate, anyway? I'll be in right lumber with this bird.'

'What's her name?' I said.

'Gemma Grice. Black bob, fishnets, heavy make-up, Roxy bird. She's in all the time.'

'You flogging to her too?' said Danny.

Macker sighed. 'There's more to me than drugs, you know. I do have a life.'

Danny scoffed and it took him on a coughing fit. He took a blast from his inhaler. 'By heck,' he gasped.

'I had that when I was little, me,' Macker said. 'Asthma. Fucking ball ache, mate. I know all about that, but can I make a suggestion? Don't smoke light ciggies - they're really deadly. Me mate's granddad died smoking Ultra Lights, and he went like that.' He snapped his fingers. 'Emphysema. Bleeding horrible way to go. With Ultra Lights you suck like buggery, trying to get that nicotine, you know? The smoke goes right into the deepest part of your lungs. So, I always say to folk with lung ailments, like - smoke Capstan Full Strength, no filters. They'll add years to your life.'

He looked at all of us. The cocky street clown always came out when he was scared.

'Does he know our Neil's in the back?' I said to Danny.

Macker's face went grey. He looked to Danny, me, then Mary. 'Oh, no, no, no, that's not me, that... Mary, Jackie, I had no idea he was down here. I wouldn't come down here, for fuck' s sake. I'd be mad to. Mary, Jackie - this is God's honest, this is.'

I kept my eyes on his. 'I was told you were outside last night... Well?'

... 'I might've brushed by.'

'You did or you didn't.'

'I did... Yeah, I did. This bird again.'

'Right. And you didn't see Neil?' I kept on him. ''Cause I was told you were seen with him as well.'

He shook his head. 'That's not true at all, Jackie. Someone's having you on. I never saw your Neil, that's gospel that is.'

I pulled the Tesco bag from my coat pocket. 'Only… I'm outside earlier and I'm looking in the alley at the back, and what do I find but that little lot.' I put it into his lap. 'Mind the needles.'

Macker looked. 'I'm sorry to see this, Jackie, but this is someone else.'

The tap behind the bar went on, startling us a bit. It was Mary getting some water. I turned back to Danny.

'Has he got anything on him?'

'Over there on the bar. Car keys, a Stanley knife and four hundred quid.'

I walked over to the pile. There was a roll of tens and fivers, a jumble of keys, and the blade. I picked up the knife.

'Planning on laying a carpet, Macker?'

'You know what it's like, Jackie, this town.'

I picked up the roll. 'A good night too.' I turned to Mary and pointed to the lad. 'He doesn't go anywhere.'

I put the roll down and walked to the stockroom. At the hallway by the toilet, Mary pulled me up.

'Listen,' she said, her voice low. 'Just take Neil home, love. He needs looking after - he needs his mam. You've got him, he's alive, be happy with that, man. Let me deal with Macker. I've got the machete over there. I'll threaten to cut his finger off - I'll put his hand on the table and spread it. I'll put the fear of God into him, I promise.'

I looked at her and she knew what I was thinking. We'd tried that before. It'd made no difference.

'I don't like this, Jackie.'

'Then leave. This stops tonight.'

✳

I turned the key to the stockroom and looked in. There, on the floor, was my son. His knees were pulled to his face and his hair hung in greasy clumps. Fingernails rimmed with dirt, jeans scuffed with moss stains, baseball shoes caked with dog filth. The disinfectant smell of the room couldn't hide the stench of the street coming from him. He didn't look up.

I relocked the door and went into the toilet where I leaned against the sink. I couldn't enjoy the relief of finding him. All I saw was the long, miserable road of detoxification. I wanted him to just vanish like a passing cloud.

I looked in the mirror. The light above the sink made my scar look deep. From eyebrow to cheek, it looked like it'd been drawn with pen. I got a sudden flash of that night, Belgium in '44.

Shells landing all round me, dirt falling into the trench. I feel him falling on my head. He recovers and looks around, his eyes growing wide - piercing blue like a bad angel, as he sees me. His face blackened with gunpowder – now his arm spinning round with the knife.

It vanished as it came. But the room buzzed about me. I breathed deep and splashed water on my face. I could hear Mary giving Danny a quiet bollocking for pulling in Macker. There was Danny's hurt response. Then Macker was asking her to let him go.

I combed my hair back from my forehead and went through

to the club.

✳

Macker was still at the table. Mary stood by the bar holding her machete, while Danny hovered by the exit. They all looked at me but said nothing. I took my time, peeling my coat off and draping it over the rail on the bar. I drank some whisky. I lit a cig. I leaned against the bar looking at the keys, knife and roll.

Some drunken girls could be heard clip-clopping by outside. They moved on, cackling like wild geese.

'This it?' I said to Danny. 'He's got nothing else on him?'

'Nowt'

I picked up the keys and tossed them to him. 'His car outside, check the dodgy panel on the driver's side.'

Danny left. Mary, still carrying the machete, replaced him at the bottom of the stairs. One of Macker's knees started to bounce.

'How did you know about the panel? Mary asked.

'I sold him the vehicle, didn't I Macker?'

I remembered flogging him the car, telling him to get a low-end vehicle like me. Flash cars were like throwing two fingers to the Peelers, I'd said. They were a dead giveaway you were on serious graft. Did he listen? Did he hell as like.

'Now, do you want to change your story?' I said.

'Jackie, I'm dealing. I didn't say I was *not* dealing. I just wouldn't do it down here and I wouldn't flog to your Neil. That's gospel, that is Jackie.' His mouth was still going. Speed.

I knew Neil kept a tape recorder under the bar. The lad used it to make compilations at the club to take home. I looked underneath in the corner, and there it was with a tape already inside. I brought it up to the bar and rewound the cassette. I pressed play. A Northern Soul stomper blasted out. I stopped it and rewound. I pressed record.

'Testing, testing, one two.'

I rewound and played it back. I could feel Mary's eyes on me, thinking torture and a recorded confession. Macker looked over thinking the same.

We waited for Danny to come back. Macker smoked and returned his stare to the floor. He held the cig like I used to, cradling the dimp between thump and forefingers, the lighted end facing the palm.

The Bombers were doing their work on me. All the edges and colours of the room were crystalizing. I looked at Macker and it was like seeing him for the first time. Who was this kid? He stood at about five feet seven at the most. His knuckles were swollen and scabbed from endless fistfights. His neck shot straight up from his shoulders, the back of his head pointing to the ceiling. He stared out from deep-set eyes as if looking over an invisible pair of specs. It gave the impression of complete control and confidence. It was unusual and disturbing in one so young.

A bushel of dirty hair was drawn back behind small ears. This was the Borstal haircut - long on top, short on side. He'd kept it. I reckoned it was because I'd always worn my hair in this forties fashion. In fact, the kid was the dead spit of some of the Waffen SS soldiers we'd faced in Europe; young lunatics that fought to the last bullet then threw themselves at you with whatever they could pick up.

I had a drink of whisky and swirled the glass. Mary was

fidgeting and puffing away like a chimney by the exit. I could hear her Docs scuff on the concrete.

Danny came down the stairs. He carried a Spa bag that drooped under the weight of its load. He put the bag on the bar and began to unload it. Tightly wrapped in cellophane, were two kilograms of brownish powder. Other smaller stashes were brought out; about a dozen ten, five and two-gram bags were piled on the larger package. We all stared at the haul. Mary shook her head as she looked over at Macker. His face was sickly white even in the darker light of the club.

'That's Bill's, that is,' he finally said. There was a tremor in his voice. 'He laid out a lot of money for that.'

'How much?' asked Danny.

'Eight grand wholesale those, if they're a penny.'

Danny looked at me and whistled.

'I know it's you who's flogging to Neil,' I said. 'But I'm a fair man so I'm going to give you the opportunity to tell me. If you just admit it, admit to supplying Neil with smack, we can all go home. You can go home without injury. I'll take this recording to Bill and a few others in town and they'll listen to it. And because of the respect I carry with these fellers, I'll be well within me rights to do with you what I want. And I what you to leave… indefinitely. You'll take your business away and never come back, never return; never show your face here again. Understood?' I looked at Mary and Danny. 'I think that's pretty bloody fair.' I turned again to Macker. I was still mulling over what I was really going to do with him once I'd gotten the confession; I was keeping that open. 'So make a choice. And make it now.'

'It's not me, Jackie, honest it's not.'

'You sure about that?'

He nodded.

'Bring our Neil in,' I said.

Danny went into the back. I could see Macker thinking of making a dash for it. Mary sensed it too and squared off, the machete rising in her grip. The light from the bar bounced off the blade and made a pattern on the ceiling.

Danny came back with Neil. The lad was a rag doll. Leaning into his stomach, his skin was a wax dummy and his eyes shifted about the room. He saw Macker and shriveled. The sight of the drugs on the bar had him mesmerized and jumpy. Before anyone could speak Macker waded in.

'Tell them, Neil, tell them I've not been near you.'

He stared at Neil expecting something from him. Neil just looked to the floor.

'Neil,' Macker said. 'Come on, mate.'

I turned to Macker and eyeballed him to silence. I went back to Neil. 'He sells heroin and does not deserve your respect. This is not about grassing someone out, Neil. So, stop playing the hard arse and tell me the truth. Is it him?'

Neil stayed looking at the ground. His reply was simple and feeble.

'No… no it's not.'

'Then who?'

He wiped a runny nose with his sleeve and coughed. 'Don't know. Kids under the viaduct.'

I drank the last of my drink. 'This is your last chance. Is it him?' Nothing. The tap dripped. I turned to Danny. 'Throw that shit down the toilet, Danny.'

Danny gathered up the kilos and smaller baggies. Neil put

head in hands. Macker paced. I could hear the lad's breathing. Danny finished packing, picked up the bag and Macker's blade, and made for the back.

'Danny stop.'

Danny pulled up and turned.

Macker said: 'You don't have to do this, mate.'

'No?' I said.

'Bill will cut me hands off if you do this.' His was voice high with tension. 'Worse. I am a bleeding dead man if you do this, Jackie.' He wiped a sweating forehead. 'Look, tax me for it. There's four hundred in that roll and chalk me up for another six. That's a grand - twelve and half percent of the value. It's yours. Take me money, give me a battering, anything, but don't flush that down the bog. Please.'

'Get rid of it before I choke him with it,' I said.

Danny moved off.

'Okay, so look…'

Danny stopped. Turned again.

Macker scratched his forehead. 'You won't do this if I admit it, is that it? You won't flush that down the crapper?'

'You can walk right out of here,' I said.

'All right, all right,' he said. He walked in a tight circle then stopped. He turned to me. 'He came to me. *He came to me, Jackie, I had no choice.*' He looked over at a cringing Neil. 'I said no at first but he kept on mithering me. Then he said he'd go to someone else, so it was best if it came from me - 'cause at least he knew what he was getting.'

I looked at Neil, now leaning on a pillar. He'd sunk down onto his haunches, his hands still covering his face. I picked up the tape recorder and came round to the other side of the bar, close to Macker.

'Yesterday was the twenty-fourth of November 1977,' I said. 'You'll identify yourself and what you did, and on what date. You got that?' I turned the recorder on and pushed it closer to him. 'Say it... Say it.'

'I sold smack to Neil Dunne yesterday... on the twenty-fourth of November, 1977.'

'Identify yourself. Say your name.'

He did. I stopped the recorder and rewound it. It squiggled back to the beginning. I played it. We listened. There was the confession I wanted. I ejected the tape, put it in my pocket, and returned the recorder to the bar. Macker broke the silence.

'Danny, can I have the gear back now, mate?'

'Down the toilet, Danny.'

Macker's mouth opened like a landed carp's. Danny looked at me. 'You heard me, Danny.'

Macker's face was a picture. 'You gave me your word.'

'I tell you what... You can have the gear, you can have it, but Mary will take your thumb first. Pick which one. Right or left. We'll take it off and you can leave with the gear.'

Everyone looked at Macker. The tap was still dripping in the sink, plop, plop, plop. The lad's head drooped like a deflated balloon. He stared at the floor.

'Danny,' I said.

Danny disappeared. Off he went. Walking to the toilet. To dump the gear. We listened. Hey-ho. There was silence for a couple of minutes then a muffled toilet flush, followed by a deep gurgle of water going down the drain. There was the faint hiss of the tank refilling. A police siren whined off in the distance. The toilet flushed again. The whole thing lasted a few minutes. Danny came back in, dusting his hands. He put the knife with the rest of Macker's stuff.

'Does the Irwell have any fish in it?' Danny chirped. 'They'll be well blotto tonight if there is.'

'Not the time, Danny,' said Mary, 'not the time.'

'Bang goes that cottage in Wales.' He saw us looking at him. 'I'm just saying.'

'You can grab your things and go now,' I said to Macker.

He slowly moved to the bar and gathered his keys, roll and the knife. He spoke low. 'You've done it now, you. You really have.'

'Excuse me?'

'You've just signed it, you.'

'Signed what?'

'Your death warrant, mate - your fucking death warrant.'

'All right, all right,' said Mary, moving to him. 'You just shut it and leave while you still can.'

'I mean it,' he said, sticking the blade out. 'I have mates as well, and Bill Shaw will throw a fucking fit over this.'

'Get out, get out now -'

'All of you! You have no idea what you've just done. That loser kid of yours - he's the one who started all this, him! On his knees he was to me, begging like a child.'

I just stared at him like he was mad, like he had a death wish. I thought he might suddenly backtrack, apologise and run away.

'It's all right, guv,' said Danny. 'We'll deal with this.'

'Stay the fuck off.' He slashed the blade. 'I'll open up the first one that touches me.' He jabbed the knife out in front of him, pointing to me. 'You think this recording will make a difference? I spit on it, I'll deny it, I'll say you beat it out of me, tortured me - you'll be back to square one.' He paced, his eyes black, mouth bending into an ugly sneer. 'Jackie fucking Dunne. You have no idea who I am! Not a clue. The money I will make - and then *I'll* say what's what... and the first ones to go will be – you - then you, then you, Jackie Dunne. And then - then... *you.*' He landed on Neil, his eyes full of hate. 'What a useless waste of space. He was on his knees to me. That's all he's good for this thing of yours - being on his knees and begging.'

I saw white. I moved to him and he swung at me. I grabbed his forearm and crushed his knife hand, snatching the weapon. He pulled away from me, kicking and writhing, trying to get free but I yanked him into a headlock where he heaved up and down, struggling like chimp in a net. I felt his wiry strength but I had him. Mary and Danny were on us trying to prize us apart, shouting for me to stop, but I tightened my grip and drew the blade deep and slow across his cheek.

A low groan came from him. I let him go and I threw the knife away, stepping back. He stood still, two hands clamped to his cheek, while blood seeped out from his fingers and ran down his sleeves, dropping onto the floor.

'Get him out of here,' I said, moving to the alcove.

I wiped the blood off my hands with my spare hanky and lit up. I listened to the commotion, Danny and Mary behind me.

'Danny, get us that bar towel over there! Quick, hurry, will you. Here, press it tight... Grab another one... quick he's bleeding like a stuck pig.'

'Jesus H...'

'He'll need stitches on the double. You'd better risk it and take him to the infirmary.'

'Can't he drive himself, the little get?'

'Are you mad? He crashes the car and dies - we'll all be in lumber. Just drop him off and leave his car, get a taxi home. Danny!'

'Fine, fine. Mr. bloody Muggins, here… Come on, you.'

'Drop him at emergency and make sure he goes in - and take the side streets.'

I could hear Danny grumbling as he rounded the corner of the stone steps with Macker. I heard Mary go into the stock room.

✳

I went round to the bar and washed my hands. Mary went by with some Flash spray cleaner, paper towels, a bucket and mop. I came back round to check on Neil, a heap by the pillar. Mary was mopping up the mess. She glared at me.

'He'll live,' I said.

'You hope. Jesus, man.' She fucked and blinded as she cleaned. 'I'll clean this up and we should make scarce.'

'He won't go to the law.'

'No, he's a right little gangster, that one.' She scowled at me. 'I don't know how useful that was, Jackie, I really don't.'

'Ah, well.' I took a nip of whisky from the optic.

'He'll love that scar; a badge of bloody honour for him, that. But they might report it at the hospital, so let's play it safe… Look at the floor. Are you going to stand there boozing or are you going to help?'

I grabbed another towel from the bar top and threw it on

the floor. Neil limped by towards the stairs. Mary dropped everything, grabbed him by scruff of the neck, and hauled him back in.

'Oh, no you don't you little sod!'

'I want me mam!'

'Will you deal with this son of yours? I'm sick of the bleeding lot of you!'

She threw him at me and he withered to the floor. She went behind the bar to refill the bucket. I watched him crawl to the bar and lean against it, clutching his head. I looked down at him assessing the damage.

'I can't deal with Brenda right now,' I said. 'Let's just get him to Hope.'

'I'm not going to Hope. They'll just stick me in a room with a couple of fucking Paracetamol!' He burst into tears.

I hauled him to his feet. 'Get up! Get up now! All the things we've given you. Private this, private that! And you end up like this!'

'I want to die!'

'How dare you! I've seen boys your age with their heads blown off, shot to bits! And you - you bloody wastrel, you make me sick!'

I shoved him off and he crumpled to the floor. He was stunned and stopped crying.

'I'm sorry, dad... I'm sorry...'

Then his chest heaved and he was off again. I looked down at him. Emotions flew around in me and I couldn't land in any of them. All I could do was watch it all happening before me. Mary put the mop down.

'I'm calling Brenda.'

'Mary.'

'Only she can deal with him when he's like this. *Someone* has to have some sense around here.'

'Mam. Mam…'

✳

There was Brenda, standing at the bottom of the steps. My wife was amazing in many ways, not least because she had a sixth sense about things. She was just tuned in, especially when it came to her lad. And now here she was, out of the blue like a descending angel. She took in our boy, the scene, and then swept in towards him, crouching by his side.

'You're all right, love. Your mam's here.' She pulled at his anorak sleeves. 'Show me your arms. Come on. How long have you been on?'

I watched her fascinated; envious, if the truth be known. How she had the peace of mind to handle him when he was like this, I had no idea. And she was still a beauty. Even with the misery of the last few years, her eyes glowed defiant in the face of it all. She kept with Neil, digging info from him.

'About a month,' he sputtered.

Now she examined his forearms like a nurse; detached, efficient. Like she'd always done before.

'When was your last fix?'

'Yesterday.'

'There's no infection, thank God for small mercies.'

'I need to go to the toilet, mam.'

'This is what happens, you can't hold anything in. Come on.' She started to lift him. 'Give me a hand here, dad.'

'I can do it myself, mam.'

'Is it through here, Mary?'

'Mam, I can do this bit on me own.'

'Your hand's shaking like a leaf, you'll just be spreading it around.'

Neil went mad. Mary stifled a laugh and I nearly cracked up as well. Even the missus had to hide a snort.

'It's not funny. Will people leave me alone'

'It's too late for that, love.'

'Mam, I can manage on me own - please.'

There was a haggle for a minute, neither of them budging. I was about to lose my rag again when Mary saved the day.

'I'll take him, Brenda.' She squashed a whine from Neil. 'Don't flatter yourself, kiddo - I'll not be wiping your arse. I'll stay well outside. Come on.'

✳

I got my fags out. I offered Brenda one, lighting us up. I wandered behind the bar. Brenda paced, her arms folded across her chest as she smoked.

'What are you doing down here, Brenda,' I said, leaning over the sink.

She turned and nailed me.

'Sometimes I just get tired of waiting. Yeah, waiting for news of that lad in there, waiting for you, waiting for men who only show up to eat, sleep and bring tragic, bloody news with them.' She looked around the room, taking it all in. 'Look at us. Am I the only one who thinks this isn't normal?'

I was with the plughole. 'Not now.'

'Course not now. Not now, not ever.' She was off again, wandering. 'How I envy the normal; folk who stay at home of a night and watch telly - together on the settee. Wouldn't that be a concept.' She inspected Mary's cleaning. 'Someone's taken a leathering over this, haven't they?' She turned to me. 'I hope you haven't done something you'll regret.'

'I do what I have to.'

'And damn the consequences. You've been throwing your weight around for years over our Neil; it's not made a blind bit of difference. All its done is make you enemies.'

'Good, I'll sort every last one of them out.'

She sighed and stepped closer. 'When will you realize it's not what's out there - this town's a bastard, it's what's in here.' She touched her heart. 'For you as well as that lad in there.' She approached the bar and leaned in. 'They're not your enemy, Jackie - Father O' Connell or the Samaritans. They do what they do and it's good work too - '

'I'm tired Brenda.'

'And I'm not? My God, there are times I could sleep for a year. But at least I have something – *someone*.'

I said nothing. But she saw something in me, some sliver of something in that moment and she went for it.

'You can't imagine the relief - the relief when you finally admit that you can't go it alone. And that it's no shame to ask for help.'

'God should spend three weeks in Manchester,' I said. 'See how he handles all this.'

She sighed. 'You have an answer for everything. But this isn't working and you know it.'

The fridge purred. She took a long drag and puffed out most of the smoke before inhaling a smidgen.

'I went to the pub at first. Old Timer told me Corey Blaine

was in, creating again.'

'He was drunk.'

'When was he not? And all the calls to the house as well; what's going on Jackie?'

'I don't want to talk about Corey Blaine!'

I came up from the sink and wandered a bit. I caught her reflection in the mirror looking at me. Her mind was just ticking away, like it did. She put out her cig as Mary led Neil from the back. Our lad was doddering like an invalid. Brenda examined him:

'Here he is, our cross to bear.'

'What are you talking about?' asked Neil.

'God in all his wisdom and mercy.'

'Kinell.'

'What have I done to deserve you two?'

'I want Horlicks, mam. Have we got any Horlicks?'

'That's a first. Come on, let's get you home.' She took his arm. 'And yes, we've got Horlicks somewhere.' She led him up the steps of the club.

'I'll be two minutes,' Mary said, returning to the stockroom.

✳

I overtook them and unlocked the car. I started the engine and cranked the heat. I fiddled with some 8-tracks and Louis Armstrong came on. 'What a Wonderful World.'

I waited by the boot of the car. The night was cold and damp and the stillness was still here. The street was strewn with puddles and the worn cobbles shone like bubbles of broken glass. A light mist rose and a rat came out of a drain. It scuttled along a wall opposite, stopped to sniff, then disappearing into a hole.

An Austin Allegro was parked down the road, two figures inside. The lights were off but I could tell from the exhaust the engine was running. The Peelers? I strained to look but couldn't see.

Mary came out of the club carrying a big rubbish bag. She locked the door, went to her car, put the bag in the back. She came up to me and gave me the key. She looked drained.

'I won't be down here for a while. I'm keeping me head down. You should too.' She lit a cig. 'There'll be hell to pay, you do know that.'

'I got what I wanted.'

'That tape?' She shook her head. 'If those deadlegs take notice you can crown me in diamonds. Think again, Jackie.'

'I've still got some on board with me.'

She looked about. 'Things are different with this smack. The chance for big money, it turns men's heads.' She came back to me. 'And him? Have you ever seen the like?'

'Macker?'

'Any other lad would've been crying for his mam. What we could've done to him. But him creating like that? That's not normal what we just saw.' She noticed the Allegro a little further off. 'It didn't take them long.'

'One of Bill's?'

'Ray's car. Looks like the big feller as well, Didds.' She threw her cig away. 'He'll have been on his way to a drop. They've been expecting him.'

'Good.'

She looked at me a bit too long. Then went to her Jeep. Once inside she wound down her window.

'I'll call you tomorrow.'

I watched her drive off. The Allegro put its lights on, backed off and did a slow three-point turn. Then it drove off in the opposite direction, leaving a plume of exhaust behind it.

Brenda wrapped on the window. I took a bit of whisky. I got in. We drove off. Louis was crooning away.

TWO

Crammed as deep as I can in the corner, curled in a ball, doubled over, helmet pulled own. Ground shakes all around me and shell bursts are everywhere – one, two, three all around me, singling me out. The ground jumps – another burst, the percussion shaking my head, making me see double. Another burst - dirt spatters down on my helmet and all around me. The slit trench is just a gaping hole, sunken and tumbled-in wall.

Where's Bill, where's Corey? They're over there in different holes. Separated all ready. Another shell burst, smoke, the smell of cordite everywhere. The man, the boy I was with has gone, buggered off. Me alone… and this is where I'll die.

More explosions, when will it end? There's a lull, just a few seconds, then it starts again – one, two, three. Eardrums are bleeding, my nose - eyes bursting out of my head. More blasts, dear God.

'The Lord is my Shepherd, I shall not want, he leadeth me into still waters...'

First day in the line, the first bloody day and I'm dead. Hardly twenty years old and I die today. More blasts, some of the wall comes in. I dig my way deeper into the ground, but I can't. My hands, my fingernails are bloody with scraping. Another shell burst and something is blown in.

It's a feller. I feel his weight and he tumbles over to the other side. He's stunned... then moves a bit. Jesus, he's a German. He realizes where he is and pulls his knife, slashing at my face. I don't feel it, even though I'm half blinded by blood. Then he squares off ready to lunge. I scramble for my bayonet... where is it? Where is the thing?! Where is it?!

I sat up in bed.

Brenda was lying facing from me. Without turning she put her hand behind her and onto my leg, pressing down. I looked at the clock. Eight o'clock. My neck and the pillow were sodden. I pulled back the covers, sat on the edge of the bed listening to the wind. I watched the shadow of the tree dance on the blinds. What is happening to me? I'm getting soft, soft in my old age.

I listened to Neil sawing logs in his bedroom.

Getting him home had been easy. He didn't even create when she made him take a bath. Being bribed with Horlicks and lithium had helped, and he lay there like King Tut in a vat of goat's milk. Then it was into bed where he was off like a light. We were good until around three, then it'd started; the groaning, the sweats, the tossing and turning. And the wife had stayed with him for most of the night.

I crept into his room. I looked down on him and he seemed half his age; a boy cocooned in a Debenhams quilt. I sat on the chair and looked around the room.

I realized that I'd hardly ever been in here. The walls were chock-full with posters of music events, Northern Soul all-nighters and dance weekends. Ray Charles stared from a poster on the wall above the bed, his dark glasses like X-Ray vision burning through to your bones. An Air-Fix Spitfire plane hung in the air in the far corner. A string was missing and it dangled to one side, where it revolved a bit. I went over to it and felt a tunnel of air coming through the open window.

I found myself looking at his bookshelf. There was a full set of Encyclopedia Britannica, grand-like on the top three rows. Just below those was an English history section. I glanced along it at titles like: *A History of The English Speaking People,* by Churchill and *Henry Livingston.* Oddly a biography of Lord Bayden-Powell was literally surrounded by dozens of Dandy and Beano comics, as if it'd been stuffed in the wrong place. Then I saw a book called *Decline of the West* by a geezer called Oswald Spengler. Who the hell was he when he was at home? Below that were typical reading like *Boy's Own*, *The Famous Five*, Enid Blyton volumes, *Swallows and Amazons* and other such books. There was a whole section on World War Two. Stuffed in between these books were stacks of 45s and many LP's: Martha and the Vandellas, Marvin Gaye, Sam Cooke, The Ronettes, Patti Drew, The Dells, Tommy Edwards, Tami Lynn, Chuck Jackson, Mary Wells, it went on. Who was this lad of mine?

I heard him groan and turned to see him shivering, doubled

up and pulling the blankets to his stomach. Panicked, I started to look for the lithium pills but couldn't find them. I went into my bedroom where Brenda was throwing on a nightgown. She brushed by me and I could hear the pills rattle as she took them out.

✳

I put the kettle on. The card of the clinic Bill recommended was by the drinks table, so I went to the phone. I called and it rang a good while before I put it down. I knew I had to get him in, pronto. We couldn't go through another night like that.

I lit up and stared out the window. The sky was a deep grey with lower lighter clouds rolling by. The lawn was blanketed with frost, typical weather for the wrong side of November.

I thought of last night's phone call from Danny. How he'd dropped Macker at the infirmary as instructed; how he was quiet all the way there, just sat with the towel fast to his face, saying nothing. His blood had soaked through and all down him. By the time they'd arrived he was almost unconscious. A frantic call brought the gurney running.

I thought of Bill, what his next move would be. Since eight grand of his had been flushed into the Irwell he'd have to do something. I wasn't worried about Neil rabbiting on to his mother, though - no matter how grieved he was with me. If he was anything he wasn't a grass. He wanted too much to be a part of it all, be one of the lads.

The kettle whistled madly and I poured. I got the cups, sugar and milk ready. Brenda came down and went into the front room.

'What are you doing?' I said.

I heard her rummaging in the cabinet. Then she came back through holding some 45s up.

'Taking requests.'

'He's got dozens up there.'

'He wants something specific.'

I watched her go and listened to her climb the stairs. Then I heard a record: 'The Sweetest Feeling' Jackie Wilson. This is what we were like with him. Everything he wanted he got. And we wondered why he was like this. She came down again and sat at the kitchen table. A couple of falling leaves danced by the window. I poured her a cup of tea.

'You look shattered,' I said. 'Are you going to be up there playing records all day? Can't you get your Nola over to help out?'

She nodded. 'Thank God for sisters. We were never close before all this but by heck, I owe that woman.'

She reached for my cigs and I lit her up. It occurred to me that she was smoking most of my cigarettes. When she smoked they was usually menthol. Now it was Senior Service, no filter. We sat for a bit just looking outside. A cheeky ray of sunshine snuck through the cloud and hit the quartz kitchen top.

'I want to go private,' I said. 'With the NHS they pump him full of vitamins and have him in the gym. Then he's out three months later, two-stone heavier but back to where he was. He needs proper professional help, counseling that'll keep him off it.'

'You, counseling?'

'I'm not talking about O'Connell or the bloody Samaritans. There's a place in South Manchester, Altrincham Treatment Centre. I know some who've used it.'

I left out the bit about Bill and his boozy wife.

She thought for a minute. 'If we can afford it, why not?'

I drank some tea. I wasn't expecting such an easy victory but tried not to show relief. Then as an afterthought, she said:

'But won't they need notice? I mean, you can't just show up last minute, can you?'

I got up and went to the phone again. It rang just as I got to it. I paused before picking it up, expecting Mary or Danny, or maybe even Bill. It was Corey.

'Can we talk?' he said.

I tried not to look at Brenda. 'Not a good time.'

'It never is.' His teeth clinked against a glass.

'There's nowt to say, mate,' I said.

There was a pause. I could hear him thinking. 'Sorry about last night... That was out of order.'

'It's fine,' I said. It wasn't but I said it anyway.

'Can we meet?'

'No.'

More thinking. There was the clink again. 'You can't put me off for forever, Jackie.'

'I have stuff to do,' I said.

'Will you be at The Antelope this afternoon?'

'Highly unlikely.' I put it down. Ignoring a look from Brenda, I refilled my cup and put in some bread for toast.

'That was Corey?' she said.

I decided to give her something. I knew she'd only push things if I didn't. I also knew Corey would open his grid at some point if he didn't get his way, so I thought it best to pre-empt him. I needed to control the story.

'He wants a souvenir from the war,' I said.

'What souvenir?'

'A German soldier's ID. It's called a dog tag.'

'A dead one?'

'We'd have a rum time getting it off a live one, love.'

'Dear God,' she said. 'A dead man?'

'There were plenty of those around, Brenda.' I could feel her examining me. 'It was just some 'at you did. We all brought back stuff from the war.'

I nearly told her of the guns and ammo and other booty we carted back. How the customs officer wanted to root through my bag and those of my platoon, and how I was having none of it, sticking a Colt .45 under his chin, threatening to blow his head off and meaning it. But I figured that might aggravate things. The toast popped up.

'I've never seen this necklace thingy,' she said.

'I stashed it at me mother's before I even met you, '47, '48, some 'at like that.'

'And why does he want it, this dog tag thing?'

'He gave it to me years ago in Germany,' I said, buttering the toast. 'Now he wants it back, it's not important, is it?'

'It sounds like it is to him.'

'He's here tending to his dying mam and he needs some 'at else to do, like mithering me.'

I didn't tell her about the German War Graves Commission that he was determined to return the thing to. And I left out the soldier's pay book he wanted back from Bill. It would only lead to more questions and I didn't need the agro.

'Well, sort him out,' she said, taking some toast. 'It's not like we don't have enough on our plates.'

I poured her another cup of tea. She nibbled the crust on

the toast. We could hear kids playing over in the next garden, squealing with delight.

'I was just looking at him,' she said. 'He just gets younger and younger. I keep seeing… a little boy.' She was dreamy, looking out of the window at the sky scudding by. The toast was dangling between her thumb and forefinger. 'I ask God why this is happening. At first I thought it was us, the way we lived, getting everything for nothing. But we're not bad people. When I look at some in this town, we live like saints.' She put the toast down and looked at me. 'I know you're no angel, Jackie, but you do your bit. You have your Legion work, the football club, the charities. It all balances out. Or at least it's something. And I know you're a good man. So, the punishment doesn't fit the crime. And I wrack me brains to look for what *I've* done to offend Him so much that we have to suffer this.'

'Not everything happens for a reason, Brenda.' I exhaled and put my cig out.

'It has to. There's always a reason.'

'Some are just unlucky. I've seen good men die horrible deaths. There's no rhyme or reason.'

'I can't believe that. Father O' Connell says it's a test of my faith. And it's the same for you. And some day we'll be there, all three of us praying together. I know it will happen.'

I got up and put more water in the kettle and bunged another teabag in the pot. I could feel her on me.

'But it has to be something else,' she said, 'some other reason.' Her cig had burned down to the end. She put it out and lit another, then looked at the cig for a minute. 'I don't expect you to tell me everything, especially if you -'

'I haven't done anything, Brenda.'

'It doesn't matter. What matters is to confess it.'

'Oh, come on, girl.' I looked out of the window.

'You've done it before, Jackie. You did it for years, he told me you did - confessed to Father O' Connell.'

'Not everything gets fixed with a few Hail Mary's and Our Father's.'

'But it's a start, isn't it.' She got up. 'These things go out to Him - to Our Lord and He listens. He listens and helps us.' She came round to me. 'We could go today to church while Nola's here. Or the Father could come over here, later on.'

I stared at the kettle, willing it to boil. She stepped closer.

'I know there's something worrying you. You don't spend the time I've spent with you -'

'Brenda, please.'

'It's win, win,' she said, touching my shoulder. 'You help yourself, you help us all'

'For God's sake.'

'I can't lose him, Jackie. Not after all the work I've put into this boy, all the praying I've done.' I could see her chest heaving and she was seconds away from losing it. Then both hands went to my chest and she just let herself go. 'I can't lose him, I can't. Help me.'

'There, there, girl - come on, now.'

I put my arms around her and she sobbed a bit, burying her face into me. Then she recovered and pulled back. The phone went. We let it ring. Then she picked it up.

'Hello?' She looked at me. 'Hiya, Mary... Fine, love fine... He's doing all right, all things considered... It was a bit of a rough night but I think he'll come along. We have plans as well, so... Oh, a place in South Manchester Jackie knows of.

That's the plan anyway... Yes, he's right here.' She handed me the phone. 'It's Mary.'

'Hiya.'

'We need to meet, Jackie.'

'When?'

'Now. This morning.'

'Can't it wait? We've got a lot on here.'

'And I haven't? We need to talk and sharpish.' I heard her inhale. 'It's started.'

'What has?'

'I'll tell you when I see you.'

I looked at Brenda. She gestured in the weary way she always did: 'Just go, go.'

'Where? Not here.'

'I've talked to Danny. We can meet at his place. It's half way between us. Can you be there at ten?'

I stifled a breath of frustration. 'Fair enough. I'll see you then.' I put the phone down. 'I have to go.'

She was looking out of the window. I could hear the song upstairs faintly.

'Honey, the sweetest, sweetest feeling... loving you...'

I went to get ready.

Brenda was always good about not asking what went on with the business and me. It was our rule and she stuck to it for years. But Neil's problems and her religious lark were making short work of that rule. I'd kept her at bay this time, but I knew there'd be interrogations worthy of the Gestapo coming down the line. Before leaving I called the Altrincham Treatment Centre again. There was no answer. Again. Brenda appeared in the hall as I was putting on my coat and hat.

'Damage control, love…' I said. 'Last night.'

'I never doubted some bugger would be out of sorts.' She was back to her old self. 'Leave us some cigs, will you?'

I did. Then I left. In my pocket I had six copies of Macker's taped confession I'd made the night before.

✳

I was soon at Danny's council house in Pendleton. It was a typical sixties effort. A slum clearance of fine, sturdy old buildings had given birth to these things. Danny had been shifted from Moss Side with his mam who had died some years back and he became heir to this horror. The neighbour next door had a car up on blocks and an oil drum sat there. There were piles of junk everywhere. The lawns were fenceless and gateless; giving the impression that the neighbour's filth was also your filth. The council would've been proud.

A couple of ragged kids chased a tennis ball across Danny's lawn and onto their own. Then they disappeared down the ginnel between the houses like ferrets down a hole. Mary's Jeep wasn't there. Instead Theo's Escort sat by the curb.

I rang the doorbell. It was a novelty Christmas tune, 'Ding Dong Merrily on High.' Danny opened the door in a string vest, a cig hanging from his mouth. His skin was pasty and hadn't seen sun in a dog's age. As a result his tattoos - dragons, hearts, women and insignia from his regiment, stood out against the whiteness. A Union Jack, with colours as bright as the day he'd had it done, covered half his shoulder.

'Hiya, guv. Come on Tiddles.' The cat patted on ahead of me, her tail high and curling to and fro at the top.

There were no carpets on the floor, just pale green lino.

The walls were covered in brown and beige dotted wallpaper, bachelor living and then some. This was why I rarely came over; every time I did I gave him a raise. I followed him into the kitchen where Mary sat drinking tea and smoking.

'You want a cuppa, guv?' Danny said.

'No, I'm cuppered out, ta.' I nodded to Mary. 'Hiya.' I sat down. 'What's that smell?'

'Coal tar lamp over yon,' Danny said. 'Me chest is shocking today.'

I knew the contraption. My mother had used one for us when we sick. A nice memory flitted by and vanished. Danny sucked on his inhaler.

'Cutting it down to twenty a day might help,' I said.

'I've told him, he won't listen,' Mary said, looking like she'd hardly slept.

The radio was playing Leo Sawyer. 'You Make Me Feel Like Dancing.' Danny turned it down to a tolerable level, which should've been off.

'So, let's hear it,' I said, lighting up.

Mary leaned forward, elbows on the table. 'I'm woken up at five this morning by an explosion. I look out the window and the Jeep's gone up. I see three fellers in balaclavas legging it to a waiting car.' She looked at us, waiting for our reaction. 'They've come all the way down to my gaff. There's not three bloody hours in a day - not three hours when it's not like Oxford Street on a Friday night down there, and they've come down, spending time and risk - to torch my bastard vehicle.'

'And you're thinking it's about last night?'

'Well, it's not the Internal Revenue, love. I heard the name Joey just before they all piled into the motor. Joey, that's one of Macker's lads. She looked to Danny. 'Right?' She didn't wait for a reply. 'He doesn't waste any time does he, Macker? He must've been putting this caper together as they were stitching him up. He'd have been on the phone to Joey at three in the bloody morning. Unbelievable. That's not just taking a liberty, that. That's... that's...' She shook her head and put her cig out. 'There's not many in this game that give me the creeps, but that Macker...'

'I know,' said Danny leaning forward, his forearms on his knees. 'I saw it for the first time last night. The way he went on.'

'He's not a full shilling that lad or I'm Diana Dors. I'm telling you, you see some rum bastards in this game, but he's a true psychopath that one. If I never move from here, he is. I've suspected it for years but last night... last night convinced me.'

'And now this,' said Danny.

'Well, this is it.' She turned to me. 'I wasn't thrilled with what went down last night, Jackie, you know I wasn't, but you was well within your rights, given what he's been up to. I'm surprised it wasn't worse. But for him to come back with revenge - in hours. He should be swallowing what we did to him and be grateful we didn't take a thumb.'

'You've had no trouble here?' I said to Danny.

'Quiet as the grave,' he said.

'Well, it's just a matter of time, isn't it?' Mary said. 'I've told him to carry something, watch his back.'

A few seconds limped by as we smoked. I considered going back home but I couldn't believe Macker would break the cardinal rule and have a go at my family. We'd had him at our dinner table and Brenda had sent him home with food packages.

A ball suddenly hit the window and it startled us. Danny

got up, went to the window and opened it.

'If that happens again you little gets I'll give you a thick ear. Piss off to the playing fields and behave proper.'

'Me dad will have you, you fat twat.'

'Just let him try.' He picked up an air pistol and fired it. We could hear the kids laughing and running away. Danny closed the window. 'Sorry about that. Bloody savages.'

'What's Theo doing?' I said to Mary.

'Don't worry, I pulled him up. He wanted to sort this Joey out, but I don't want this spinning out of control.' She supped some tea. 'We need to talk to Bill. Work some 'at out.'

'Like what?'

'I don't know, some kind of a compromise.' She leveled her eyes on me.

'Jesus tonight,' I said. 'Maybe I should pay the bastard back.'

'Well…' She must've seen my jaw drop so she went on. 'Eh, listen - not in cash, in trade. Bung him a car, some 'at to shut him up.'

'I can't believe I'm hearing this.'

'You got what you wanted, Jackie - you sent a message. Let's all move on.'

'I want Macker out of this town, that's what I want.'

'Then throw that into the pot, but let's have a confab.'

'And offer him a couple of cars for compensation?' They just looked at me. 'Why don't I reshingle the bastard's roof while I'm at it.' The cat was rubbing herself against my legs.

'You know what we're saying,' Mary said.

'I do and it's mad.' I turned to Danny. 'Is this you as well, this? Danny?'

'Guv, I flushed eight grand of Bill's drugs into the Irwell last

90

night.' He started to fidget and flick his cig with his middle finger. 'That's wholesale. That's forty thousand quid when it's flogged off in bits. I was working it out.'

'You were working it out.'

'Well, I was. Puts things in perspective, doesn't it. I'm not saying we shouldn't have done it, but it's different for you. No, no listen. You know as well as I do Bill might well give you a pass. But his pride won't let this go. So chances are it's us two who'll cop it.'

'I won't let that happen, you know I won't let that happen.'

'You couldn't stop last night, Jackie,' said Mary.

I said nothing. The cat jumped up into my lap. She just stared up at me.

'Jackie, what *you* do, *we* do,' Danny said. 'It's the way it works, you know it is.'

I looked at them both. 'How long have you two been talking about this?'

'Just now,' said Mary.

Another fib. They'd been pondering this for a while. My back was getting up so I said: 'Look, I know this is about Neil.'

They both sighed and shifted in their chairs.

'No, I know it is.' I tried to stay calm. 'Look, I know there's been ructions. It's been a barmy year, I know. But there's bigger stuff here. It's bigger than our Neil.' They just looked through me or away. The cat started kneading my waistcoat. I lifted her, got up and paced a bit. She wriggled off and patted to the floor. 'Alright, I've been a bit of a wild card but I've held up my end.' I turned to Mary. 'Haven't I done right by your Jez? He's still got Alan Boyle looking out for him, come hell or high water. So, don't say I haven't done my bit as well.' I had. Mary's son was safe as houses while he was in the nick and Mary knew it.

'We're just scared of this spinning out of control, guv,' Danny said.

'Last night, Jackie, you lost your rag,' Mary said. 'You let him get to you. I've seen this coming for months - years - and it could've been much worse. And that's the problem with this whole thing. It's too personal. We don't know what might happen.'

'You make me sound like I'm losing it.' I looked for some reaction, some flexibility, but they were stony faced. I stewed for a few seconds about this proposed meeting. I looked out of the kitchen window. 'All right, all right,' I said. 'I will talk to Bill Shaw *if* Macker is on a train by the end of tomorrow. Monday night. If he promises to make that happen I might consider bunging him a package deal to Llandudno. That would be generous as well as ridiculous, but I'll do it if it keeps you two happy.'

So, I relented but with strings attached. If there was any confab it had to be my gaff. I'd already been to Bill's place so he could show me a similar courtesy. I also thought his pride wouldn't let it happen. So we'd all be saved the embarrassment.

Danny agreed to set it up. Then he had a coughing fit. It was so bad he had to lean over the sink, as if going to be sick. Then he had to use his inhaler four times. I glanced at Mary and she shrugged. I looked outside again. The view from Pendleton hill showed Broughton and Salford in all its glory; cold, remote.

✳

I was on was my way to my car pitch. The rain was on again and the wiper needed changing. It was a long drive to Altrincham and I couldn't be doing with the racket. I threw on one of Neil's compilations and The Miracles came on with 'Going to a Go-Go.'

I'd left two copies of Macker's confession with Danny and Mary. I gave instructions to make copies and dole them out to those thinking I was out of order. They'd been stony-faced, having little faith it would make a difference. I knew some would take the piss. I didn't need to go to such lengths for approval on anything. If I felt aggrieved, I acted and folk could deal with it, end of. But the tape was just added insurance. Mary and Danny thought it was wheedling away at my street cred, more proof that I was losing it.

I'd promised a new Jeep to Mary but there was still resentment. It was their loss of faith that was really nagging me.

I arrived at the lot and got a dog treat from the glove box. I knew something was wrong immediately. Rodney was usually going mental by now, barking and wriggling at the gate. I opened up and looked into his doghouse. He was dead. He was lying on his side and there was sick near his mouth and foam round his gums. There was a piece of meat, half eaten, lying close by. He'd been poisoned.

I went straight into the office and called Brenda. Everything was all right. Mary had just shown up. This surprised me.

'Mary?' I said. 'What she want?'

'She brought some Lucozade for Neil.'

'Don't let her smoke that crap in my house. I was just checking in. I'm off to the clinic now.'

'You're not gone yet?'

'It's complicated… nowt to worry about. I'll see you at tea time.'

I put the phone down. Knowing Mary was at my house was some comfort, but I suspected other reasons beside the Lucozade.

I went back outside. I got a piece of tarpaulin and pulled Rodney onto it by his tail. I pulled him to the back and put some bricks on him. Then I went into the office and phoned Jimmy Mac. I told him about the dog and to bring a shovel on Monday. I fumed a bit as I reckoned this'd been done in the early hours, after the incident down at Mary's.

I went to the parts rack, found a wiper for the car, and went outside. Bill's Mercedes pulled up in front of the Ford. Ray, Didds and Bill all got out and inspected the Cortina. I stood there watching them.

'I hope your stock's in better nick than this demmick,' said Bill. 'It's a bloody disgrace, this. You're giving us all a bad name, man.'

I looked up and down the street for traffic.

'There'll be no agro, Dunne,' said Bill. 'I'll keep my head. One of us has to.'

I knew right away it wasn't Bill who'd killed Rodney. Macker was working behind his bosses back, I could see that now.

Bill buttoned up his sheepskin and got out his flask. 'We're supposed to have a confab tonight at your gaff. Is that right?'

'Are we?' I said.

'Why, has that great lummox Danny Simms dropped another bollock?' he said, taking a nip. 'I'm glad I stopped by.'

'Danny called Wally at The Shamrock,' said Ray, stepping forward. 'You want to see us at your boozer. Nine o' clock, or are we mistaken?'

I said nothing.

'Stop pissing about Dunne,' said Bill. 'There's no pride lost in apologising, making amends.'

'Amends?' I shook my head.

'You did a right job on that lad,' Bill said. He put away the flask, lit a cig. 'Just been to the infirmary. Thirty-eight stitches. I haven't seen that from you in years.'

'He's been warned umpteen times.'

'He was going by the club, nothing more.'

'He's lying.'

'The Peelers were following him. He ditched the car to look like a punter.'

'He told me he was waiting for his bird. Tell him to get his stories straight.'

Bill blew smoke out. 'Why would he go there when he had a drop to do, tell me that, Dunne? It was a big night, important folk. You've made me look a right cunt, you have.'

'Here, listen to this. In Macker's own words.' I pulled out a padded envelope and tossed the tape to him. It dropped at his feet.

'A confession, is it?' he said, looking down at it. 'He told me about this… said Mary threatened to cut his fingers off.'

'I thought he'd say that. Are you going to pick that up? I'm not talking to anyone unless you take that with you.'

Bill signaled to Didds and the big feller picked it up. Bill sneered at me.

'What the hell is this, the bleeding Old Bailey?'

'I want Mary and Danny square,' I said. 'What happened was my doing, so sort it with me.'

'You're in a rum position to make demands, you.'

'Macker's already throwing his weight around. Did you know

about that?'

Bills eyes narrowed. 'What's he been doing?'

'He's got that Joey kid running around down at the crescents. And Rodney's been killed… poisoned.'

'The dog?' He looked at Ray and Didds. They all looked at one another. 'He wouldn't. He loved that dog.'

'Then who the hell did it, Soft Ned?'

'The dog, eh?' All three of them craned their necks to see.

'I buried him. You want to watch Macker. He's playing dirty hands behind your back.'

'Eight grand wholesale, forty on the street,' Bill said, throwing his cig down. 'You owe me. That's the bottom line to all this.'

'You might get it back in some 'at, but there'll be nowt unless Macker goes.'

'And I give up a million over the next few years?' He snorted. 'I'll have to think about that one.' He leaned on that with great irony. 'Nine o' clock at your gaff - have your cheque book ready.'

They got in the Mercedes and drove off. I went back into the office. I called Danny and all was well with him. I told him about the dog. He was mortified.

'Jesus,' he'd said. 'I'll never be able to watch Rodney Marsh play again. I'm so sorry, guv. Bloody savages.'

'So, we have this meeting at the pub tonight. Nine o' clock, eh?'

'How do you know?'

I told him of Bill's little visit, the talk of Macker etcetera. I didn't tell him I was going to the infirmary.

'I'll see you at The Antelope around one,' I said. 'Get some ale in if it looks like I'm late.'

I hung up and got down behind my desk. I pulled back some of the carpet to reveal a small compartment. I popped the lid and pulled out a German army-issue dagger. I replaced the lid, the carpet, and put the dagger in my overcoat pocket.

✳

I drove over to the infirmary. Mary had a point when she said I'd lost my rag. I'd let Macker get to me. It was the taunting, saying Neil had been begging, begging for his life. The very idea made me ill. I'd seen men and boys begging for their lives, I'd seen it plenty and it was the stuff of nightmares. In the car park I found Macker's Capri and parked close to it.

I arrived at the ward. I looked in the long room through the glass partition but I couldn't see him. Then I saw that curtains had been drawn round one bed, so I walked down and had a decko. Macker had his back to me and was pulling on his trousers.

I slid in. He turned, saw me and nearly fainted. I shoved him on the bed and leaned over him. Now I could see his face. He was bandaged up in great swirls of grandeur. It came across one side of his face and under his chin, then it whipped around his crown and across his forehead and round the back of his head. He looked like he'd been in the battle for Berlin.

'Hold your horses,' I said. 'I'm talking, that's it.'

He was wearing a hospital gown and I could see his bare arms. They were riddled with track lines from injecting speed. On the inside of his right bicep there was a blood-type tattoo, the kind the SS used to have. It said 0 +. On his forearm he had a tattoo of the SS Death's Head. Charming.

'I know you tried it on down at Mary's,' I said. 'And I know you had Rodney killed.'

'I don't know what you -'

'Shut it,' I said, putting the knife to his throat. 'I should cripple you right now. But what good would it do here, where they could fix you back up in no time? But I could *kill* you, couldn't I.' He turned his head away from me so I pulled it back, grabbing the stitched side. He grimaced. I leaned in and whispered. 'I've just seen Bill. If he digs his heels in about you going you'll leave anyway. You'll pack your things today and you'll be gone by tomorrow night. If you don't leave - if you don't - then I'll do what I need to do. And if you think Bill can stop it you've another think coming. As God is my witness, you will be sorted good and proper... and forever.'

He looked at me for some seconds. 'Will you do it? Will you sort me?'

There was no irony or challenge in the lad's tone. I suddenly had a chilling thought he wanted me to do it, to actually kill him.

'No, I wouldn't,' I said. 'I wouldn't soil my hands. We'd get someone and it'd be up to them how they did it. And I know some nutters, believe you me, I do. Some cellar men who like to take their time, get the ale in, order some take-away, bring their fucking toothbrush. I don't think you'd want that, would you? ... As soon as you get out of here, pack your bags and fuck off... by tomorrow night. Is that crystal? I said, is that crystal?'

He nodded and I put the knife away. I left, pulling back the curtains and nearly bumping into a nice-looking nurse.

'Sorry, love.' I walked on.

'Excuse me, sir. Excuse me.' I heard the curtains squeak.

'Mackenzie? Are you all right?'

I went back to my car, popped the boot and rummaged for the tire iron. I went over to the Capri and smashed in the windscreen. Then I smashed the side windows. Then I did the headlights and rear lights. I took my dagger and did the tires. It did occur to me, as I obliterated the first window, that I was destroying the lad's only means of escape. But then I thought, bugger it; he can take a train like the rest of the population. Yes, the little bastard can take a train.

I was on my way back to the Cortina when a Vauxhall Viva screeched to a stop beside me. Two blokes I'd never seen before bailed out carrying Rounder's bats. Who the hell were these buggers? I couldn't leg it back to the hospital, they'd have me before I got ten yards. They started towards me so I yanked out the dagger and squared off. I had the iron in my left hand and the blade in my right.

'Are you sure you want to do this, fellers?'

They puffed themselves up and were soon circling like hyenas. We feinted and dodged for some seconds before they both came at me. I veered, letting them overextend and nearly collide. I cracked one with the iron across his forearm, leaving him yelling like buggery and dropping the bat. I spun and slashed the other across his mush with the dagger, and kicked his mate under the chin as he was retrieving the bat. I felt the bat from the mush feller slam into my shoulder and I lost my rag. I dropped the iron, spun and grabbed the mush's arm, twisting it and kicking him in the gonads. Then I slammed the hilt of the dagger into his solar plexus. He was done. I yanked him round as the other one was coming back at me, colliding them together. This tatty clump I now rammed into the back of a parked car, where I nutted the mush and kicked his cods again. He crumpled and crawled off to be sick. I had his mate by the throat and stuck the dagger under his chin. He dropped his bat and started yammering.

'No, no, it's all right, don't, don't.' He had a Scouse accent.

'Who are you with?' I said. 'Tell me or I'll cut you.'

'I don't know what you mean.'

I stuck the dagger up his nostril and pulled back. A half-inch flap appeared with blood and all and he howled like a banshee.

'Jesus, tonight, no, no.'

I put the dagger back to his throat. 'I'll take out your gizzard next. Now, who are you with?'

'Macker,' he said. 'Mac Collier.'

'Are you the one's he did time with?' I said. 'Don't fucking lie to me.'

'Yeah... yeah, that's us. Sorry mate - we made a mistake, it won't happen again.'

'Were you down at the crescents this morning?'

'Eh?'

'Were you down at the crescents? Hulme crescents?'

He looked at me all puzzled. 'I don't know what you mean.'

'What about a used car pitch over Cheetham Hill way?'

'No, no, you got the wrong men. I don't know these places. That's the truth, guv.'

I knew he wasn't joshing me. I shoved him off and he scrambled after his mate.

'Handy you're next to the hospital.' I picked up the iron and headed to the Ford. I got in, wiped the knife on my hanky, and stuck it under the passenger car seat. I started her up and watched those bloody amateurs hobble off to emergency.

I didn't hang about but scarpered as soon as I could. I parked the car in Whalley Range and took a nip of whisky. I lit up and sat until the adrenalin had leveled out and wiped away the blood on my cheek. I was getting too old for this. I rummaged in the glove box and through my stash. I pulled out a couple of diazepam and necked them.

As I drove, I thought about these men. They were the Liverpool crew Macker had done time with in Walton and were his drug connection. Macker, we found out, used to go down to Liverpool to pick up the smack. So what were these fellers doing here?

I got on The Princess Parkway and whipped down to the M56. Being on the motorway after weeks of ferreting around Salford was like a breath of fresh air. Small pleasures. I could see the lay of the land, rural South Manchester to the left and right of me. The clouded sky emphasized the winter green of the embankments.

Despite the Valium the pain in my shoulder was nagging. The dust up had cost me. So I threw on one of Neil's compilations. I got 'SOS' by Edwin Starr, 'What Does It Take' by Junior Walker, 'Hold Back the Night' by The Trammps and 'Your Love Keeps Lifting Me Higher' by Jackie Wilson.

I soon got tired of the newer stuff and bunged on a real oldie. 'In the Mood' by Glen Miller. Music always took me away, no matter what it was. And I often found it fitted the mood or reflected what was happening at the time. It was funny that way, music. It was like a parallel universe was operating, watching us and throwing its oar in from time to time - to frustrate or fancy us.

I got off the motorway and made my way through the fluffy lanes of Altrincham. I entered an upscale neighbourhood dotted with large '20s and '30s detached homes. I soon pulled up outside a mansion; mock Gothic, I believe is the style. The place looked like it once belonged to some important toff. Apart from a few ugly fire escapes, it still had most of its former glory. It was surrounded by manicured lawns and fenced grounds all polished to perfection, a Garden of bloody Eden. Chesnutt trees and rhododendron bushes dotted the area. The leaves on the trees had long started to drop, but they had been piled into small heaps, and gardeners were corralling them into bags. It looked like it was going to cost me a bomb.

I sat in my car looking at it all. The place looked grand enough, but June Shaw's endless visits were no vote of confidence. Her relapses were legend about town. She was a poster child for addicts. Booze, gambling and sex were all her specialty. She was a real handful and even when things had soured between Bill and me, I still felt sorry for the bastard, all this on account of his wayward wife.

I drove up a winding path and parked the car on a gravel roundabout. I got out and entered through the large oak door, one side open. A hall led to a large, vaulted room. I felt like a tradesman entering on the wrong side of the building. A middle-aged secretary, with a bouffant hair-do lacquered to a helmet, looked up from her paperwork.

'Yes, can I help you?' she said, looking completely disgusted by my presence.

'Hiya. Is there someone I can talk to about my son?'

She looked at me over cat's eye glasses like I was a maggot.

'Is he a patient?' She was putting on a stockbroker-belt drawl, but I could hear a Wythenshawe council estate a mile away.

'No, not yet,' I said. 'Soon to be. I did call today but there was no answer. It really is quite an emergency, love – miss - ma'am.'

'Sorry, but we don't take appointments on Sunday, I'm afraid.' She forced a smile that sent cracks through caked-on pancake.

It went downhill from there. In brief, I pleaded, cajoled, insulted then back peddled. I finished by bribing her with a tenner, which I floated onto her desk. That had the desired effect and after snatching it up, she made an internal call to a doctor and told me to wait down the hall.

The waiting room was a small paneled room with pictures of important looking folk on the wall. I sat and lit up. A couple of what looked like clients walked by. Suddenly I saw June Shaw, Bill's wife. She sauntered by, glancing in my direction. She was wearing a tracksuit and her hair had been dyed a different colour. She moved on, not wanting to say anything. I got up and looked down the hall. She was walking on.

'Excuse me, sir. Are you the gentleman Deirdre told me of?'

I turned and there was feller in his early forties. He was blond, tanned and looked like a Beach Boy. He wore a white doctors coat over a Ben Sherman shirt and flared slacks with a wide waistband. His shoes were suede and he sounded like a yank.

'That's me,' I said.

'Dr. Leigh,' he said, clasping his hands in front of him. 'Jonathan Leigh. I'm the owner. What can I do for you?'

'Jackie Dunne,' I said, offering my hand. He hesitated

and then complied. I figured old Witchy Poo up front had mentioned my temper. 'It's about my son. He's a drug addict, that's the long and short of it.'

He looked at me and slowly nodded. I went on, rabbiting like a shop girl.

'We've tried the NHS, the hospitals a couple of times. They do a good job, don't get me wrong, they clean him up, make him well - but a few months later he's back on.'

'I see. Well, I'm sure we can accommodate you, Mr. Dunne, but we won't have any vacancies for at least week.'

'A week?' I felt sick. 'Jesus, I'm desperate here. *We're* desperate. Can't you check for any cancellations?'

'I don't need to check, Mr. Dunne. I know all my patients. We only have ten people here at a time.'

'I have money, doctor, plenty of money. I don't mind paying, I don't.' I pulled out my roll and it fell onto the rug. I bent down to pick it up and my hat fell off. I picked that up, put the roll in my jacket pocket, but when I brought my hand out my fags came with it and they fell on the floor. I picked them up. 'Jesus H...' I finally stood up. I could see him looking at me like I was a mad. 'What?' I said.

'Mr. Dunne, we have no room, sir.'

I was looking like a prize twat. Then I got ratty. 'All right, fine. No room at the bloody inn. Let the little bugger suffer. Sorry I mithered you, mate. Half a bleeding day wasted, but fine.'

'Mr. Dunne. I understand how you must feel -'

'Sorry doc, I didn't mean... Look, I'll be honest with you, mate, I'm losing the plot here. I've been through detox with him at home and it's bleeding awful. I just thought... anyway, forget it. I'll take him to Hope Hospital and the little get can deal with it. End of.'

'Jackie...'

I turned and there was June Shaw, smoking one of her dark cigs. She spoke to the Beach Boy.

'He can have my space, doctor. I can leave early.'

We both looked at her.

'I'm not sure that's wise, June,' said The Beach Boy.

'Jonathan, I've been here for nearly six weeks. I'll be fine. You'll be seeing me again in three months anyway...'

Oops. The good doctor shuffled in embarrassment but June kept on him.

'Honestly, let the lad have my place. I'll start packing.'

'Just hold on a second, June.'

'Doctor, I'm fine. Let him have it. I want him to.'

We both looked at him. Obviously miffed at this sudden turn of events, he sighed.

'Well, I'll need to check with Deirdre to make sure there's no one else on the waiting list. But I can't make any guarantees, Mr. Dunne. I'll need to do an assessment of his case before taking him on.'

He went through to the reception. I turned to June.

'I think we owe you that one,' she said.

A few awkward seconds hobbled by.

'I don't like what he's doing... my Bill,' she said. 'I see folks in here struggling with it. It's an evil drug, heroin. I never thought I'd say this but I hate him sometimes.'

'I don't know what to do, June. Things are getting bad between us.'

'Don't I know it. Well, we'll start with getting Neil sorted.'

She smoked. 'I'll do my bit with Bill, I'll keep on him, but I've tried before and it's like talking to a brick wall. I'm no help, with the debts I run up. I know what I am. But it's still no excuse for this....'

I looked about the room. It was like something from a BBC Murder Mystery. It was hard to believe it was full of smack heads.

'So, there's a lot of heroin addicts in this place?' I said.

'We're sworn to secrecy but between you and me it's a lot more common than you think.'

I didn't need to hear this. 'There can't be that many addicts in Greater Manchester, can there?'

'You'd be surprised. It's new here, yeah, but it's growing.' She saw the look on my face. 'Oh aye, in the past it was family doctors that treated addicts. Yeah, wrote them prescriptions and everything.'

'Gave smack on prescription?'

'Not six years ago. '71 was the last year, I think. And most of these addicts weren't deadlegs. Just folk with chronic pain; doctors, dentists, anesthetists, you name it; you'd be surprised, Jackie.'

'Bloody hell.'

'Yeah. But then the government outlawed it. Some Dangerous Drug Act or some 'at. So addicts couldn't get it legally anymore. So, they got it illegally.'

'Robbing chemists.'

She nodded. 'Then dealers started popping up. That Macker swine and sadly... my Bill.' She scrunched her cig out in the sand ashtray. 'It'll all end in tears; I just know it. And I can't apologise enough for him.'

106

The Beach Boy was coming back.

'Give my best to Brenda. I do miss her.'

'Aye. I'll do that.'

The doctor arrived. 'Can you come this way, Mr. Dunne?'

June nodded to us and walked off. It was strange meeting her like this. What a bloody fishbowl we all lived in. Trouble was there was no getting away from one another when things went sour.

✳

I was led down a paneled passageway and ended in a large room, a doctor's study. It smelled of leather and old wood. The odor of expensive cologne was not far behind – definitely not coming from the skeleton hanging in the corner. I was invited to sit in a fat chair in front of his monster of a desk. He sat and took out a notebook, flipping a page. He clicked open a pen. I felt like a kid about to take an exam.

'Now, Mr. Dunne. How long has your son been using heroin?'

'About a year,' I said. 'Before that it was speed, barbiturates. He was injecting those as well.'

'And he's had what…? Two hospitalizations?'

'Three. A couple with the barbs and speed and one with the heroin.'

He took down some notes. Then he looked up, tapping the pen slowly against his thumb.

'Well, we do like to supervise the detoxification process. And after a period of rest the psychological assessment can begin and a treatment plan worked out.'

'I'm sold on all that,' I said. 'And you actually have drug

addicts in here that you help?'

'Most of our clients have issues with alcohol. But the twelve-step program associated with alcoholics has also been very successful with drug addicts. Are you familiar with that program?'

'Well, not myself but I do know some pissheads - drunks – *alcoholics*, sorry. And I've seen it work,' I lied.

He leveled on me. 'I'd like to ask a couple of questions about Neil.' He positioned his notebook and poised his pen.

I was getting nervous that whatever this grilling was, I wouldn't measure up or meet the bleeding criteria. 'Righto,' I said.

'There are many reasons for the addiction. We need to identify some possibilities. Do you have any ideas why your son may have… fallen into this behaviour?'

'Well, it's the lifestyle, isn't it?'

'His lifestyle?'

'It's these all-nighters they go on. They want to stay awake so they take speed; slimming pills, really, that's all they are. Keeps them dancing for hours. Then it's the barbs, barbiturates to bring them down so they sleep. It's a vicious cycle. The heroin just got in under the radar. Looking for new highs and whatnot.'

'And the relapses,' he said. 'Has there been anything in particular that has brought them on? Has there been a bereavement -?'

'No, no nothing like that.'

'A failure? Exams?'

'Nope.'

'Failed business ventures?'

I stalled a bit.

'Has there been anything like that, Mr. Dunne?'

'Well, no not really.'

He tilted his head to me. 'Any information will help, Mr. Dunne, it really will.'

'Well, there was a trip, I suppose.'

'A trip?'

'To America.'

'To America? My country? What on earth was he doing there?'

'Well, you can get records, see, in warehouses for next to nowt. Twenty cents, half a dollar'.

'Really?'

'Places like Philadelphia, Detroit, Chicago. The DJ's from here have been doing it for years. You find a good song, some 'at that did nothing in America in '67, you bring it back here, start playing it in the clubs - Wigan, Blackpool, and it can be a massive hit with the kids and make a DJ famous. Mad, isn't it.'

'And so he went on a trip to buy these records.'

'Yeah, he was... *we* was opening up a shop for him, a record shop. Kind of a present for getting clean after the first heroin... do. I wanted to keep him busy.'

'A way of giving the lad a task, some responsibility and a mission.'

'Right, right.'

'That's sensible. And you went with him?'

'Yeah. Yeah, I did.'

'A kind of father-son bonding trip.'

'Well -'

'No, it sounds great. Hanging out in dingy Detroit bars

talking with locals, a pilgrimage between father and son. Sounds wonderful.'

'Well, if you put it that way.' I was feeling confident he was hearing what he wanted. Then:

'And how did that go?'

I looked at him. He was full of expectation and I could see where this was heading. It'd gone this way before. In the one and only Samaritans meeting with Neil and Brenda, it'd taken this turn. But that's what they do. Some polytechnic twat had backed us into a corner and it was all 'this relationship and that relationship' all that stuff. I'd figured he was getting at the root cause of all this dysfunction, as he called it, and that this *dysfunction* was shaping up to be me. I'd felt it coming down the tubes a mile back. *I'd* just said Neil's troubles were a case of too much dancing and drugs and that was about it. He had a choice and he chose the easy route, and now he's a drug addict, end of. It's not fucking brain surgery, or words to that effect. In a barney with the wife afterwards she'd said some 'at like 'he just needs to know that his dad loves him.' I'd nearly thrown my dinner at the wall over that one. 'Needs to know?' I'd said. 'What the lad *needs*, love, is a ten-mile run with a fucking sixty-pound backpack. That would sort the little get out. I'm his dad not his fucking nanny.' Well, the evening had been kyboshed and I was the bad guy again. So *now* with the Beach Boy staring at me, I suspected something similar was coming down the barrel. Now, I knew I had to answer the questions to keep him happy, so he felt all right about taking Neil on. Why we needed this rigmarole was beyond me. I didn't think it was relevant to our Neil, or in fact, any of his bleeding business. So I said:

'It went fine, doc. No problems at all.'

'No problems at all?'

'Not a sausage worth, doc. All tickety-boo. We're opening a shop on Tib Street as soon as he's done here, or sometime after -'

'Yes, you wouldn't want to overload him -'

'Absolutely. But eventually we'll get it up and running and sell off the Detroit haul. So, there are plans afoot. How long will you need him? For the detox and the counseling?'

He paused, wanting to plough on with the interrogation. 'Well, at least a month.'

'That sounds magic. And when can you take him?' I pulled out my roll and started flicking through it. It was time I took control of the interview and I figured the tactical move of flashing the dosh would seal the deal. 'And what are we looking at?'

He gave me a figure that nearly made me shit. I flipped it out of my roll and threw in an extra hundred in case he was still on the fence.

'Oh, that's really not necessary.'

'In case of any extras,' I said. 'And if he comes out smiling there'll be a big, fat gratuity as well -'

'Really, Mr. Dunne -'

'No, I insist. So when can we get him in?'

The doctor eyed the money. He knew I was pulling a fast one, but decided against fighting it. So, with a knowing smirk:

'Well, let me see.' He picked up a leather-bound book that looked like The Book of Kells. He flipped through, scrolled down and scribbled. 'Tomorrow around noon then?'

I was so chuffed I got up and shook his hand like an anxious boy. 'That's fantastic, doctor. I'm thrilled to bits. The wife will be tickled as well. And Neil, well, I can't thank you enough.'

'And in the meantime,' he said, closing the book, 'search everywhere in the house for drugs. His bedroom specifically, of course.'

'He's not lived there for ages.'

'It doesn't matter. He may have hidden the drug and forgotten where. We don't want him suddenly coming across it.'

'Right, I'll do that'.

After giving Neil's details: age, birthdate and some other necessaries, we wrapped up the registration. I handed him the cash and he coddled it for a few seconds before sticking it in his drawer. He wrote me out a receipt, which I pocketed, then he picked up some leaflets.

'Please give these to your son,' he said. 'They're very helpful in explaining what we do and what the twelve-step program is. He should read it thoroughly before coming in.' He handed them to me. 'Would you like to take a look around the facilities?'

I suspected another grilling, so I said. 'No thanks, doctor. I'd better push off. The wife will want to go to mass at some point, it being Sunday and all.'

I'd swear blind I saw another knowing look on his face.

'She's religious then, your wife?'

I was beginning to wonder who the feck we were booking into this place; the wife, Neil or me. The twat was doing my head in, so I said:

'Not fanatical, doctor - just habit on her part. More for community, you know.'

I folded up the brochures, shook his hand again and left. He stood and watched me go. I went out of the door and down the hallway, past old Frosty Drawers, the bird with the cat's eye glasses, and out to the car.

✳

As I got into the car I could see him peeking through the lace curtains. I could imagine the Beach Boy sitting, wanting to hear the confession of Jackie Dunne. Wanting me to say I'd messed up the Detroit trip. That I'd gone across the border from Detroit to Windsor, Canada to see Corey Blaine, to blow off some stuff that was bugging me; that army mates are the only ones you can talk to about some things, no one else gets it. So, I'd pretended to be sick and told Neil to go off and explore the usual warehouses to add to the records we already had. And I came back in a black mood, as I always did when seeing Corey, and that I was distant and snappy, but never told Neil why. So that no doubt festered with him, thinking I was mad at him or whatever. So a few days after we got back, him being a soft and overly sensitive little bugger, he dumped the project, the shop all of it. The shop lease was cancelled and the fucking records bunged into a warehouse gathering dust and getting warped with the damp. And then this *sulk* had turned into counseling with the wife, the Samaritans, the religion and then the drugs, the drugs again - all over a few crabby days in Detroit. No, Mr. Beach Boy, it was all *my* fault - that's what you wanted to hear because I can see you eyeing me through the curtain. But I wasn't going to say it, was I. No, a ten-mile run with a bleeding sixty-pound backpack, that's what the kid's short of. I started the car and put on some music. I got Martha and the Vandellas. 'Heat Wave.'

On the snake-like drive down to the gates I saw a phone box on the corner. I parked the car and went in. There was no urine reek in *this* phone box. Brenda answered the phone.

'It's me. I've booked him in, tomorrow at noon for a month. Be happy, this isn't your National Health knockabout.'

'And it's nice?

'Lovely. I've brought some brochures. We can all have a gander tonight.'

'Are you here for tea?'

'Yeah. You won't be going…?'

'No, not tonight. No mass for me, I'm shattered.'

'Alright.' I could hear music in the background. 'What's that?'

'Mary's still here. We're having some sherry, and listening to some tunes. Don't worry, we won't clean out the drinks table.' She laughed.

'I'll see you later then.'

I hung up. I got back in the car and drove off. I didn't mind the wife necking some booze. She needed the blowout; I knew that. But I didn't want Mary filling Brenda's head with mad ideas about shifting Neil to her relatives on The Islands, or mine in Dublin. She'd brought this up with me the last time Neil was bad, and I'd made it known *then* what a duff idea it was. So, I never mentioned it to Brenda. Then again, if Brenda was gassing with Mary it was the lesser of two evils. If Nola her sister had been there Brenda would've been down at church with O' Connell, rattling away at the Psalms. And he would've been prodding for dirt the way they do.

✳

I got back on the motorway and started back.

I knew the old get was mystified as to why I hadn't been

114

to confession. The last time I was in that suffocating booth I'd been wearing a uniform, thirty odd years ago. You'd have thought, after all this time, he would've given up. But I could feel him operating behind the scenes through Brenda. It was understandable, I suppose. Being the villain he'd always known I was, given to every petty crime known to man, it was confession for me every Sunday; come hell or high water. And there I was that time in full kit, sweating and itching in that little cubicle.

'Bless me Father for I have sinned.'

'What is it, my son?'

'Well, I battered a yank who was chatting up one of our Salford girls and throwing his money around. So, I clocked him one and nicked his stuff.'

'I see.'

'Then I robbed the Quartermaster's store and swiped a carton of cigs, some sugar and powdered eggs to give to my old mam.'

'Anything else?'

I'd told him more of the same or words to that effect. And he'd given me the penance and all the rest of it. Then I was carted off to Europe and nine months of slaughter, and then a year dealing with starving civilians in the heap of stinking rubble that was once Hamburg. I hadn't seen O' Connell since. So, he was wondering why. But use your loaf, mate; use your bloody loaf.

✳

It was about one o' clock at The Antelope. By the time I got a pint I needed it so bad it was gone in three gulps. I had another at the ready. I got half way through that and calmed a bit. Between that and the Valium, I was well sorted. I stood at the bar looking for Danny.

I was in a decent mood because of the detox victory. But the pub was driving me spare. I'd been completely ruined by recent renovation. They'd ripped out all the old wood, lamps, everything that'd made the place a cozy watering hole, and slapped up off-white plaster that housed invasive top lights. Having a conversation within three feet was like being inter-rogated by the Abwehr. Metallic high chairs and rounded plastic-like tables had the place looking more like an airport lounge than a local. I wanted to bludgeon to death the land-lord, the brewery, or whoever was responsible for the vandalism. But if you threw a fit every time you went onto a pub in Manchester that had been destroyed, you'd be in in a mess twenty-four seven.

It was already filling up. Suddenly next to me, ordering a round of drinks was Brian King; just the bloke I wanted to see. He was in his late thirties and ran a successful real estate company. He'd nearly leased the record shop to us six months before, the one that went tits up when Neil pulled out.

'Jackie, how are you?' he said, shaking my hand. 'It's been a while since.'

Brian always had smile on his face, an upbeat positive feller. So, he bore no ill will at being mucked about. I also knew Tib Street space was still empty.

'Brian, good to see you,' I said. 'How's the family?'

'Running me ragged,' he said. 'Thank Christ for work. How's Neil doing, still into the records?'

'It's like an illness with them. We've got about ten thousand sitting in a warehouse in Ancoats gathering dust and damp.'

'That must be costing a few bob.'

'It's endless mate.' The drinks came; two pints and a whisky. 'Let me get those'

'Are you sure? Ta, mate.'

I'd known Brian since he was a teenager. When he tried to flog me a stolen car nearly twenty years ago, I gave him such a kicking that he quit crime on the spot. I got him a job doing custom paintwork on cars and he took it up with gusto. Five years later and his real estate papers firmly under his belt, I fronted him money to open an office. The rest was history. He was married with two kiddies, had a semi-detached house in Prestwich and two cars. Life was good.

'You know I'm thinking,' I said. 'I'd like to have another go at the shop.' I saw his eyebrows rise. 'I can get a committed team to work it and flog these records we have, you know - and go back for more if it goes well. I know we can do it. What do you say?'

He was surprised, chuffed and wary all at the same time. 'Yeah, why not,' he said. 'Give is a call on Monday and we'll set something up.'

I thanked him and we exchanged more pleasantries. Then he rejoined his party. Two things off my list.

I was tickled with how things were panning out. I wanted to celebrate and was about to order a large whisky, when I heard a commotion. I turned to see punters being knocked aside like bowling skittles, bodies lurching and angry cries everywhere. I soon saw the culprit. Danny had his eyes fixed on something to my left and was scrambling in that direction. He was shoving folk aside, sending them careening into tables, spilling over drinks. I looked to my left to see a big feller, frozen in terror, looking at Danny blaze towards him. As Danny got close, the geezer put his arms up in submission and stepped back to brace himself. Danny slowed and stopped. He'd seen what the man was holding up. It was the Racing Post. Danny stuttered and looked about at the mess he'd caused. Folk were cursing, picking themselves up, wiping themselves down and looking at Danny as if he was mad.

I instantly knew what'd happened. So did the man, so did Danny. The great lummox had come in and seen the big feller moving towards me, his arm reaching into his pocket – for a weapon, no doubt. So, like the faithful bulldog he was, he'd set off to save the day.

'No worries, mate,' the man called out. 'Everything's fine.'

Danny held up his hand in apology and grabbed his inhaler, taking a blast. Then the wave of embarrassment was full upon him.

'Sorry, mate,' he grunted. 'Err… thought you were… What you drinking?'

'No worries,' was all the other feller could muster. 'I'm on me way out.' He edged round Danny and headed for the public telephone to place his bet.

Danny turned to the pub. Punters who'd been gawking, quickly looked away; brushing off sodden dresses and beer-soaked shirts. The jukebox still droned on. It was Slade 'Merry Christmas.' Christmas tunes and it wasn't December yet.

'Sorry folks,' he said.

'You bleeding maniac, Danny Simms,' shouted some woman. 'You need your bloody head feeling, love. Not right, that's you.'

Danny took it like it came from his mam. I shook my head.

'Drinks all round,' I said. I turned to the barmaid. 'My tab,

Joyce. You'd better get him his usual as well.'

I turned to see Brian and his party looking in my direction. Not a good start to a working relationship. Danny and me escaped to the lounge as the wave of punters approached the bar for compensation.

The atmosphere of the lounge was empty and cold. But a break in the clouds saw the low, winter sun casting a bright rectangle on the floor. A couple of old girls sat close to a radiated fire. Hunched over glasses of stout and puffing on Woodbines, they nodded to us as we went to the corner. Danny plumped into the leatherette side seat and a noise of air escaped from a hole to his right. I sat opposite.

'Well… there's a hundred quid down the Swanee.'

It took a while for Danny to get his breath back. I felt for him. He'd always had asthma, blaming the defoliant they'd used when he was doing National Service in Malaysia. But it'd never been this bad. He used to stop a kerfuffle in ten seconds, barely breaking a sweat; just threw fellers around like they were rag dolls. But nowadays, any grapple beyond that, had him gasping and helpless. This'd come home to us when he took a leathering from a couple of pissheads from Little Hulton. They'd firmly won the day. All this was spelling the end of Danny's career.

'We have to get you into another line of work, mate,' I said.

'Like what?'

'We're having another go at the shop, the one on Tib Street. You could work there.'

Danny looked at me like I'd asked him to deck out in women's clothing. 'Working in a bleeding shop? I don't know, gov.'

'Think about it,' I said. 'I'm going to close the club.'

'Close the club?'

'Neil's going into rehab, so he'll be gone for at least a month. And we've all those records in the warehouse from the Detroit trip. Plenty of inventory.'

'At the Ancoats place?'

'Yeah. Plus it's a day job. This nightlife, I don't know. We're like vampires. I'd like to alter me hours as well as Neil's. It might help you as well.'

Danny took a drag of his smoke and exhaled. 'So, the club's closed from now on?' he said.

'Some 'at tells me we're going to see ructions. If there's trouble down there kids could get hurt, then the Peelers are involved. We don't need the agro.'

He nodded reluctantly. Then he saw something on my overcoat. Blood. I told him what had happened in the car park outside the infirmary.

'Liverpool?' he said. He thought for a bit. 'Macker's planning to pull a fast one on Bill.'

I nodded. 'He'll bring the Liverpool crew in and Bill will be edged out... that's if he's not bumped off.'

'Should we say some 'at to Bill?'

'I think we have to. We can use this to our advantage. We can use it to - what's the word - *negotiate* Mr. Collier's banishment.'

We drank. The rectangle of bright light was edging up to the wall as the sun sank lower. The room seemed to be warming up, so I took off my overcoat and Danny shed his sheepskin. Then I saw Corey. He was passing in the vault but he hadn't seen me. Danny saw my expression change. I told him about

Corey's little performance at the pub last night.

'Old Timer told me,' said Danny, shaking his head. 'Totally out of order that, chief. I'm sorry I let him in.'

Corey appeared at the doorway. He was already blotto.

'Hiya Jackie,' he said. 'Thought you weren't coming in today.'

Corey weaved in and sat down with a thump on the wall-seat leatherette. He got out his fags and lit up.

'Eh, you,' said Danny, 'if I'd known you were going to kick off last night I wouldn't have let you in. Unacceptable, mate; totally out of order.'

Corey stared at the ashtray. 'Some things just have to be said.'

'Get stuffed,' Danny replied.

Corey tilted his head and looked at him. 'You served, didn't you Danny?'

'Malaysia '58, '59.'

'I heard that was nasty.'

'It was no picnic. Why?'

'Jackie and me were in Belgium then Holland and Germany… fighting Hitler.' He inhaled.

'I know that.'

'It was a noble war, wasn't it, Jackie?' Corey went back to the ashtray.

'I know that too,' said Danny.

Corey leaned into the table and put his cig out. 'You ever kill an unarmed man… a prisoner, Danny?'

I put my pint down. The old biddies cranked their heads slightly in our direction. Danny put his hand up to say he was dealing with this.

'I wouldn't tell you if I did,' he said.

'Only I have.' Corey stayed with the cigarette dimp,

squashing it in the ashtray as if it wouldn't go out. 'And it's hard, you know… to think about what you did, when you see the kid's face every day… a 15-year-old kid who just wants to go home. 'Cause a Lufwaffe cadet isn't an evil man, he's not Hitler, he doesn't deserve to die… any more than a baby in Bremen.'

'That's the same as a lad in uniform, is it?'

'It is when you just see him on his knees… crying, begging for his life.' Corey slumped back against the wall. He kept looking at the table. 'And you do it anyway, you shoot him 'cause your mates are egging you on. 'Cause they've done theirs, shot them point blank and now… now all eyes are on you.'

I got up. Danny got up ahead of me, went to Corey and grabbed his arm. Corey was now aware of Danny, as if waking from a dream.

'Are you kicking me out? Is he kicking me out, Jackie?

Danny hauled him up. 'Get out, come on.'

He started to usher Corey to the door. They were about to leave the lounge when Corey burst into song. It was 'Jerusalem.' They were into the vault and disappearing through the crowd as he got to 'these dark, satanic mills.' Then the song was drowned out by the jukebox sounds of the Top Ten.

I sat, furious with the bastard. I'd never told Danny any of this. We'd shared stories before but I'd never mentioned this episode. I knew I'd have to elaborate once he got back.

'You're all right, love,' said one of the old girls. 'My brother was killed in France in '17. I hope you got as many of the bleeders as you could. Bloody swine's, they are. Now they want to be friends with us.' She smoked aggressively through nicotine fingers. 'That Roy Jenkins wants his head feeling. And that pillock Ted Heath, got us into bed with them in the first place… words bleeding fail me.'

I nodded and studied the dried foam on my pint pot. I got up and went to the bar and got us two more pints. Brian had left and the pub was thinning out as folk made their way home to Sunday dinner. I knocked back a whisky while at the bar and took another with me, along with the pints and some peanuts for Danny. I got to my seat as he was coming back.

The brilliant block of light coming through the window had crept up to the wall and across a bit. We sat.

'I'm sorry about that, chief,' he said. 'You all right?'

'Why shouldn't I be?'

'Eh, you don't have to explain to me. I know how it works.'

I sipped my pint and lowered my voice, conscious of the ladies not far away.

'I'm alright with it,' I said. 'We had three of them - Corey, Bill and me… three POWs. The NCO asked us to "take them for a walk". *I* knew what it meant, but Corey was oblivious until it started to happen.'

'He didn't know?'

'No. He had this camera he'd found in some burned out half-track. Completely knackered, it was, but he was that clueless he was taking pictures with it, like we were all at Blackpool pier. Mucking about, like - posing with these fellers like we were best mates. Bill and me thought he'd lost the plot until we figured he'd no idea what was expected. What a bloody shambles.'

Danny drank. I did likewise. The oblong shone like a bar of bullion as it moved up and across the wall.

'His was a kid?' Danny stroked his pint. 'Is that what he was saying?'

'Luftwaffe ground crew. Young teenager. We could've spared Corey the trouble, I suppose. I'd already done mine, an officer. Bill had a Waffen SS geezer. Corey, with this kid, was like a bunny in the headlights. Gave the kid time to realize what was going on, and it just got worse.'

'That's war, isn't.'

'He's not built for it. I mean, they were the last of a scratch unit that'd killed a lot of our fellers. We'd been pinned down for twelve hours. They gave us a right kicking. The SS feller had shot some of our lads who'd been taken prisoner. We knew this 'cause one lad escaped and pointed this bastard out when we got the better of them. Tit for tat.'

'Sounds about right.'

'The other two just happened to be there. We couldn't do one without the others… Unfortunate, but that's the way it was.'

We drank. The light hit one side of my face and I had to squint. I could feel the old biddies listening as they stared at the radiator.

'You never told me,' Danny finally said.

'It's not the kind of thing you write home about, but hey, I had a job to do, so I did it. But poor, old Corey… he's not built for it - never was. Even blames his lad's death on it.'

'Patrick? His son who died of cancer?'

'Fifteen, he was. The same age as the cadet.'

'Give over,' Danny said. 'So, what does that have to do…?'

'You're not religious are you?'

'I'm not mithered, me - Church of England. It's like being an atheist.'

'Well, Corey is. Catholic.'

'And he thinks…?'

'All that shite they taught us. Bloody priests… and it's that guilt festering in him. That's why he blames everyone else; the RAF, Churchill, Bomber Harris, whoever.'

The light was full on my face. I held my hand up to shield my eyes. I got up from the wall seat, pulled a chair round, and sat with my back to the sun. I could feel the heat on my neck. I knocked back the whisky.

'What does he want from you, though?' Danny said.

I told him how we'd taken the ID from these fellers. The dog tags, pay books, medals, the lot. How Corey couldn't handle it, so gave the cadet's ID to Bill and me, sometime in late April '45, four weeks after the incident. And how now - *now* he wants them back. I told him about the German War Graves Commission; how they identified dead soldiers and made a grave, informed the family. I told him all this. By the end of it I was sweating. The winter sun was burning the back of my head, and the room felt like a bleeding sauna. I could smell myself.

Danny thought for a minute. 'Are you going to give it, the kid's dog tag?'

'I might if I could find it. But I'd stashed all that crap away when I got back in '47. As far as I can remember I put it all at me mam's in the loft, though I can't be sure.' I finished my pint. 'What time was this meet again?'

'Nine o' clock. The pub.'

'I'd better get home. See what's happening with our Neil.' I turned to the biddies. 'Sorry, ladies. You didn't need to hear all that. But… bad times, they were, very bad times.'

'You're all right, love.' She smiled and her false top pallet slipped a bit. She closed her mouth and went back to her stout. I noticed that the other biddy's eyes had welled up. She had to dab them to stop a tear rolling down.

✳

I left the pub with a bad taste in my mouth. As long as I didn't hand over the ID disc Corey would be a pain in the neck. One side of me just wanted to find the bloody thing, give it, and get him off my back. The other side hated the man - to bring all this up now, to do this after all these years? And after I'd saved your life, man?

I sat in the car fuming. I could see it all, even now. That day I saved your life, Corey Blaine. The abandoned factory complex we thought had been cleared. Shells of factories, smaller buildings and the remains of an army in retreat; burned out half-tracks, staff vehicles, suitcases, clothes, typewriters; shells, blown-up field guns - a junkyard of crap - smells of burning rubber and flesh.

Me, Bill and you, Corey - the Bren gun team, a little back from the fellers up front. The front fellers walking over that small heap of rubble, not two feet high; all spread out as was the way; and the deathly quiet, not even birds twittering.

Then… then. Tracer bullets zipping towards our right, arcing over and bouncing up, bringing down those up front. And us diving for cover like rabbits, pinned down with nowhere to go. And it's going to go on this steady slaughter. Until I stop it.

I started the car. If you, Corey, had given thought to *that* day you wouldn't be giving me this grief, you wouldn't. I drove and turned on the music. 'Let's Dance' came on by Fred Astaire.

✳

Opening the front door, I heard soul music playing loudly on the Hi Fi system. Then I got a whiff of cannabis. I took off my coat, hung the Trilby and walked into the living room. There was my wife and Mary Brown, pickled to the nines, slow jiving to the music. Neil, in his pajamas, was full length on the settee with the stump of a massive joint perched between his fingers.

'What the hell is this?' I said.

They stopped dancing and looked at me. 'Yes, to the Lord' The Stoval Sisters,' Brenda announced.

Both women snorted with laughter. I went and turned the music down.

'We didn't hear you come in,' she said, still giggling.

'I can see that.'

'Well your dinner's burned to buggery.'

'Look at the state of him,' I said, looking at Neil. I turned to Mary. 'Is this you, this?'

'Oh, have a drink and calm down, Jackie,' chirped Brenda. She went to the drinks table.

'Are you stoned as well?' I said to her. I turned to Mary again. 'Have you been giving her drugs as well?'

'We should thank her,' said Brenda, weaving at the drinks table. 'His stomach was killing him. He'd been drinking Milk of Magnesia like it was Boddingtons Bitter, and he was at his limit with the Paracetamol. I didn't know what to do, so she gave him a joint.'

'They give it to cancer patients on The Island's, don't they Mary,' said Neil, digging his way out of the settee.

'Get upstairs now,' I said to him.

'And how many have you had?' asked Brenda, pouring another sherry.

'I've had three pints. Is that all right?'

'That means six.' She started over to Mary with the sherry.

'I'm all right, love, no more for me.'

Brenda halted then turned to me. 'Why are you so late?'

'I've been kind of busy, Brenda,' I said, moving to the drinks table, 'booking him into this place in Altrincham; doing this, doing that. I was going to go to his place in Didsbury to look for dope, but I forgot.'

'There's nowt there,' said Neil.

'But there could be some *here*. You could've stashed it months ago and forgotten.' I poured some whisky. 'It could be rolled up hidden in socks. He told me all this, the geezer at the thingy. So, I'll be up there rooting in a minute.'

'There's nowt here,' said Neil.

'Will you get him upstairs?'

'I'm not going,' said Neil. 'I'm going to Jamaica.'

I looked at him. I looked at Mary and Brenda. They'd just exchanged looks. The Stoval Sisters were still singing ever so low.

'What was that?' I said.

'He's hallucinating,' said Brenda. 'Leave it with me, love.' She pulled at Neil's housecoat. 'You upstairs now.'

'I'm going to Jamaica.'

'I'll be off then,' said Mary.

'No, you won't,' I said. 'You've been yakking to him about Jamaica, haven't you?'

'And it was Exuma not the mainland,' Brenda said. 'There's a civil war going on in Jamaica, we're not that daft. We were just talking about *Exuma*, and he overheard that's all.

'Well, I'm talking now and no bugger's going to Eczema, whatever it's called.' I was trying not to lose it. 'Is that clear, all of you?'

'It were just a bit of chatter about holidays,' said Brenda, 'after the clinic, like.'

'I know what it was about,' I said, eyeballing Mary. 'Buggering off for a year until things calm down, right?' I turned to Brenda. 'Well, running away don't solve owt. He's staying here and having another go at the shop when he gets out.'

'Out of where?' said Neil.

'Have you listened to a blind thing I've said? I've been schlepping all over Cheshire for you. It's a private centre.'

'I'm not going.'

'You bloody well are. It's been paid for all ready.'

'He knows he's going,' said Brenda. 'But the shop, when did all this come up?'

'The shop…' Neil shook his head. 'Kinell.'

'Language, you,' I said. 'I've been talking to Brian and we're going to do it, end of. Thanks all the same, Mary, but Eczema's out.'

'I make me own decisions on that shop or not,' said Neil. 'It's my life.'

'It'll be your life when you're not a bloody addict. The dance club's been a bleeding bust, so it's the fucking shop, alright?'

'Just one day,' said Brenda, 'one day, Mary, without a bit o' language in this house, that's all I ask.'

'I'm not doing the shop and you messing it up again,' said Neil, 'I'm not.'

I nearly pitched the bottle at the wall. But then I just said to myself that I messed up nothing. He - *he* was the one that threw in the towel.

'Who's messing what up, love?' said Brenda.

'I'm sorry I started all this,' said Mary. 'I didn't mean -'

Neil suddenly got animated, but his eyes were red and unfocused.

'Detroit was a great idea, Mary. "Let's go to America buy records like the DJ's are doing. Open a shop." Brilliant. We're not there two minutes and he fucks off to Canada.'

This brought me up short, I don't mind admitting. I was about to put the top back on the bottle but this stopped me dead. I had no idea he knew I'd gone. I looked at him, and for the first time through his wandering, hazy eyes, he looked at me.

'And he didn't think I knew, did you, dad. But I did and he had.'

Brenda looked to him then to me. Mary looked at all of us.

'Canada?' Brenda said.

'Comes back, mam,' he said staggering, 'comes back and he stays in his room for the rest of the trip.'

'It was half a day,' I said, taking another drink.

'You're not interested. You couldn't care less about a record shop. I'm going to Jamaica to scuba dive.'

'You spoiled, little get.'

'Fuck off.'

I threw the drink down and moved to him but Brenda stepped in. 'Alright, alright, that's enough from both of you!' She swung round to Neil. 'You upstairs now.' She grabbed Neil and ushered him to the door. I watched them go.

✳

There was an awkward silence. Then I turned to Mary and broke it.

'In future talk to me before you start interfering.' I lit up.

She went and got her coat, putting it on as she came back. 'He needs to leave this town, you stubborn bugger.' Her voice was low. 'Exuma, Dublin, it doesn't matter but he must -'

'He's not going anywhere!'

I sat on the settee. Mary moved to the end and leaned in, still keeping her voice low.

'Do you want that woman or that lad up there - do you want them standing at your grave, or visiting you in jail for killing someone? I'm sorry, Jackie, but that's what's coming and you know it, don't tell me you don't.'

'Jesus, no bugger's dying woman. Get a grip.' I waved her away.

'I've known you for twenty-odd years and I've never seen you like this, so far out of control.'

I got up and poured some ginger ale. The heat in the room was like a furnace. Mary followed me.

'And you're being played as well, like a fiddle you are.'

'By who?' I turned to her.

'Macker,' she said. 'Have you no idea what's going on right under your nose? Why is he the only one selling to your Neil? Eh? - Because you were too good to him, Jackie, too good. To a lad who's got no dad that goes a long way. And he's jealous, he's jealous of your Neil.'

'He'll be gone by tomorrow anyway, and all this'll be behind us.'

'Oh, give over, man. If Bill Shaw drops that lad, I'll eat coke. He's a cash cow and a half, and he's not going anywhere.'

'Oh, he will, I'll sort it out'

'Like you've been doing for the last two years?' she said, her voice rising. 'I'm surprised *any* of us are alive, given the bloody agro you've caused.'

'Well, they'll be in jail by the end of the year, won't they!' I shouted. 'I'll make sure of that!'

Mary paused. She looked at me like I was mental. 'You won't go to the coppers, you can't.'

'I'll go to the press, The Evening News.'

'You'll what?'

'I know the editor down there. Shadrack. He's done dozens of stories about the Legion, local interest stuff. I'll go on record, tell him there's a growing problem in this city. Heroin. I won't mention names, but by Christ I'll stir up a hornets nest.'

'That's as good as going to the law.'

'But it isn't is it?! I am *not* one of them!'

Mary went very quiet for a bit. Then: 'But I am. And so are you, even if you won't admit it.' Then she buttoned her coat up. 'I'll put what you just said down to the drink.' She got to the door. 'Send him away, Jackie. It's the only thing that'll keep that lad alive… or any of us for that matter.'

She turned and left. I helped myself to some more ginger ale. The row had given me a headache so I opened the French doors for some fresh air. I'd not done a jot of work on it and the back garden was thick with old, dead leaves. I strode around kicking them aside, quietly boiling away gabbing to myself. What a mental idea leaving Manchester, and to my bloody relatives in Dublin? Give it a rest. Being around a bunch of Micks who hate this country, that'd do him a lot of good. Bringing all that shit back with him. I don't think so. It's family, it's community, it's city and it's country - in that order. You start mucking with that and you're done, it all crumbles to dust. I've seen it when a nation is wiped off the map. The Germans had nothing. Unconditional Surrender? Not on my bleeding watch.

I mumbled away to myself until Brenda came back into the dining room. She looked at the glass on the floor and glared at me. She picked it up and went into the kitchen.

I knew Neil's revelation about my Canadian visit was fermenting in her head. It would bubble over any minute, I could feel it. I thought I should get it over with, so I threw my cig away and went into the kitchen. The kettle was on and she was brewing up. I lit up and pulled the ashtray to me on the kitchen island. Sure enough:

'Why did you visit Corey Blaine?' she said, putting tea bags into the teapot. 'That's why you went to Canada, right?' She turned to me. 'What other reason is there to go to Windsor or wherever this place is, but him?'

'Yeah, I did go if the truth be known. Is that a crime?'

'And came back in a foul mood.' She dumped some sugar into the cups and turned. 'Why didn't you tell Neil it was Corey that spoiled your day and not boredom with the trip, like he thinks it is? He thinks it was all his fault you were in a crap mood.'

'And that's brought us all to this, has it? Neil's bad again 'cause the trip was ruined?'

I walked past her to the tap where I ran the cold water for a few seconds. I filled a glass and drank my fill. I could feel her looking at me.

'Did you talk about Patrick?' she asked. 'His kid who died -'

'I know who Patrick is.' The kettle started to whistle so I turned it off. 'He always talks about Pat.' I refilled my glass. Brenda let it fill up and I drank some more.

'What else did you talk about?'

'Look, I'll go upstairs to him,' I said, putting the glass down. 'I'll set the record straight about Detroit, alright?'

'No, no, that's not a good idea Jackie - not when you're both like this. Leave it for tomorrow when everyone's settled down and sober. Please.'

'Fine.' I drank the water.

I could feel her backing down.

'I'll make you something to eat,' she said. 'You've probably had nowt but a packet of pork scratching's, right? Right, turn the telly on and I'll bring you something. We all need to just settle down.'

✳

In the living room I slumped down, turning on the TV. There was nothing on so I turned it off again. I watched the little dot get smaller and smaller on the screen.

I thought about what Mary said, Macker's jealousy of Neil, all of it. I always suspected it, but you sweep stuff under the carpet. I couldn't kill the kid, I'd seen too much of that. But if Bill refused to stop this heroin game, kick Macker into touch, I'd find my own way to solve things. And sending Neil away was not one of them.

I watched the telly cool down and listened to the static. It was a daft idea to get into anything with Neil right now. It would just blow up into something, so I settled down to wait for tea. Then I remembered what the Beach Boy had said about searching his room. It was hardly the time, but I didn't want to risk him finding drugs he'd stashed months ago. I looked in the direction of the kitchen. Brenda was pottering away.

I knocked on Neil's door and walked in. He was sat up in bed with his portable turntable on his lap. 45s were scattered all around him and his forefinger was wrapped around a joint like Churchill with a cigar. Blue smoke billowed and joined the line of haze hanging across the room. His head was back, looking upwards through half-closed eyes. Marvin Gaye was singing, 'Mercy, Mercy Me.'

'Mind you don't fall asleep with that thing burning.'

He didn't answer. I went to the window and let some air in. Then I got the brochure from my pocket and put it on the bed.

'You're in here next week. That's the best in the north of England. You get the month then we'll get stuck into the shop again.' He ignored it. 'I'll leave it there.'

I went to the sideboard and opened it. Clothes were hanging, and there was a built-in drawer unit. I started going through them. He turned the music down.

'I'm worried,' he said.

'What about?'

'Macker... How is he?'

I stopped and turned. 'I don't want to hear that bastard's name in this house again, do you hear? Never.'

'Is he going to leave?'

'I'll make sure he does. I'm not having you leave because of him. This is our town, you belong here; let no one tell you otherwise. Can you imagine listening to all that diddly-diddly rubbish in Dublin, or that reggae shite in Jamaica? You'd go mad within a month. No, this city is the place to be if you're into Soul, R and B, any of the yank stuff.' I tried my usual tack of looking for common ground between us. 'It came over with the yanks after the war -'

'It's all right, dad, you don't have to sell me the shop. I'm over it. There's more important things in life.'

'We'll talk about it tomorrow when you're not so... tired.'

I went over and took the joint from him. I put it in the ashtray. He looked bleary-eyed in my direction. I continued my search.

'You went to see Corey, didn't you?' he said. 'When we were in Detroit.'

This stopped me, pronto. I turned and he went on.

'I saw a taxi receipt to Windsor on the side table. What else is there, beside Mr. Blaine?' He looked at me as if expecting an answer. 'It's none of my business. It just shows how stupid it all is... this record stuff, compared to what you deal with.'

I looked at him a bit closer. 'What do you mean?'

'The war, all of it. I know Corey's got shell shock, everyone knows.'

I relaxed a bit. 'No, you don't understand.'

'I know I don't. At my age you were fighting a war. What have I done? Wasted me life with music, poisoned me body. No wonder you're disgusted.'

'You're stoned.' I went back to rummaging.

'I *am* a wastrel. And I make *myself* sick.'

I turned back to him and his head had sunk to his chest. He looked pale and tired.

'I didn't mean to say that.'

'I *haven't* got a clue.' He shook his head. 'I *don't* know I'm born.'

'Stop it. You can't compare yourself to me.'

'I never had a chance to become a man.' He looked up at me. 'You, Corey... you're fucking heroes.'

136

I breathed deep with frustration. 'We knew nowt. We were just replacements.'

'I studied that campaign, dad. I know the regiment you were in. You were fighting the Waffen SS, paratroopers as well as the ordinary army. And even *they - they* were like our special forces. Veterans of the Eastern Front and they wouldn't surrender. That makes you even braver.'

'Thank you, Mary Brown.' I turned and went back to my job.

'I have to be stoned to talk about this? I'm not stoned, I'm as clear as crystal. Your lot saved England… for what? A bunch of druggies dancing in basements.'

I folded up a T-shirt I'd been rifling through. Neil fiddled with his records, idly shifting them around as if they meant nothing to him.

'Well, I think it's a bit rum to bring up Detroit now.' I put the T-shirt back. 'Why the heck did you wait all this time to say owt?' I turned to him. 'Eh?' He didn't answer, so I went back to the drawer.

'Ashamed… Always have been.'

'Ashamed of what?'

'You saw terrible things.' He looked around the room. 'I've been given everything and wasted it. Northern Soul, who gives a shit? There's bigger things in life.' He tossed the record across the room.

'What are you doing?'

'You went to see Corey Blaine, you came back and you had to deal with me and all this, this stupid shit.' He waved his arms, dismissing everything. 'No wonder you wouldn't talk to me.'

'Now wait up,' I said. I laid it out for him. 'It had nothing to do with you, or the record shop.'

'Of course.' He slumped down facing away from me.

'No, no, honestly. I was in a mood because Corey...' I dried up not wanting to go there.

'You don't have to butter it up -'

'No, no, he has these ideas about the war, see...'

'Like what?' He turned and looked at me. 'See. Don't sugar coat it, dad. I know I'm a waste of space.'

'Will you stop talking like that. It's not helping.'

'I know what I am, dad.' He sat up. 'I'm an addict and it's all getting boring. Everyone's had enough. I've had enough.'

I couldn't tell him the root cause of Corey's madness and my part in it. So, I thought of Corey's other complaints, the stuff that made even rear echelon soldiers mad. But I didn't know where to start. I could smell Wesel, Bremen and Hamburg even now, as I stood in that room. But how could I explain it to him? *A mile away* we could smell decaying bodies still trapped in the rubble, the clouds of flies, burst sewage pipes, burning petrol and the disinfectant used to kill any disease that might come from this mess. How could I explain the sight of orphaned kids scampering about, skeletons with ghosted eyes, and the women selling themselves for cigarettes bartered for food, how could I explain it? And even now thinking about these things, I felt guilty for allowing them into my mind and stealing my outrage, stealing my anger for the misery inflicted on the warden by the Luftwaffe. And it made it worse knowing that there was no comparison in the size of the slaughter. We had killed as many in a night as they'd done in the entire blitz. How could I explain this? And it did do all our heads in at first. But you got over it, as much as you could. But some couldn't let it go. So, I said:

'All you need to know is that Corey put me in a mood. That's what I brought back with me - that. It wasn't you, or the records.'

I thought this might keep him happy. He looked at me then he said:

'Why did you visit him in the first place?'

'He's still a war mate, isn't he?' I tried to keep a lid on my frustration. 'You want to make sure he's alright.'

'I know about soldiers and their mates. That bond.' He stared at the quilt, his face pale and lost. 'No one can compete with that, not even family.'

Jesus, I can't win with this kid. He started to toss the records across the room. They sailed through the air, spinning like flying saucers and landing in a heap.

'It's all crap, all of it. It's all a waste of bleeding space!'

'Neil.'

'Ric Tic label. What does it all mean? Nowt.'

Brenda was suddenly there. 'What is going on in here?'

'You talk to him. I bloody can't.'

She turned to Neil. 'Why are you doing this?'

Another record went wobbling through the air like a Frisbee. Then she looked at me.

'What have you said to this lad?'

'I've said nowt. You can thank yourself and Mary Brown for this! I kept rooting, more to avoid a confrontation than anything, just going through the motions.

'I can't leave you two alone for five minutes,' she said. 'It's always got to end in a squabble, without fail it does.' She took the ashtray and put it by the door.

I picked up an old, stained shoebox from under a pile of old Air-Fix boxes. It looked vaguely familiar.

'It's all life and death this music, mam.' Whizz, another record went flying. 'The centre of the universe, it is.'

Brenda had her hands to her temples. 'My God, we've all gone mad, my family.'

I opened the old box. It was pure reflex, but I dropped the lid. Brenda looked in my direction while Neil carried on rambling. I saw the contents of the box and just stared. Brenda noticed and moved to me.

'What is it? Is it drugs?'

I picked up the lid. 'No, no, just some old...' I started to put the box back.

Neil saw it and pointed. 'I haven't seen that in forever,' he said, throwing back the covers.

I put the box down and the Air-Fix boxes back on top of it.

'What are you doing, dad?' He was crawling out of bed. 'Give them here. I thought I'd lost them.'

'What's he talking about?' Brenda said. 'What is it?'

I let him get to the pile. I turned and lit up a cig, wandering away. I heard him rifling through the boxes. Then I heard the shoebox lid go. There was a pause. Brenda spoke first.

'What are they?'

'German medals, mam.' There was pride in his voice. 'They're the Iron Cross Second Class, the Wound Badge and the Close Combat Clasp. When he was alive that feller... he was a highly decorated German soldier, mam. Dad squared off with that bloke and he won. That's how I know how brave you are, dad. That's how I know.'

He cradled the box, turned and shuffled back to the bed.

✻

I went down into the kitchen and drank more water. I hovered there for a bit, staring at the leaking tap. I heard Brenda come down stairs.

'You're dinner's in the dining room.' She came by me and started to wash pots.

'Has he calmed down?'

'He's looking at them medals.' She kept with the sink and the soapy water.

'I don't know how he found them.'

'He just told me. He used to hide his drugs at your mother's. One day he found them.'

I poured some tea and took it to the island where the milk and sugar was. I waited for her to say something. It didn't take long.

'Those two soldier's ID things… is one of them what Corey was asking about?

'He can have it back and we get some peace. Won't that be nice?'

She stayed at the sink. I could hear the soapy water slushing gently about.

'There's a book there too,' she said.

'Right, yeah, that's a soldier's pay book. The one who won the medals -'

'I don't want them in this house.'

Her tone was short and sharp. I didn't know what I expected, but it took me aback.

'Suit yourself.'

141

'It's a grave, that is… a dead man's things.'

'A bunch of tin love, nowt more.'

'I don't want them here, Jackie!' She spun around and the brush she was holding flicked soapy water across the kitchen floor. She stared at me, her eyes glassy. The brush dripped.

'Fine. Fine.'

I left. I grabbed my coat and hat from the hall and went out, closing the front door behind me.

✳

I drove to Corey's, my head buzzing. So, my wife's ashamed of those things, is she? She thinks the medals are something to be embarrassed about, that I shouldn't have taken them? Well, there're certain rights that come when you vanquish another man, certain privileges; and war booty is one of them. That's the world, my love.

I walked to the front door and knocked hard. Seconds later Corey appeared. I pushed by him through the hallway into the kitchen.

'Who is it?' Corey's mother called from upstairs.

'Don't worry ma, I'll be up in a bit,' he said.

Corey closed the front door and joined me in the back. I hadn't been in that kitchen for forty years but it still looked the same. There was a wooden table with two chairs in the middle of the room. An old light hung above it, casting a stark beam onto a greasy tablecloth. A half-empty bottle of scotch lived there with a glass, and an overflowing ashtray. The sink was full of unwashed pots and the place smelled of fried chips. I let him get in and he just stood there studying me.

'Close the door,' I said.

He did. His movements were slow and deliberate. He turned to me.

'That Luftwaffe cadet,' I said. 'The dog tag you wanted back... I found it.'

Corey's expression didn't change. 'Do you want tea?' he said, moving to the stove.

'No, I don't.' I lit up and paced. I could feel him studying me. 'German War Graves Commission, eh?'

'They identify dead Germans. They tell the family, Jackie. That's all.'

'Thirty-two bloody years ago - I think they would've figured it out by now.'

'He won't be just another missing soldier, will he. His family will get...'

'What? What will they get, Corey? Closure? Is that the word for grieving folk and their dead? Closure?'

I exhaled aggressively. The smoke rolled out and filled the triangle of light between us, making a fog.

'Yes, that's it,' he said. 'They have a funeral for him. He'll finally have a proper grave, a headstone.'

'That's nice.'

'Jackie.' He shook his head like he was talking to a naughty kid. I wanted to thump him.

'Shut up.' Then it was my turn to shake my head. 'All this palaver over a dead kraut.'

I put my cig out and lit another. I could feel Corey staring at me. He seemed maddeningly calm.

'Tell me again what you said to me in Canada,' he said.

'Excuse me?'

'Tell me what you said about all this... and your Neil -'

'I don't give a toss what I said in Windsor, or whatever shit hole we were in. I was blowing off steam, nothing more.'

'Seeking redemption is not -'

'Oh, shut up with your shite! Three lousy, bloody krauts - fuck off.' I walked away for a second. I turned back to him. 'And I'm supposed to do that as well am I - turn in my feller's pay book and ID tag? Bung in the medals as well; so his family, wherever they are, can sing hymns? Is that what I'm supposed to do?'

'That would be up to you. But it wouldn't hurt, would it Jackie? Might take a load off.' He moved into the table and poured himself a drink.

'You've been mithering Bill Shaw as well, haven't you? Haven't you?'

'I spoke to Bill, yeah.'

'About getting this kid's pay book as well; but he won't give it, will he - won't part with it?'

He just looked at me.

'No, I didn't think so. And I'm with him on that one. About the only damn thing I agree with Bill Shaw on - is *that!*'

'Don't stoop to his level, Jackie -'

'Shut the fuck up!'

'Corey.' It was a faint voice from upstairs. He opened the door and shouted out.

'It's all right, ma.' He closed the door and turned back to me. 'You won't give it back... is that what you're saying?'

'What do you think?'

'Why? Why won't you give it back?' He came closer to the table; his head forward a little, his eyes narrowing.

'Because if I do that it means I agree with you, and there's no bleeding way, mate. German War Graves Commission, sod them. What about our lads? How many of their bones are still out there in Europe? No, no.' I paced. 'You can whistle for the bastard thing.' I threw my fag end down on to the lino and crumped it. 'And if you ever pull a stunt like you did at The Antelope today, I'll knock your fucking block off.' I threw up my collar and made to go.

'I'll never give up, Jackie, until I do what I have to do. And you help me do it. Because you did this... created me, all this -'

'Oh, go away with you, man.' I opened the door to the hall.

'We were supposed to take them to the field hospital!'

'Corey...' It was his mother calling.

I closed the door. I stood facing the door with my hand on the handle. He stepped right up behind me and spoke low. I could smell the booze.

'I'll never forget that day. I can't shake it, I try but I can't. Our orders were to take them along the supply road, back to battalion. And there - there they'd go to a field hospital to be treated for their injuries. Then on *your* orders, corporal Dunne, we moved off the road, down in the valley, where we could be alone with them, where a gunshot wouldn't be noticed.' I heard him take a drink. 'And I remember that field and that gulley. It was beautiful... patches of snow, the river and the willow. I will remember the weeping willows, hanging into the river, for the rest of my life...' He drank. 'But at that point I had no idea what you'd planned. I just thought we'd do *what Sarge said to do!* So, I thought I'd have some fun. Even though the camera was duff. "Stand next to me, mate, like I've known you for years, have a photo taken, lads. Share a fag while we take you to the rear, hand you to the doctors. You're brave, you've fought well and will be treated properly." I heard him drink. 'They didn't bank on running into three yobs from Manchester, did they?'

I stepped back, pulling the door open, knocking into him. I left.

✳

I drove east. There was no one on the road. Even for a Sunday the roads seemed empty. I felt like the last man on earth, or was driving through some people-less limbo. You bring this up, Corey, after all these years, to what? Well, it won't work. I am a hero, mate. I saved your Irish arse and the rest of the bloody section. I can see it even now, as I drive; it's all as clear as crystal in my head. Maybe you should remember, Corey; maybe you should.

The evil arc of tracer bullets, I saw them that day, coming over from that abandoned factory two hundred yards at two o' clock - that day you could've died, Corey. Dust flying up everywhere, and we're hitting the ground, hiding behind that small heap of rubble, protecting us from the bullets. But it's hardly enough, is it Corey, and the bullets are hitting back-packs, shredding them. You and Bill scrambling for cover with the Bren gun, me separated, realizing that *I* have the tripod! But we'll never get a shot in anyway, we're that pinned down. The buzz-saw sound of that German MG42, the fellers behind dashing to our spot for cover, piling in, scrambling for safety. And the tracers are bouncing off the rubble flying up in the air behind us for hundreds of yards, whipping in all directions. Then the trench mortars, Corey, landing all round us, red-hot splinters flying everywhere, and a lad's phosphorus grenade goes

146

up, hit by shrapnel or a bullet. We watch helplessly as he dies, burning to death, wriggling in agony, his high shrieks making us mad with hate.

And any minute your grenades will be hit and you'll go the same way as the last lad. And you're crying for your mam and I can't stand it - I won't have it, no. Us telling your mam you've died like that, not when I've told her we'll look after you, no.

So, I'm up now. Legging it to the left, but feel like I'm in deep sand like a dream, feel like I can't move fast enough, single bullets zipping past me. I'm at a stand of birch trees now, and the grenade is out. Hands shaking, I yank the pin and run to the window - run, run fifty yards away. Trip! I'm falling. The Mills Bomb falls, handle somersaulting away, and the thing rolling ahead with four seconds before - three, two - down on the dirt.... Bits hit the birch tree behind, feel the heat but I'm not hit. I'm up again running, but don't pull the pin until close, just keep running. Legs are like jelly but I reach the building, and I pull the pin and toss the grenade in the window. A second goes by and the thing is lobbed back out. Throw myself down... Can't believe I'm not hit and I get up. Unhook another bomb, pull the pin and let the handle ping away. I wait two seconds, hand shaking - I throw it in then... Then fellers here from our section shooting into the window... It's like a dream. I'm sick, puking. You and Bill screaming in my face, mad with joy.

✳

I pulled in next to a massive hedgerow and got out. It was thick and tall, almost like a wall. Walking down the road, it started to rain. I'd left my Trilby in the car. Bugger it.

I stopped and looked up at a grand Victorian job with big windows. The light from Bill's telly flickered blue in the front room. I pressed a button on the gate and heard a buzz. My watch said seven o' clock. Bill would be home. He was religious about watching The Golden Shot with Bob Monkhouse. I buzzed again and Bill's voice came back at me.

'Who's this?'

'Me.'

Silence. 'What do you want, man?'

'To talk.'

'I'm seeing you in two hours.'

'I'll be at the end of the road.'

'You're taking the piss, you… Who's with you?'

'I'm on me tod.'

He rang off. I buzzed again.

'I'll keep pressing this,' I said.

I could hear him railing on the intercom as I walked away. It was chucking it down now, but I didn't care. I waited at the bottom of the street, looking at the rain. It was hitting the road, splashing up millions of little explosions.

A few minutes later Bill came down under an umbrella. He stopped ten yards away and looked around. The street lamp couldn't penetrate the cover of the umbrella. He seemed to be a man without a head. I was talking to the devil himself.

'Always unpredictable, you,' he said. 'I have a shooter. I'm telling you in case you get funny. I'll use it.'

'Please yourself.' I wiped the water off my face. It was dripping off the end of my nose.

'Look at this weather. What's so bloody important that it can't wait 'til nine o' clock?'

148

'Macker's got feller's in town from Liverpool,' I said, raising my voice above the rain. 'He's planning something.'

'Give it a rest. You'll say anything to get that lad out of town.'

I could faintly see his head shaking. Steam from his breath was coming out.

'You won't do it, will you?' I said. 'Will you? Send the lad packing.'

'What did you expect?'

A car went by sending out a spray. Bill stepped aside. I stayed put and let it soak my legs.

'Did you listen to the tape?' I said.

He pulled it out of his coat.

'You told me he'd be in lumber,' I said, 'if you caught him flogging to Neil. That was our bargain, Liam Shaw.'

'He'll be punished. But I'm not kicking him out.'

'So things won't alter.'

He said nothing.

'So, it's all about the dosh?' I said.

'What the hell else are we doing this for?'

I said nothing at first. I saw him pocket the tape. 'I've seen Detroit,' I said.

'When? On Panorama?'

'I went there with our Neil for records. It's a war zone, that's what some call it. People are shot left, right and centre; ten shootings a day. That's what heroin does to a town.'

'We're English, not batty bloody yanks like them lot. It's guns that have ruined that city, not a bit of brown sugar.'

I could see him fidgeting and looking around. He was seconds from leaving.

'In ten years we won't recognize this place,' I said.

'And I give a bollocks? Manchester's a shit hole. Always was, always will be. You can't make a silk purse out of a sow's ear, that's what my old man used to say.'

'You're still quoting that Republican twat.'

'Steady, man.'

'Cheering for the krauts during the war. Bombs dropping all around us, and he's going on like that. Bloody disgusting.'

'You're already on shaky ground, mate. Don't push it.'

'Anyone normal would be embarrassed by him. But you…'

I heard him curse and he turned and started off. I shouted after him.

'I served my country!'

'And I was knitting?' He kept going.

'I did it willingly.'

He stopped and half turned. 'What is the point to all this, Dunne?'

'I'm proud of this country and this town.' I wiped the rain from my eyes. 'But you and your lot… There's a lot said about what the English did to Ireland, but not enough said about what the Irish have done to England.'

A car approached again. The headlights shone on him, show-ing his broken nose. He wasn't even looking at me. His breath billowed out like a dragon's. I raised my voice.

'Not even animals shit in their own back yard. But you lot… I won't let it happen.'

He looked at me. His body was still half-turned. 'Don't forget where you come from, Jackie Dunne.'

Rain was spilling into my mouth. I felt like I was drown-ing. I wiped my face again. 'I know who I am; an Englishman surrounded by Micks. Micks who want to tear it all down.'

He said nothing. I could hear him thinking underneath that umbrella. Then he turned his body to me.

'There's something not right with you, Dunne. Look at you. You're still dressed like it's nineteen fucking forty-four. Stuck in the past. But you can only pity a man who's lost the plot for so long. Patience runs out. Then he's just in the way. So, don't force my hand, Dunne. You repay your debts.'

'It's odd for a man to protect his community, his country?'

'You think a few bloody charity events can change the colour of your spots? Think again. You're one of us and don't forget it. So play by the rules and make reparations. That's how it all keeps going. Co-operation.'

I saw his finger peep out from the darkness of the umbrella, pointing at me.

'Eight grand, Dunne - I want it at this meeting, tonight. I know you're good for it. That's pocket change for you. So nine o' clock... think on. As for this thing...'

He pulled out the tape and dropped it to the pavement. He stamped on it and kicked it into the gutter. The rainwater carried it down to the sewer grate, where it swirled for a few seconds and then disappeared.

'That's your answer, is it?' I said. 'I thought I'd give it one last time.'

'Don't do anything daft. There's certain things I won't forgive. Nor will anyone else.'

'Don't bother coming. The meeting is off.'

I turned and walked. I heard him come up and snap a round up the spout of his Walther pistol. I felt the barrel in the back of my neck. He pulled the umbrella to the side to hide it.

'You steal from me - make me look like a fucking idiot and I just take it?' He pushed the barrel harder. 'You think I'll snap to because corporal Jackie fucking Dunne, Military Medal holder and chief cunt tells me too? You have another think coming, matey.' He shoved the pistol again into my head. 'I'll drop you, man. I will. You have a *day* to get that money. A *day*.'

I heard him walk away. I let the rain flatten the hair to my head. The number twelve bus floated by, throwing out gallons of water on either side. I watched it disappear like an amphibious vehicle on a mission.

✷

As I got back to the car, I noticed a phone box on the corner. I went in and got out some coins. I put what I had on the phone unit, and got out a card from my wallet. It read:

Robert Shadrack, Editor. The Evening News.

I picked up the phone and called Danny, cancelling the meeting. He had a conniption. I calmed him down and he begged me to call Mary. I did. She went ballistic as well, so I hung up on her. I then dialed the number on the card and waited while it rang. It took a while but it was picked up. I put the coin in when a man answered.

'Robert Shadrack, speaking.'

'Jackie Dunne. We met at that fundraiser this summer.'

Silence. 'It's late, Mr. Dunne.'

'Sorry to bother you at home… Remember we talked about what was going on? There'd just been a run of overdoses, folk dying from heroin. The papers said it was kids bringing it back from holidays in the east.'

'I remember.'

'Well, it's not. Certain parties are organized. They're the ones bringing it in. I want to talk to you about it.'

'When?'

'Now. It won't take long.' There was a silence. I looked down at the floor. I was standing in a puddle of my own creating. 'Mr. Shadrack, are you there?'

'I think you should give this some serious thought first, Mr. Dunne.'

'That's exactly what I've been doing. You thinking this is about self-interest on my part, is that it? It's all right, that's the first thing I would think, someone like me calling you at this hour. He's had a row with certain parties and wants to see them go down, right?'

'It crossed my mind.'

I could feel myself shaking with the cold, my teeth chattering. 'Look, Mr. Shadrack - when all's said and done I'm a citizen, someone who cares about what happens in his community. There's wheeling and dealing, then there's just wanton destruction. Murder. It won't do, not for this town. That's how I see it.'

'I see.'

'We need to get the attention of the coppers, the council. They seem oblivious to what's going on. Are you interested?'

'Are you sure it can't wait until tomorrow?'

I knew I'd change my mind if I did that. So would he. I couldn't have him hanging up, so I made a decision.

'Use my name. You can quote me. You can't say it's about self-interest now, can you? 'Cause that would put me life in danger, wouldn't it.'

'I wouldn't want that.'

'Or are you thinking what might happen to you? If you spill

the beans, as it were…. Mr. Shadrack?'

'I'd be a liar if I didn't consider it.'

'That's fair enough. At least you're honest.'

'But I do understand duty. I am a journalist. And I live here in this city, as well.'

'Duty. I like that. We're on the same page then. Self-sacrifice, sir. Some of us don't mind taking a bullet for things we believe in. There are still fellers like that, Mr. Shadrack. It's not as rare as you think.'

'I know about your military record, Mr. Dunne.'

'I don't give a two-penny fuck about that, sir; excuse my French. But it's useful at times like this, if it gives me credibility and means you'll listen.'

I heard a woman's voice in the background. 'Robert, who is it?'

'It's all right, Susan, just work.'

It was now or never. 'I've got enough coins here for about twenty minutes. It's all we'll need.'

'Let me get organized here.'

I looked down and saw that the puddle was now the whole floor of the phone box. A woman was outside standing with an umbrella. I popped my head out.

'Love, I'm going to be here for a bit. Can you come back in twenty minutes? Go home, keep dry and come back. Can you do that?'

She looked at me like I was mad. Then she just turned and walked away. The rain was making a spray on the top of her umbrella; it was coming down so hard. I closed the door. The windows were steaming up. I lit a cig and pulled out my mickey. I leaned and got comfortable. He came back to the phone and

I heard the rustling of paper. He told me to go ahead. I did so. I talked to Robert Shadrack of The Evening News as the wind and rain howled about outside.

THREE

The Staff Sergeant looks at us all.

'Right, Dunne, orders are to take these bastards back to Battalion HQ.'

I look at the three prisoners, a sorry looking bunch. Then I'm back with the Sarge.

'That's two miles back down the road here,' he says. 'We can't spare any vehicles. Just stay on the road, there'll be traffic to and fro, and don't wander into the fucking fields. Some of them aren't secure. This area's still lousy with Waffen SS and the bleeding Werewolves. Is that clear?'

'Yes, Sarge,' I say.

'Once at HQ ask for a Captain Hughes, he's the MO and he'll register these cunts with Lieutenant Colonel Harwood. Then he'll take the prisoners, treat them, tart them up for questioning.'

'Yes, Sarge.'

'Hughes will direct you to SQMS Francis who'll make sure you're fed and will give you the necessary supplies and send you back on the next available lorry. Don't forget the fucking fags and brandy.'

'Yes, Sarge,'

'Here's your travel documents, signed by the Lieutenant. Don't make a bleeding pig's ear of it. See you shortly. Carry on.'

'Very good, Sarge.' I say.

I turn and examine the prisoners. One's a boy soldier, no more than fifteen, wearing a Luftwaffe uniform. He's uninjured but ragged and filthy, his face blackened by gunpowder. The other is an SS Rottenfuhrer and his head and one eye are band-aged. He's also a mess. The other soldier is a young Wehrmacht officer, an Oberleutnant. His arm is in a sling and he's in the same state as the others. The soldiers look completely haggard, years older than what they probably are. I look again at the Oberleutnant and he looks…. familiar. But it's impossible, I think.

'Hande hoch, you bastard's,' says Bill. 'What's Jerry for about face?'

'Get fucking moving,' says Corey, grinning and gesturing with his Lee Enfield. 'Bewegung - bewegung!'

The prisoners start moving ahead of us. It's slow going. Vehicles pass us moving to the front, 3-tonners, 15cwt trucks, half-tracks and field artillery being towed. I keep looking at my prisoner, this Oberleutnant. As we get further from the lines soldiers thin out. Apart from the odd lorry, we're alone. I keep my eyes peeled left and right for any enemy activity out in the fields. We hear the odd spatter of small arms on both sides of the road.

Corey starts to take photographs of the prisoners. First it starts with him photographing them from behind.

'Look at the state of him with that bastard camera,' says Bill about Corey. 'The bloody thing's shot to buggery, Blaine.'

'I'm making a day of it,' says Corey. Click, click, and click again. Then he stops them and lines them up. 'Come on Freddie, Mike and Arnie. Get in a row.'

'What the feck are you doing, Corey?' I say.

'Oh, I do like to be beside the seaside,' he sings, 'beside the seaside, beside the sea.' Click, click, click.

'He's lost his marbles,' says Bill.

'Let him do it,' I say. 'We need a bloody laugh.'

'Get in, lads,' Corey says to us. 'It's the swimming arcade at Southport.'

'No, it's not, you bastard,' Bill says, 'It's the fucking central pier at Blackpool.'

'Come on, Uncle Jackie,' Corey says.

Bill and me line up just behind the prisoners, our guns still trained on them. They are sheepish and look to the ground.

'Smile, you Jerry bastards,' Corey says. He goes to one, the young one, and lifts his head and grins at him. The kid smiles. He does the same to the others. The SS man shifts his head away from Corey's hands. 'Touchy bastard, isn't he,' says Corey. 'Smile, you cunt.'

'Leave him be,' I say. 'Mind that rifle, Corey. Swiping the bloody thing and taking *us* prisoners.'

The Oberleutnant voluntarily lifts his head and stares ahead. He is stoic and dignified, even as a prisoner. They're tough men.

Corey clicks away on the ruined camera.

Click, click, click, and click. I look to the side to see the Oberleutnant. *I suddenly recognize him.* It's unbelievable. I think I'm just dead wrong; it just can't be. My imagination is messing with me. I tell Corey to stop arsing about and get us going again. We walk along.

We stop to rest. They drink water and we smoke cigarettes. As we're about to set off again, I catch the Oberleutnant looking at me. He quickly looks away.

We walk along some more. He'd quickly looked away; yes, he'd quickly looked away. I've lost at least a stone in weight since Belgium, and endless fighting has hardened my features and changed my face. But he looked away. Yes, yes, it's him. *And he recognized me.*

'Over here,' I say. I point to a gully next to a river that leads off into a field. 'Move,' I say. I shove the Oberleutnant.

'What you doing, Dunne?' says Bill.

'Shortcut,' I say. 'The road curves round up yon. We'll get there quicker.'

'But Sarge -' says Corey.

'Yeah, there's still enemy out there - the Werewolves, Dunne!'

'Shut it!' I say. 'I'm the fucking corporal, I'm in charge.'

Corey and Bill look at one another, shrug, and then guide their prisoners, the Luftwaffe cadet and the SS man. We walk down from the rise of the road onto the lower level of the field and gully. We walk. The ground's hard and frozen, and there's still un-melted snow. We can hear the sound of our boots crunching underfoot. I look to Bill as he follows the SS soldier. His helmet is set at a jaunty angle and he's grinning. He knows what will happen. He knows what we're going to do.

I opened my eyes and sat up slowly. I was rough. The booze and the Nembutal's were getting their own back. I reached for some aspirin on the side table and necked about six, chewing them like they were Jelly Babies. I was in the spare room and the clock said it was seven in the morning. Brenda had been up and down all night with Neil, so I'd come in for some peace.

I shuffled to the bathroom and downed about four glasses of water. I danced a toothbrush around my mouth and went back to the room.

The wind moaned outside and the open curtains quivered a bit. I looked outside at the dark as I had a cig. Then I felt sick. There was a couple of crackers and a crumble of cheese on the side table, remains of my midnight, boozy nosh-up. So, I fought my way through them, washing them down with water. I eased into my clothes like a leper.

I tiptoed into Neil's room. While he snored like a dragon, I picked it up the shoebox from the side of his bed, opened it and checked the contents were all there; the Iron Cross, Wound Badge, Close Combat Clasp, pay books and dog tags. I limped downstairs with the box. I got my coat and hat and left.

✻

There was a light but chilly breeze fiddling its way up from the Irwell valley. Not the usual arm-wrestling bluster, but the gathering clouds looked dark, unfriendly.

I drove over to Cheetham Hill Road, parked the vehicle and went into Mavis's Café. I ordered a fry up, gagging at the thought of it. Mavis knew not to pester me. She'd seen me in some states and just kept schtum, placing my order down with a nod and a wink. I wolfed down a gallon of tea and a couple of Black Bombers. I needed the amphetamine. So, down they went with strong, sweet tea.

I began to feel human again, but Shadrack and the article were playing on me. Even though I'd mulled it over for months, I still got the flutters. In the sober light of day I was having second thoughts. I considered calling him and cancelling, something I was ashamed to even think of, but then I read the morning papers. A kid had died over the weekend of a drug overdose. Heroin.

Shadrack told me the article would be in tonight, or it could be held for the weekend. Reading of this latest tragedy, I knew it would be today, so I couldn't stop it now if I tried. I was edgy. The response wouldn't be good from friends as well as enemies. I had about six hours to smooth the way, if that was possible.

If all this wasn't enough, I started to think about Corey and last night; him looking at me like he did across the kitchen table.

'What did you say to me in Canada, Jackie?'

And I thought about that trek across the border from Detroit. So what if I went to unload, share some shit that was bothering me. We all have these moments. We'd nearly lost Neil for the umpteenth time, for God's sake. I was vulnerable, man. And in that taxi, going through the Detroit to Windsor tunnel, my mind had been spinning.

I'd always managed to deal with the war. For years it was just an inconvenient memory. I had the fidgeting, the boozing, the odd nightmare; it was standard crap really. Most times the war was like a dream, someone else's life. The memories were covered in gauze that made everything fuzzy and out of focus. Sometimes, in the past, images would come a bit clearer - in dreams or even during the day. But recently, after Neil's first heroin overdose and withdrawal, the sight of him scrunched up in pain… it had kick-started some rum shit.

It was as if this gauze was suddenly ripped or sliced through, pulled apart, and these memories were there in Technicolor. And with them came the gut feelings, the smells, the thoughts, the reactions. There'd been times when I thought I was going mad.

I'd see Alfie Church dying of his belly wound, suffering so much that we killed him with morphine. Then it was Reggie Warburton dying in that barn, bayoneted by a Waffen SS Panzergrenadier. Then Alan Pankhurst dying of typhus in the field hospital in Germany. All of them curled up and clutching their stomachs, faces contorted with agony. Then Neil's face would replace theirs, and it went on and on. These phantoms would just appear in the middle of the day. I could be doing anything and suddenly there they'd be, as if they were happening now.

Then I'd thought I was just going soft and I'd get livid at myself for this bloody weakness. It was inexcusable to be this feeble, so I just buried it again under work and play.

But then… then I'd started seeing Neil in that German uniform lying on the floor, twisted, grotesque as dead soldiers lay. The uniform was bursting with fat, bloated legs. Sausage fingers were claw-like with black fingernails. *Then* I knew I had to talk to someone. And it happened to be Corey. After all, he was thousands of miles away. I never thought I'd see the bugger any time soon. But it was a mistake telling the bastard all this. His mother got sick and here he was, using all this for his own ends.

I read the paper some more and played with my breakfast. I ate one sausage and half an egg.

✳

I set off for Neil's flat. The ructions of the last forty-eight hours were flitting in my head like bees round a hive. I was so mithered by it all – Macker, the drugs, Bill, Corey, my German Shepherd, Mary, Danny, the Scousers and a Partridge in a bloody Pear Tree, that I took a wrong turn. I was heading east on what was left of Market Street.

I would usually keep clear of the street at all costs. I'd never forgiven the council for destroying what the Luftwaffe had failed to do. The Arndale Shopping Centre had gutted this famous boulevard, replacing it with a monstrosity that pained me to even look at. Suddenly, there it was looming like something from Stalinist Russia.

I threw on some Sinatra to sooth my approaching conniption. 'My Kind of Town' came on. That was better. I could've taken a right on Cross Street but to conquer my ill will, I continued up the ruined road. The next minute I was navigating an abortion of unfinished roadway, fenced-off ditches and diversionary signs.

I was soon back on tarmac and continued through Piccadilly. But it didn't stop me fuming about what the developers had done to my city. In truth, it'd been downhill since the late fifties, when Manchester couldn't be matched by any city in Europe. This had been my time. And we turned this place into something special.

I cast my mind back to that time. It was nostalgia, sure enough, but all my shenanigans back then affected what was going on right now. And what the outcome might be.

I'd just been demobilized in '47 from Germany and showed up to a madhouse of black-market opportunity. I was blotto for two years, but the scrapping had been far from a waste of time. It made my name with the scallies. So, by the time I'd got cracking and started with the scrap metal yards, no bugger would touch me. These bankrolled coffee shops on Oxford Road then later a small jazz club. Still chocker-block with yanks of every colour, race and creed, all with money a-plenty, we pulled in a lot of gelt. Gambling joints and gentleman's clubs, all reeking of cannabis, followed. The effects of this bonanza spilled over into Salford and surrounding areas, where the local lads cleaned up as well. The cops had all been bought off. It was paradise. And so it had been right up until the early sixties, when all but a few yanks had left. But still, the soul of the city had vanished, and the destruction of Market Street rung the death knells. It was the end of an era that was not to be seen again. *But*, and this was important, many of my mates were still here. I knew that most, whose fortunes I'd made during that time, who respected and feared me, would back me up through thick and thin. I was gambling on it at least. I would need them. In the wake of this article, I would.

I could feel the Bombers kicking in. Even the dirty grey of the smog-caked buildings were taking on a rosy hue. As I got off the Mancunian Way, I got out the mickey and I took a nip. My headache was fading. Frank had finished, so I threw on another tape. First up was Ray Charles, 'I Don't Need No Doctor.' I sure didn't. I was driving like bleeding Mario Andretti.

Ten minutes later I was in Neil's flat. I went into the living room to get the medals. My medals. If Brenda had a problem with my Jerry souvenirs, maybe seeing *my* service medals on the wall of my pub, would give her some perspective.

I looked at the mantelpiece and the wall. They were gone. My service medals and my Military Medal had all done a runner. The portrait of me as a young corporal had also been swiped. The photograph of Brenda and me with baby Neil had been smashed to buggery. The frame was in bits and shards of glass were scattered on the carpet.

I sat down, lit up, and looked around. I sat there looking at this crummy flat. The Hi-Fi was gone and his records nicked. The place was a hodgepodge of furniture that'd all come with the flat. There were hardly any personal touches of his anywhere. It was as if he didn't even live here. The only evidence he'd been here *at all* was the photos and medals. Seeing them gone, it felt like he'd disappeared all over again. Vanished into thin air.

I sat there grinding my teeth and thinking who might swipe the things. My cigarette was still burning as I got in the car and set off for Longsight.

✻

Macker lived off Stockport Road in an old slum at the end of a row. I drove by the place and there was his Capri, still bearing the scars of my vandalism. I drove round the corner.

I parked the car, took the dagger from under the passenger seat, and a dog treat from the glove box. I went round to the front. Looking through a small gap in the shabby curtains, I could make out the midden that was Macker's front room. I strained my eyes for details, and thought I recognized the frame of my service medals on the settee.

I checked my watch. It was barely nine o'clock and the upstairs curtains were closed. Macker was a night owl, and nothing short of a nuclear holocaust would raise him before two in the afternoon.

I went round to the back. His pokey yard was walled and the door bolted on the inside. I pulled a rubbish bin to the wall, got on it, and launched myself from one to the other. I threw my leg over and jumped down, landing on a small shed that once contained the rabbits that he fed live to his pet python. The snake had been killed when it strangled one of his dog's puppies. That was it for Sir Hiss, the python. He was beheaded with an axe, leaving his body wriggling for a full five minutes until it was dead.

I slid the bolt open on the door in case of a quick exit.

Delilah, his Rottweiler, peered through the curtains at me. Knowing me she didn't bark, but whined like a mad weasel. I pulled out a dog treat and showed it to her. I was her signal to shut up. She did and just slavered on the window. As I got to the door, I pulled out my tools and went to work. I fiddled at the lock for an embarrassingly long time, but eventually I was in. The animal sidled up to me, its bobtail buffing the linoleum floor. I fed her and moved on.

I went through the washhouse to the kitchen, stealing about as quietly as I could. The house was the disgrace I remembered, but with a few added atrocities.

The kitchen was a disaster. A fortnight's worth of pots billowed out of the sink. All surfaces held odds and sods of every variety, and there was the reek of festering rubbish from somewhere. The tops were sticky and stained. The lino curled up at the ends, leaving dark spaces behind that were clogged with matter and filth. There was even a petrified dog turd lurking in the corner.

The front room was no better. Sad, half-closed curtains hung ragged, casting the room in an even darker light. The furniture was the usual circus of poor taste. A dirty-white leather three-piece sat on the outskirts, while a glass and metal-tubing coffee table stood abandoned in the middle. Dried and sticky powder covered part of its cracked top. Coffee mugs, spoons and plates with half eaten scraps on it, scraps that even the dog seemed revolted by, covered the rest. An off-white shag pile rug lay rotting like a dead animal underneath it. Records were everywhere; LPs, 45s stacked and fanned out in fallen piles. Drug paraphernalia was all over the place. Three or four bongs were scattered about, upright and horizontal. Rubber tourniquets lay hither and yon like dead grass snakes. Plastic baggies, cellophane and syringes lay next to beer bottles and tin foil.

But among this catastrophe of clutter, the display cases containing my medals were stuffed. One was leaning up against the back of the settee; the other that held my Military Medal was next to it, laying flat. The photo of me as a corporal was on the side unit, staring out from between two piles of magazines.

It was disturbing to see my photograph in Macker's house. To say it was creepy wasn't in it. I was reminded of the row I'd had with Mary.

I gathered them all up. Delilah had been following me religiously up until now. Now, she turned and looked at the stairs, cowering. I couldn't see anything right away; but I followed the line of the stair rail up to where it joined the ceiling. Pointing at me was a sawn-off double-barreled shotgun.

'Don't move, Jackie.'

It was Macker's voice. I felt like a prize twat thinking I could pull this off.

'I could shoot you, Jackie.'

'Aye, you could, but what good would that do?'

'Make me feel better.'

I said nothing.

'I didn't want the dog to die,' he said. 'I'm not a monster, Jackie. I told Joey to do some 'at to your car pitch. I thought he'd smash a few windows. But the dog… fuck… the twat got some steak and put rat poison in it. That's what he told me.'

I said nothing.

'I'll punish him for it, I will,' he said. 'Making me look like a psycho… a poor, innocent animal.'

I couldn't see him, just the nozzle of the gun. Without his face I could tell he was talking from side of his mouth, the other side from my cutting. He was angry, unpredictable.

'Put it away, Macker.'

'You killed my car.'

'It'll get well again.'

He snorted. 'You're breaking and entering.'

'Just getting what's mine.'

He said nothing.

'What do you want with a bunch of medals?' I said.

'Souvenirs. You have souvenirs as well, don't you… souvenirs of a dead soldier? Maybe when you're dead I'll put them up at The Shamrock next to Bill's.'

How did he know about my war booty? Bill must've told him. I heard him cock one of the trigger hammers.

'How long do you think you can pull the wool over Bill's eyes?' I said.

'As long as I want; he just sees the money, blinded by greed.'

'It won't take long for him to work things out,' I said. 'Those two deadlegs you've got lumbering around town, they won't go unnoticed.'

'They looked after me when I was inside.'

'And they'll do the same to you as you plan for Bill. Mark my words. They're just using you.'

He shifted slightly. 'You think I'm thick, don't you?'

'I'm older. I see stuff you don't. You can't trust a Scouser. You're always an outsider to them. They hate everything east of the M57.'

He clicked the other hammer. He was planning on giving me both barrels, or was he posturing. I couldn't be sure. But I had to think fast.

'If you're planning on making some money don't blow it by killing me.'

'Why would that mess up my plans? That would help me, with you out of the way.'

'Murder - it's not you, Macker.'

'How do you know what's me?'

'You'll get caught in the end. Folk always do.'

'Only if there's evidence. Have your body in bits in no time. Get some acid. No evidence, no crime.'

I felt a trickle of sweat meander down my back. The lad was enjoying this. I had to get the barrel away from pointing at me. The shotgun was fickle, sometimes with a hairpin trigger. I'd seen them go off when they weren't meant to, the slightest movement sending them blasting.

'Put the shooter down, Macker. We can talk more sensible without that pointing at me.'

He scoffed. I flinched as the barrel moved.

'You're quid's in where ever you are,' I said. 'Norwich, Sunderland - it doesn't matter what city - you can make good graft. Take your trade and the Scousers and bog off where there's no agro. No Jackie Dunne. I wouldn't be mithered. Why don't you do that?'

He started to sing 'Purple Haze.'

I let him get through the first verse.

'Purple Haze,' I said. 'Your favourite.'

'Johnny Jones and The King Casuals. Their version knocks spots off Hendricks's solo effort.'

I began scouring my brain to find common ground, trying to think of the record label, but my mind was blank.

'When I drive down Oxford Street to Whalley Range,' he said, 'where a university professor cuts the smack for us, the pavement's lined with students mad for a Saturday night on the town. I look at all these kids and I think there it is, the key to my fortune. Why the fuck should I piss off to some pokey shit hole, when in five years I'll own this bleeding town. Why?'

He started to sing the second verse. When he'd finished he said: 'What label, Jackie - the label for the record? Johnny Jones and the King Casuals.'

He was playing with me. The stress and the speed had my heart coming out of my chest. I cursed myself for bottling out under the pressure. I thought of legging it to the back door, but I knew the shotgun would get me. I heard a car pull up outside.

'That'll be me mates,' he said.

The Scousers had turned up. I didn't need a crystal ball to

guess what was coming if those two got the better of me.

'Better start praying, Jackie.' We heard the car doors closed. Then the doorbell rang. 'Avon calling.'

He pulled the barrel from between the slats up to the banister. I saw my chance. I threw the picture frame at the gun and made for the kitchen. Macker was thumping down the stairs. I got to the door and threw it open. The wall next to my shoulder exploded. I was already out, my ears ringing. I made the yard door in seconds and was out into the alleyway.

I legged it down to the Cortina. I fumbled with the keys until it was open and the medals tossed in. I turned and there was a Scouser rounding the corner, brandishing a knife. The other came careening from the alley, holding the Rounder's bat.

I pulled the dagger out and squared off. The two ground to a halt. I grinned, pointed out their injuries. There they were; the filleted nose, the carved-up face.

'Here we go again, lads. Sucker's for punishment, you two.' I pointed the dagger at one then the other. 'What happened yesterday - nowt compared to what I'll do now. Take a step closer fellers.'

They started posturing, chins out, legs going. It was a sight and a half. I stepped closer, the speed boiling in my blood.

'I will cut out your throats and bury the fucking pair of you, here and now, so let's go. Come on!'

The two of them wavered, but fucked and blinded to make up for doing sod all. Macker showed up, sans shotgun. Despite the wound, he carried a shit-eating grin that would've suited the devil himself.

'And you,' I said to him. 'Come on – you all right now – I'll have the lot of you. Just give me the bleeding excuse - please.'

Macker put his hands up to call off his dogs.

'You never told me, Jackie,' he said.

'Told you? Told you what?'

'Johnny Jones and the King Casuals. You never told me what the record label was.'

I walked up to his smirking face. I could feel the Scousers fidgeting in my periphery. I'd laid myself open but I didn't care. I got to him and put the blade to his chest, right where his heart was.

'Why don't you tell *me*, kiddo?'

'Purple Haze.' He paused for effect. 'Peachtree Records. Produced by William Bell. Supervised by Henry Wynn.'

I nearly laughed. The kid was pots for rags mental. I shook my head and walked away. I got to the car to see the three of them dribbling off.

'We will get you, Dunne,' said the one with the nose.

I waved him away like he was a naughty child. Then I got in the motor and hit the wheel in triumph. Driving off I felt amazing. I'd terrorized the deadlegs, put the kid in his place *and* gotten the medals back. My humiliation at the hands of that cocky, little swine was erased. It was like being twenty-three again; riled up and punchy - back in the bare- knuckle days with the gypsies - when me and Bill got paid for leathering fellers - in the old fruit market in Ancoats, a ruin from the bombing.

My heart thumped and raced. Speed. It'd come in handy, by God it had; and we'd found it in the war of all places. Some lippy SS Panzer bastard who'd surrendered, and after we'd beaten ten colours out of him and brought him to heel, 'cause he was a lippy swine and well out of order - fearless even, we

172

found out why. Little blue pills called Pervitin. Panzer Sweets, they called them: 'Vor staiyin' avake.' And so we took them and by golly-me, Jeez, it was no bloody wonder the krauts had the jump on us. In a thirty-six-hour battle you needed no sleep. And they made you mad with bravery.

I slammed in the 8-track and got a stomper 'The Champion' by Willie Mitchel - surprise, surprise.

✳

After my adrenalin leveled out, I got somber. Macker had no intension of going anywhere; that much was obvious. And his plans made me shiver. But I did feel better about the article. Justified again. So, as I drove over to Brian's office on Peter Street, I plotted. I'd tuck my kid away in detox and hone in on Macker. Enough was enough. If the article didn't have the desired effect, I'd sort this out my way, just like Frank - come hell or high water.

I took a bit of whisky, parked and bounded into Brian's office.

'You all right?' Brian said. 'You look a bit frazzled, Jackie.'

'Standard stuff, mate.'

We talked about the details of the lease contract. I decided on a year, which meant there would be a rental review. But given Neil's history, I didn't want to mess Brian about again. We agreed. He said he would make the contract up, and I could come over tomorrow and sign it. We shook hands and had a nip of whisky to celebrate.

After I was done at Brian's I made a quick phone call to Jimmy Mac at the car pitch. True enough, he'd buried Rodney. Mary had been in and had left in a Vauxhall Magnum, the temporary rental. She'd looked at the Jeep I'd offered. She'd been quiet, which meant she was still stinging from yesterday.

I came back from phoning Jimmy, sat in the Cortina and had a cig. Time was getting on. I'd planned to stick the war booty in the safe in my office, but with all the rigmarole of the morning, I'd forgotten to do it. I got out and stuck the shoebox, along with my medals, in the boot of the car under the carpet. I set off home. I had an hour and a half to get Neil to Altrincham.

✳

The morning frost was still there. The blades of grass on my lawn looked like little sabre-teeth, crisp and sharp. The wind from the valley was steady, low and cold. The bulbous clouds were a blunt dark-grey and drooped like sacks. We were in for an almighty deluge.

The house smelt like a shebeen or a drug den. The whiff of hash was well out of order. I went through to the kitchen. Brenda was dressed and drinking tea. She now had a packet of Silk Cut cigarettes. She probably had a tot of sherry in the tea as well.

'How's he doing?' I said.

'I think he's through the worst of it,' she said. 'He really is.'

I could sense resistance. She was getting windy about him going, I could tell. I ignored it.

'He won't be able to smoke that stuff over there, you know.' I said.

'Where've you been?'

I told her about Brian and the lease. I left out the other stuff.

'He's looking for those German medals,' she said.

'You wanted them gone, so I took them to the pub. I'll stick

174

them in the safe over there.'

She took a puff of her Silk Cut. I knew what she was thinking, so I said:

'I'm not throwing them away, Brenda. They're collectors' items, those. I'll flog them at some point, all right?'

'Did you give Corey the dog tag thing?'

'Soon,' I lied.

I could tell she wanted to get into it. I wondered whether or not I should tell her about the article. Ease the way. But I bottled out. After we'd sorted Neil I'd tell her; one thing at a time.

'What?' she said, reading my mind in that way she could.

'Nothing. Just a bit rushed.'

I escaped upstairs. Music was coming from the room, and the reek of cannabis made my eyes sting. I knocked and went in. The place looked like someone had stuck on a fog machine. He was sat on the chair nice and smart, his hair combed and parted. There was a big suitcase and a smaller one open and full of records. Next to that was the portable record player. It was playing a record.

'Are you ready?' I said, opening a window.

'Aye,' he said, his eyes like saucers. 'I'm nervous.'

'You'll be fine. What are you playing?'

'Something New to Do.'

'Don't tell me, don't tell me… Bobby Sheen.'

'What label?'

'Are you joking?'

He grinned. I told him about seeing Brian and prepping the contract. We talked about the record shop, but he was elsewhere. He nodded and stared at the floor.

175

'What's up?' I said.

'I do admit, dad - I do… that I am powerless. Powerless over drugs and that my life has become unmanageable.'

'Okay…' I said, nodding. 'Well, I'd have to agree with that.'

'And I've also come to believe that only a power - a power greater than myself… can restore me to sanity.'

I started to panic a bit here, because it looked like he'd lost it; gone off the deep end. I nodded nervously. He went on:

'And I've made a decision to turn my will over - over to the care of God as I understand him.'

He looked at me for approval. I suddenly realized he was quoting the twelve steps of the detox program. He'd been studying the pamphlet. I sighed with relief. At least we hadn't fried his brain, what with the lithium, the hash, the sleeping pills and the bloody Paracetamol.

'Don't rush those steps, you know,' I said. 'You're supposed to take your time with all those. There's twelve of the bugger's.'

'I can't muck about, dad. Not after the time I've wasted. I've made "a searching and fearless moral inventory of myself." I've done that, and I've a list here of my wrongs. Do you want to see them?'

'Not right now, mate. Have you been through any of these with your mam?' I said, thinking there was a lot of God in there.

'No, no,' he said, his eyes brightening up. 'She doesn't know I've been studying. I'm going to surprise her.'

'Right.' I checked my watch. 'Look, sort this record case out and come down. We need to get going here.'

I took the clothes suitcase downstairs and put it in the hall. Brenda was outside feeding the birds. I went through.

'We should get going, love,' I said.

She emptied her hands onto the lawn.

'He's still stoned, Brenda.'

'At least he's comfortable.'

'He's ripped out of his head. They'll know at the clinic.'

'It's for drug addicts, isn't it?'

She was dithering. I could feel it coming.

'What?' I said, expecting the worst.

'I'm getting nervous about...'

I sighed the breath of the world. She went on:

'I'm sorry but I am.'

'He's got to go, Brenda... Brenda.'

'But does he?'

It was amazing that I didn't throw something at the wall at this point. Considering I was jazzed on speed, it was nothing short of a miracle. I breathed.

'Love. We talked about this and we decided. It's all paid for.'

'I'm sorry but I do think we're through the worst of it.'

I was grinding my teeth like a cow on a cud. I knew that winning the argument now would be impossible, so I said:

'Why don't we wait until we get there and you can see for yourself, eh? Just give it a chance. You can see the facilities and we can make the call then.'

'Wait until we get there to make a decision?'

'Yeah, we can.' I got her coat. 'Come on, we're late. Help him down the stairs. He'll break his bloody neck.' I went back up and got the suitcase full of records he'd just closed. It weighed a ton. Brenda came up. 'Hand me that portable. Give him a hand, love. Please. We can't be late.'

She dragged her heels but she did it. I was fair fuming by

now at this sudden development, but I ploughed on. I took the record suitcase and the portable downstairs and put it with the clothes suitcase. I took the clothes suitcase and the portable out to the car and stuck them in the boot. Then Neil staggered out with the record suitcase. Brenda looked at me with a face like a smacked arse. I sighed, walked up the path, and took the suitcase. I stuck it in the back and we all piled in. I set off for Altrincham.

✳

Brenda's resistance was a thick atmosphere in the car. I knew I'd have to play this wily.

'Tell your mam more about this twelve-step thingy,' I said to Neil.

'You're both on my list, you know,' said Neil, 'of folk who I've harmed. And I will make amends, mam - dad.'

'Tell her about the - what was it - the higher power.'

'Oh aye. "I'm entirely ready to have God… remove all the defects of my character." Entirely ready, mam.'

I looked at Brenda. 'This is all the stuff they do at this centre.'

'I'm going to ask Him to remove all my shortcomings later. It's top of the list, that is.'

'And what's that one,' I said, 'where you admit stuff to God and to some other geezer?'

'Oh aye. "Admit to God, to myself, and to another human being the - " what the feck is it… ah yeah – "the exact nature of my wrongs." I have admitted to God, mam. Now I'm admitting to you about the nature of my wrongs.'

'Right now?' she said, looking at me.

'I have to start sometime. I've been selfish, immature. And

I've led you a dog's life.'

'Well, I couldn't disagree with that.'

'See?' I said. 'This is what this place specializes in. You won't get this at Hope Hospital.'

'Oh, look at that cloud, mam.' At this point Neil was drooling on the window. 'It looks like a face. The nose, the thingy... chin... amazing.'

He shut up for a bit so I let it settle with Brenda. She was too clever not to know that I was playing her, and I knew this wouldn't be easy. We got on the motorway at Worsley and drove in silence to the flyover. We could see the expanse of the land before us; the warehouses of Trafford park to our left and the parks of Urmston to the right. In front the Cheshire plains stretched as far as we could see, all the way to Jodrell Bank.

Neil started up again.

'There's a lot of soul songs that are about God, you know,' he said. 'You think they're singing about a bird or a feller but they're not. It's their love of God.'

I heard him rummaging through his rucksack for 8-tracks.

'I doubt you can crank music to the level you're used to,' I said. 'There's other people to consider, you know. Not everyone wants to listen to Northern Soul stompers.'

'I'll get out the smoothies,' he replied, '...the softies. It'll help folk relax.' He passed an 8-track to Brenda. 'Put some 'at on, mam.'

She stuck it in. A soul song came on. It played for a bit.

'A fiver goes to anyone who knows what this is,' he said.

'Lucky to Be Loved By You', Brenda said, without missing a beat. 'Willie Hutch.'

Neil erupted in the back. 'Aww, mam. 'Kinell. Mam's the

179

star.'

He chuckled and rolled around. I looked at her.

'I'm not entirely gormless, you know,' she said, lighting up. 'I'll have that fiver when you're ready.'

'Dad, pay me mam, will you?'

We drove for a while listening to the music. I noticed she got teary as the song went on. Neil was stretched out in the back oblivious. The song finished and I bunged in one of the older compilations he'd made for me. A song came out. It hadn't got to the end of the first bar when Brenda and mine eyes met. It was 'My Happiness' by Jon and Sondra Steele. I went sailing back twenty-seven years in a few seconds.

The first time I'd met her. 1950. She was dancing with some feller at the Plaza. The shop girls would do this. They'd come dashing down on their lunch hours from Deansgate and Market Street to the Plaza to dance swing. I was down there cutting a deal with the manager about one thing or another. Suddenly there she was, this creature out there on the sprung dance floor, doing a slow one to 'My Happiness.' Her hair was like Liz Taylor's in style but blonde, and she had on a pale blue chiffon dress. Up top she wore a pink cardigan. She didn't see me until I cut in. They say you know the one you'll marry as soon as you meet her 'cause you see your children in her eyes. And it was that way with Brenda and me. By the end of the song I was in love with her.

Now, twenty-seven years later sitting in that crappy, little Cortina driving our son to detox, the rubbishy Manc weather battering all around us, I could still feel it. We listened to the rest of the song and I knew what she was thinking. The rest of the tracks had Tony Bennet, Dinah Shore, Johnny Mathis and

Vic Damone. Neil had shut right up and was also in another world. He was stretched out on the back seat like King Tut. And during that car ride, listening to them golden oldies, Brenda and me were back in the fifties, and I felt happier than I'd felt in years.

✳

We reached the detox centre half an hour late. It was a similar performance getting in and settled, with me doing most of the schlepping, whilst his mother escorted Neil in like he was a sick royal.

I still had some work to do on her, but I kept things moving and avoided conversation. After we got to his room she sat distant and moody and refused to unpack for him. I forged on, setting up his record player and opening the suitcase. After that we all just sat and had a fag.

'It's nice, isn't it,' I said.

She gave me a look that told me she knew I'd pulled a fast one.

The Beach Boy saved me when he showed up to introduce himself. Neil was still stoned and I was well embarrassed. After the pleasantries the Beach Boy showed some interest in Neil's records and Neil stuck one on. The doctor listened for a few bars and said:

'Very nice. I recognize the song. 'Crystal Blue Persuasion.' He thought for a minute. 'Originally recorded by Tommy James and the Shondells.'

Neil turned to me stunned. He turned back to the doctor and said: 'This is the Kelly Brothers version. Excello Label.'

'Nice horns,' said the doctor. 'Piano suits it as well.'

'You have a good ear, doc,' said Neil. 'I can't believe you know the song.'

'Do you know what it's about?' the doc said.

'Yeah, yeah, it's religion, isn't it?'

'Yes, it's Tommy James's spiritual awakening. The crystal blue is the crystal of the lake in the Book of Revelations. It's symbolic of the soul and the purity it searches for.'

Neil's jaw went slack. 'I knew it was about God but I wasn't sure what this - this symbol was, and all. That's why I played it for you.'

'It's a beautiful song. Maybe we can play it at one of the group sessions.'

'That's A-one that is. Isn't it, mam?'

Mother nodded. I nodded. Neil went on.

'I'm going to have a spiritual awakening when I'm here, doctor. You'll see. I've told me mam and dad. I'm entirely ready to… "open myself up to a to a higher power." It's long overdue, that.'

'All right, mate,' I said. 'We should let the doctor get on.'

'I see you've studied the leaflet, Neil. I'm glad to see you're motivated.' The doc turned to me, knowing I was embarrassed by Neil's clumsy enthusiasm. 'This is a good start, it really is. He's ready to take the next step. It's half the battle.' Sensing Brenda's mood, the doc turned to her. 'Perhaps I can show Mrs. Dunne around the facility.'

'If you want,' she said.

He wanted to quiz her about us, the family. I wasn't bothered at this point because I knew *he* knew he had to win Brenda over. So I was glad to hand him the reins. They left and Neil and me sat looking about the room. I got my cigs out again and we smoked some more. There was an awkward silence.

'Anything else we need to do before we leave you?' I said.

'Where are the medals, dad? The German ones?'

'I took them to the pub.'

He nodded. I looked out of the window. Leaves were drifting down from the Chestnut tree outside.

'I have a confession to make, dad.'

'What?'

'I used to hang about at Bill's pub with his lads.'

'What, even after we fell out?'

'Yeah, we talked about the war sometimes.'

'Oh, aye?' I tried to hide my concern.

'He told me how brave you were. He told me how you saved the platoon and got your Military Medal.'

'You do some rum shit when you're scared.'

'You saw that him and Corey were going to die – like some other lad whose grenades went off and burned him to death.'

'I was scared for all of us. I'd been pretty useless up 'til then; too many acts of cowardice. I was sick to death with myself.'

He looked out of the window for a few seconds. 'You know what else Bill said about the war? He said that when the war was over you had no doubt… that you were now men. Is that true?'

'Never thought.'

He paused and scratched his forehead. 'What do you think of me joining the army?'

Where the hell did this come from? I hid my shock and surprise. 'Can't we get you off drugs first, kiddo, before you go joining up.'

'But what do you think?'

'What do you think I think? I don't like it.' I inhaled and

blew out aggressively. 'They'll cart you off to Northern Ireland, that's the first place you'll go.' I leveled on him. 'Don't romanticize it all, son. It's not what you think it is.'

He paused. Then laid this out like it was the law of gravity. 'All young men need to fight a war. Hitler said that.'

'Oh, that's alright then.'

'You know what I mean.'

I got up and looked out of the window. Some client was jogging round the lawn. 'There's better ways to grow up,' I said.

He looked outside. 'That German was a tough bugger, who owned that pay book. Close Combat Clasp in Bronze... *fifteen* close encounters with the enemy. I did some research and that means hand-to-hand fighting, trench attacks and stuff. And his Wound Badge in Silver.' He looked at me. 'That's three wounds and over. Over three wounds, dad, Jesus.'

'Well, they were tough buggers some of them.'

'I translated what it said in his pay book. He was nearly two years in Russia,' he said, getting more and more animated. 'And Jesus, get this dad, he was wounded in Stalingrad. And they flew him out for treatment, so he survived the encirclement – got out just in time. All his assignments are there in his pay book.'

'You should be concentrating on what you have to do,' I said, trying to veer him away from this. 'Forget this geezer, he's been dead for decades. What are *you* going to do, *here* and *now*.'

'I know, I know but that's why it's important to look at a bloke like him. I mean, an Iron Cross in Holland when he was twenty... I mean, when you've had a life as cushy as mine, it makes you think. And I need some perspective to give me - what's the word - the *push* really – yeah the push to sort myself out.'

'He's not someone to imitate, Neil. He was a killer in an enemy army. He killed a lot of our fellers.'

'But wasn't he just doing his job? I'm sure he hated it, just as much as you did. He wasn't SS; he was Wehrmacht. I'll bet he wasn't even a Nazi. A lot of them weren't.'

I took out my mickey and had a nip. I finished the last of it. He looked at me expecting me to add to this, but I didn't. I was getting angrier with Bill. The time Neil had spent with him had obviously started this fascination.

'I know he was tough and maybe a bit of a bastard,' Neil said. 'But he just looked ordinary, just a young feller. When you see all that information about this one man, all there in his pay book, and then his *picture* - his photograph - it's like you know who they are. They're not just one of the bad guys, the evil German. He's just a geezer caught up in a bad situation that he had no control over. He could've been me.'

He could've been me. That exploded in my head like a Mills Bomb.

'I mean, you and him are similar in a way - well, you are really. You're both brave, served your country. In another time and place you could've even been mates.'

'Jesus, I don't know, lad.'

'He must've fought like buggery… Did he put up a scrap?'

I wandered a bit, looking out of the window.

'Sorry to ask, dad but…'

He just waited stubbornly for an answer. I couldn't get away from his questions this time. To him all this was part of his cure, he thought, or *our* cure. Honesty. But it's overrated, honesty. It can be shocking and cruel.

'I can't remember a lot of it, son,' I said.

'You don't want to talk about it; I get it. I know it must be hard to have to kill a man.'

I looked at him. I'd always kept him at bay before. He'd always been sensitive to my discomfort, my reluctance to talk about it. But the cannabis had made him bold.

'It doesn't change you for the better,' I said, looking outside again. 'If that's what you think.'

'Are you sorry you killed him?'

I could see his reflection in the window looking at me. I was considering telling the lad that he had to go, that man. It was revenge for the warden's family, and for all my mates that had been snuffed out by these bastards. But I'd killed so many at that point that whatever revenge I needed had long been satisfied. And I couldn't tell him the *real* reason why this man had to go. I couldn't tell *anyone* that. Not even Bill and Corey. I needed to put an end to this.

Listen,' I said. I stiffened, turned and nailed him with my eyes. 'We had a job to do and that was that. If you start questioning things it becomes a slippery slope. It was a war. It doesn't do any good to dwell on it.'

'I'm sorry to go on like this, dad. I want us all to be happy. There's so much sadness. I've created so much… misery… I want –'

I was saved by a knock at the door. It was the receptionist who'd forgotten to get him to sign something. She sorted him out and left. I used this as my opportunity.

'I'd better find your mother.' I shook his hand. 'Work hard, mate.' We stood there stiffly. 'I believe in you, kiddo.'

He looked at me with such emotion that I was thrown.

186

Then his eyes welled up and he threw himself at me and gave me such a hug. I hadn't held him since he was about five. It felt strange. I could feel the strength and muscles in his back. He was a man, my son nearly twenty-one-years-old. Close to the age of....

I pulled myself away and left.

In the hallway I met the Beach Boy and Brenda. They were finishing up. Brenda looked mollified. We said goodbye and walked out to the car.

'Are you alright?' Brenda said.

'Fine, fine.'

I excused myself and went back. I was suddenly worried about how he'd take the article, Neil. He was in a rum place. I thought he might take it hard; be disappointed in me, or something. I wanted to go back and talk to him about it, but I found myself collaring the doctor as he was returning to his study, asking questions about security. There was *some,* he said, but the building was open and folk were able to come and go at will. This got me even windier.

'You'll look after him, won't you?' I could see the surprise in his face. I babbled on. 'He's serious about this. I know he comes off a bit flighty.'

'Not at all.'

'No, he does, he was always like that. Couldn't keep an idea in his head for longer than two minutes. It was this, and then it was that – hopping from one thing to another, like a bee in a clover field. We thought he was retarded when he was a kid. But he's very bright, see.'

'I can see that.'

'But he could never sit still. And he learns things by rote and

187

it looks like he's skimming over them, but he's serious. It's the way he is. It was the music that calmed him and the dancing – it transports you like - into another world.' I was running off at the mouth like a kid.

'I know you're concerned,' he said. 'And you're a clever man yourself, perceptive. I see that. But don't worry. Addicts are very bright. They're searchers. They're looking for... for wholeness, oneness. They're searching in the wrong place, but they just need to be guided. The addict's *soul* is unconsciously bringing about a crisis through abuse and oblivion... so that enlightenment can come... break through... to clarity. Crystal clarity. And they can live in peace. Joy.'

This stunned me, and I just stood there looking gormless. I excused myself and left, feeling like an idiot. Why does it get worse as we get older? Why does it all get worse?

✳

On the way back Brenda was quiet. I was glad for that because I could compose myself. I was still preoccupied with Neil's questions and my clumsy answers. I got the feeling that he knew more than he was letting on. I turned to Brenda to get my mind off it.

'What did you talk about with the doctor?'

'This and that.' She turned to me. 'He showed me the success rates they have with this twelve step thingy - the figures. They're impressive.' She shifted and crossed her legs. 'I was glad Neil played that song for him. It struck some common ground. I think they'll get on, and that's everything.'

I nodded. We drove for a bit.

'I used to curse it something rotten, his music,' she said,

looking out of the window. 'It's what got him into drugs in the first place - those all-nighters. But his first time in hospital, remember?' She turned to me. 'You were getting me some 'at to eat. He was just lying there; pale, sick, he was so poorly. I put on one of his 45s.' She looked back out of the window. 'We had the portable in his room. So, I put on one of his records and it played. I thought it might wake his brain up, you know. And do you know what it was?'

'What?'

'Lucky To Be Loved by You.'

It was the first song we'd played on the drive down. That's how she knew it. That's why she got all teary.

'Willy Hutch is the singer. He's no one anyone would know,' she went on...'but I put it on and listened. Then I sat there and cried. I blubbered my eyes out, I did. And this song about God, and his love for this boy; this love "Being as sweet as mother's love," Those were the words. Well, that was me, I was in bits. There he was like a lost angel, my boy was to me then. And I was the Virgin Mary. I had the whole thing going on in my head.' She wiped the mist off the door window. 'So I started to pray. That was the first time since I was a girl in church during the war. I prayed. And what happened?' She turned to me. 'What happened, Jackie?'

'I know, I know.'

'He got better; after a lot of prayer he got better. But that's what got me praying again, that bloody song. Stupid, I know, but there it is. So, that's what I do, love. I pray that God will get us out of this mess. And eventually you'll both get it, my son and my Jackie. And you'll pray too. You'll accept God's love. I have to believe that.'

I put on another 8-track that I knew she'd like. It was Johnny Ray. 'Walking My Baby Back Home.' I looked at her and she caught me eyeing her legs. I wanted to make love with her right then and there, but I couldn't because we were half way over the Barton flyover. She knew it and looked back at me.

'What?' she said. As if she didn't know.

'It's been a while. And the house…'

'Give me five minutes when we get home.'

I perked up a bit then. It'd been a while. Speed shrivels your privates and sex is usually out of the question, but with my tolerance and the fact that we hadn't had a go for months, I was up for it and then some. I kept the oldies cranking out to keep the mood alive. For the rest of the journey neither of us spoke. We hit a Johnny Ray medley. The next was 'It's All in the Game.' Followed by 'I Miss You So.' We just listened, each not wanting to come back to reality and kill these feelings. As we pulled up to The Cliff 'Destiny' was just finishing.

✳

Approaching our house was a picture; that was something, at least. The rich merchants once lived here, and large Victorian homes lined the cobbled street. The historic lampposts added to it all. I knew this was some comfort to the wife. She'd loved the beauty of the place when first seeing it years ago. So she got it, I made sure. I was glad of it now because this bit of beauty was a relief from all the other stuff.

When we got in Brenda went upstairs. I went to the drinks table and got us a couple of sherries. I sat down, sipped and looked at the living room. My wife had done a lovely job, spending wisely, getting in a high-end interior decorator. The result was a classy place that could have been the home of a University professor or a doctor. The twelve-foot ceilings had the cornicing and all the trimmings. The curtains were heavy, draped in the period of the house. The furniture was the same, late Victorian with tasteful smatterings of the modern. There was no gaudy décor that might be associated with folk like us. Some of the fellers I knew, their houses were horror-shows of poor taste. Not so here. It was her pride and joy, a perfect nest for her perfect family.

The article came into my mind, nearly ruining it all. I hoped she would understand that it was the only way I could see to preserve all this. She had to see that. I thought of telling her because I knew there would be hell to pay. But I'd set up the next hour for us, just us. I didn't want anything to mess with that.

We lay there after, looking up at the ceiling, her head on my chest. There was the usual gentle scratching of the tree on the window, as it swayed to the wind. We both drifted off for a spell before a snort from me woke her up. She raised her head and put it down again. We had a smoke.

'So, the Virgin Mary, eh?' I said, taking a risk.

She knew I was joshing her. But then: 'Is that sacrilege, me thinking I was Mary?'

'I don't think so.'

She smoked a bit. 'When I started praying again, I'd only been at it a few weeks when I asked him something, Father O' Connell.'

'Oh aye?'

'I asked about praying to the Virgin instead of God the Father.'

'How did that go over?'

'He was flummoxed at first.'

'I'll bet. Did you get the flannel about The Father, the Son and the Holy Ghost; the Holy Trinity, eh?'

'I did, yeah.'

'Yeah, no room for Mary in that lot,' I said, blowing out smoke to the side. This is some rum pillow talk, I thought.

'I asked if the Blessed Virgin wasn't important,' she said. 'He said that Mary's glory is in her *nothingness*. Some 'at like that. She's the Hand Maid of God, and this Mother of God is acting in - what was it... "in loving submission to *His* command." Pure obedience of faith.'

'Did his face go all beamy and flushed?'

'Be quiet. I didn't give up. I asked if I could pray to the Virgin, so She could talk to God *on my behalf*. Then I wouldn't feel so shy talking to the Almighty Himself.'

'I'll bet that did him.'

'He went to the baptismal font for a bit. But he did come round. Now he encourages me to pray to Her.'

'Amazing what half a bottle of Jameson's can do,' I said, putting out the cig.

She shook her head at me. 'I was proud of myself because of that.'

Why couldn't it always be like this? It had been so long, so much stress and misery. We'd completely lost one another.

She got up. Neil's bed needed doing and she wanted to get cracking on the washing. She got dressed and went downstairs. I heard her in the kitchen with the washer. As I lay there, the closest to contentment I'd been in months, I knew it wouldn't last. How could it? I looked at my watch and it said three o' clock. They'd be loading the papers onto the delivery vans by now. By four o' clock copies would be all over town.

I got ready. I told her I was heading back to the pub for a spell and would be home for tea. As I left she was playing some Frankie Laine on the Hi-Fi, the Hoover drowning it out a little, but not too much.

✳

Outside the clouds looked fit to burst, and the wind had died down ready for the deluge. It was so dark that I had to stick on the headlights.

On the way to the pub I could see the papers being delivered in bundles to stores and newsagents. I stopped and looked at one. The front page read:

'Heroin Crisis: The Future of a City.'

I left it and set off again for my pub.

There weren't many in; Old Timer, a couple of the old guard and Lippy, the kid with the red hair and the missing front tooth. Danny was noshing some peanuts at the end of the bar. I nodded to them all and went upstairs with the war booty. I also had the case holding my service medals and the Military Medal, all hidden in a Spa bag. Once upstairs, I stuck the German medals in the safe.

I looked down at the display case that held all my tin. Not three hours ago I'd had grand plans to put them up above the bar downstairs. They needed to go up in answer to Bill. Having kraut medals on his wall, even in a private office, was beyond it. Now I was having second thoughts. Annoyed at myself, I huffed, puffed and paced like a bear in a cage.

I had a nip of the red whisky and refilled my mickey. I

smoked and went over the speech I had planned for when my tin was to go up.

'I'm not being big headed by putting these medals up,' I muttered. 'This display case is a *reminder* of what happened. World War Two was the biggest conflict the world has ever seen. And it's in living memory. Our memory. And it's important we keep it alive. Because our resistance, by that I mean England's - Great Britain's resistance to that man, that bloody lunatic... our resistance changed the course of European history - for the better. No other way of putting it. It was painful and bloody, but it had to be done. It's more important than the defeat of Napoleon. And it has cost us, this nation... 'cause it bankrupted us and killed off our empire. It destroyed us as a world power. And this country's self-sacrifice... our *self-sacrifice* is significant and should never be forgotten.'

I was surprised and well pleased with myself. It wasn't bad for on the fly, like. So, I got out a pen and paper and tried to remember it. I sat at the desk and scribbled away. Then I checked my watch. I knew Danny would be back with the Evening News in five minutes.

I looked out at the croft. There was the warden, burning his oil drum. He was looking at me. I'll swear he was. Just staring right at me.

The phone went. It was Brenda.

'I want you to come home....'

There was a silence as I listened to her breathing. Something was up.

'Oh, aye?' I said.

'I've just seen The Evening News. How could you do this, Jackie? How could you?'

Here we go. 'We don't order The Evening News. How did you see it?'

She said nothing.

'Brenda.'

'Corey Blaine called me, if you must know. Told me to get it. So I called the Newsagents and they sent it over. When did you do this?' Her voice was shaky. 'Did you ever consider talking to me first?'

'And what would you have said?'

'What the hell do you think I would've said?'

'What else did Corey have to say?'

'I'm not talking about this over the phone.'

I was conflicted. I either had to stay here and explain myself to the lads or go back home. I had a premonition of Corey going to the house unloading his woes on the wife.

'I'll be right over.'

I put the phone down. I went downstairs and told Old Timer I was off home but would be back after tea. As I drove over I saw Danny reading the paper by the stand down the street. His face was a picture. Not a good one.

Close to home I saw Corey on the corner of Great Clowes Street and Cheetham Hill Road. He looked like he was heading up to my house. I stopped the car and got out. He backed off as I approached him.

'Where are you going, Corey?'

'Just walking.'

'Thinking of paying Brenda a visit?'

'No.'

'You've been talking on the phone though, haven't you. What did you say?' I pushed him to a privet hedge and I stood over him. 'Well?'

'I told her what I did to that boy.'

'The cadet?'

'I told her, Jackie - and why I wanted the dog tag back. I left out as much as I could about you, what we did. But she was pushing me, so I told her my story.'

He made to go and I held him back.

'You stay out of my business. I will not tell you again.'

'It's my business as well,' he snapped back, throwing me off. I grabbed his collar but he stuck his chin out in defiance.

'That article isn't going to save your lad, Jackie. If you need redemption then do it. Don't just shove it somewhere else. You want to atone, you know what you have to do – and it isn't this.'

'Stay away from Brenda.' I pushed him off, got back in the car and drove up the street.

※

Brenda was holding the paper when I got in. I took it from her and read the opening lines. Then I gave it back.

'I'm not apologizing. Someone had to do something.'

'You knew all today this was coming out and you've said nothing, nothing! You drove us to that centre and back, you lay there with me and you said nothing. God, Jackie.'

'I'm not doing this for the good of my health, woman.' I took my coat off and threw my hat on the settee.

'Do another article. Retract it. Jackie, please.'

I walked away and got a drink. 'In the last six months two kids have died on Oxford Road, one in Gorton. This weekend

196

they found a kid dead in the canal basin. I was just down there Saturday, looking for Neil. It could've been him.' I knocked back the whisky and got another. 'The Peelers are saying these deaths are isolated. It's well-to-do kids coming back from travelling Nepal, bringing drugs with them, that's what they said. Now folk will know different.'

'Dear god.'

'They read this and there'll be letters, phone calls to the paper. If someone on town council doesn't pick this up, I'll eat my hat.' I knocked the drink back again. 'And then the Peelers will have to pay attention. Won't they?'

'Meanwhile we suffer. Neil's got a mountain to climb, we all have, and now we've got this to deal with. 'Cause don't tell me there won't be ructions because of this, because there will be Jackie, and you know it.'

'If owt happens it'll be me they go for, not you. Or Neil.'

'And that's supposed to make me feel better? You've just committed suicide, Jackie!'

'What did Corey say?'

'What? He told me to get the paper.'

'Did you call him when you read the article?'

'Yes, I did!'

'And what did he say about me?'

'I don't need Corey to put that bit together. It's normal for a bloke to feel lousy about killing another feller. Even in a war.'

'You don't understand, Brenda, you don't know anything.' I waved her away and walked to the French doors.

'I think I do,' she said, coming after me. 'You've always been a restless bugger; up and down all night, the boozing - all of it. But nowt like the last few years. Our Neil getting bad and your tossing and turning and constant yammering.'

'About what?'

'Nowt I can understand but plenty I can guess at. I can't make judgments, but whatever you did -'

'Did?' I spun round and shouted at her. 'We won a war, Brenda, that's what we did. Saved the world from Hitler. That's all you need to know - it's all anyone needs to know.'

I opened the French doors and went outside in the back garden. The feeding birds scattered and flew away. It was cold and I thought she wouldn't follow me, but she did.

'It's not as simple as that though, is it love?'

'Jesus, don't you ever get tired of this?'

'Yes, I do! I want to spend time on this - men and their war misery?' She stood on the concrete porch, arms going. 'You're not the only ones who suffered; we all got bombed. Twelve years old I was, hiding under the stairs or outside in the ginnel and take your chances with a direct hit. My God, my dad served in North Africa for six years. He never saw a shot fired. Me, me mam and our kid saw more action than half the bloody English army.' She stepped in to me, her face red. 'I remember running to the park, to the deep shelter during a raid. We started under the stairs and it got worse - so we went to the ginnel and they'd all gone to the deep shelter in Mandley Park. It were that bad we ran down there with bombs dropping all around us. Me little sister was three – she had a piece of shrapnel taken out of her leg.'

'I know all that.'

'So, yes I do! I do get tired of it all. But I'm a mother and I've carried that lad for nine months and he's a piece of me now, as big as he is. And he's coming on finally, making headway, and you go and do this. I'm still holding that lad's head above water and you're splashing around like an idiot - and I'll not stay quiet no more, I won't!' She slowed down getting her breath. 'And I'm starting to see now, I'm starting to see it as clear as crystal. You're doing these things because you've never dealt with any of this.'

I stepped in to her - ready to tell her how many men I'd killed, so many that I'd lost count. You get a squad of men in your sights you take the lot down. You throw a grenade in a room the lot goes up, you stab a man through the neck because he's trying to kill you. You have no sympathy for these bastards because they want you dead. That's the way it was, that's the way it is. But all I could say was:

"I've killed, Brenda. Plenty.'

'But there's something about this one man, something that's different... because when you shoot a man in cold blood that will weigh on you. It has to.'

I just looked at her. She didn't waver.

'I'm sorry. But I got it out of him, and you can't blame him for telling me. He's trying to help you.'

The phone went. We let it ring. Brenda finally went back inside and answered it. She listened, then:

'He's not well, Danny. He can't be held responsible. I'll call the Peeler's if anything happens to him, I will, I don't care.'

I snatched the phone. 'Danny?'

'I guess she's seen it. It's creating a bit of a stink down here as well.'

I heard the phone in the other room get picked up. I knew Brenda was listening. Danny seemed oblivious.

'I've just talked to Mary,' he said. 'She wants to have a

meeting tonight.'

'Where?'

'Down here at the pub. At least she's not just written you off.'

'Tell her I'll be down at eight.'

'Right.'

I hung up. Brenda came through to the other room. She was softer than before.

'Don't go.'

'They're me mates, Brenda.'

'They're villains first and last, and they won't forgive you for this.'

'They want an explanation, they'll get one.'

'And then what? What do I get? What does Neil get? A father whose found dead in the gutter.'

'Brenda, calm down.'

'Even if your lot does nowt, there's plenty that will.'

'I'm going out.' I picked up my hat and coat.

'Where? It's early. It's only half past five,' she said, following me. 'Don't you hurt that man, Jackie. Don't you dare hurt Corey. I'll never forgive you if you do, you hear me?'

I was down the path. I drove. I shook my head at the innocence of Brenda's assumption; that it was the shooting of a bloody prisoner that was doing my head in. I was so numb by then with the killing that I could've popped off the Pope himself and felt nothing. No, love, no. I felt the scar, the dent on my cheek and forehead. It was damp with sweat.

✳

Corey's house was dark, but a dim light peeped from a bedroom. I went down the ginnel to the back yard. The kitchen light was on. I tried the door and it was open.

I went in and there was a cig smoldering in the ashtray. He'd left in a hurry after Brenda had called him. I was about to go when I saw something on the floor. I walked up to it and looked down. It was a photocopy of a photograph. I picked it up and felt the blood leave my face.

The drawer above it had the corner of another photocopy sticking out, as if stuffed there in a hurry. I pulled it out and looked at them both.

One was a picture of me, the Oberleutnant, Bill and his SS officer and the Luftwaffe kid. We were standing next to one another, posing to the camera like on a day at the beach. I looked at the other photo and it was similar. Corey was in it and I was now missing from the picture.

I swallowed as I realized what'd happened. The German camera, the one that we thought was duff, which Corey had found in the burned-out half-track, *had actually worked.* Corey had developed the pictures - or had them done. I couldn't believe what I was seeing.

The light from above was naked and cold. It cast a sickly wash over the sad room, and there were dead flies in the ceiling lamp.

I thought of the other photographs Corey had taken that day. He'd taken them all through the hike down the supply road, and then into the valley. He'd snapped away until the shooting. *Then he'd taken photos of afterwards as well, as they had lay there.* He would've developed *them* as well. My guts churned at the thought. I scrambled through all the kitchen drawers. Nothing. Where would he stash the camera itself? The negatives might be with that. I went through the hall and got to the bottom of the stairs. I started up, trying not to make a sound. I got to the top and saw the dim light coming from Corey's mam's room. I made for another door. The floor creaked. I stopped.

'My God… my God help us… help us…' It was Corey's mam. Her voice was low, pained and feeble. 'Corey… Corey…' I started back down the stairs, but stopped when I heard a groan and a thump. 'Corey… help me…'

I went to the room and looked in. Shauna Blaine, Corey's eighty-year-old mother, was lying on the floor.

'Oh my boy… help me child.'

The room was a suffocating stench of illness. I went to her, bent down and touched her. She groaned. I got my arms under her and lifted. She was all bones. She had no idea who I was as I placed her back onto the bed. She turned over, away from me.

'Drink… water…'

I got the glass from the side table, went to the jug and poured her some water. I bent down and guided the straw to her mouth. She sucked feebly but she got some. I put the glass back, took the blankets and pulled them over her. She whimpered as I looked down at her. I hadn't seen her since Patrick's, her grandson's funeral. That'd knocked Corey's madness onto a whole new level. She was barely recognizable now. Wizened away to nothing, she looked close to death. I needed to go, get out, away from the house. I turned to go, but she brushed my hand, trying to grasp it. I pulled away and she flailed in the air, feeling for touch.

'Corey… Corey…' I let her take it and she clamped onto me like a woman drowning. 'Pray for me… son….'.

I just stood there not knowing what to do.

'Pray for me… my boy… pray for me…'

'*The LORD is my shepherd… I shall not want.*' Dear God, give strength to remember it.

'Pray, my boy, pray…' She gripped me harder. Her breathing was still shallow.

'*…He maketh me to lie down in green pastures…*

He leadeth me beside the still waters.

He restoreth my soul… he leadeth me in the paths of righteousness for his name's sake.

Yea, though I walk through the valley of the shadow of death, I will fear no evil: for thou art with me; thy rod and thy staff they comfort me….'

Her breathing was getting calmer. I went on.

'*Thou preparest a table before me in the presence of mine enemies: thou anointest my head with oil; my cup runneth over.*

Surely goodness and mercy shall follow me all the days of my life: and I will dwell in the house of the LORD forever.'

I exhaled with relief. I'd remembered it, and the prayer seemed to give her comfort. I put her hand under the covers and she started to breath evenly.

I went downstairs, picked up the phone in the hall, and called Brenda. No answer. The church, that's where she'd have gone. Maybe Corey would be there too with photocopies… of the other pictures.

✳

I drove to the community centre and O'Connell's church. On the way I thought of the state of Shauna Blaine. I should've phoned 999.

I arrived and parked on the road. I walked up the path to the centre, an early sixties job glommed onto a Gothic building. I looked up at the Church. The spire reaching high into the night sky, looking like it was touching the low, rolling clouds. Lights from the housing estate over the churchyard wall threw shadows among the gravestones.

The Rectory was off to the side, a Georgian building bordered by a fence that kept the housing estate at bay. I could see what the place would've looked like two hundred years earlier, before councils, committees, and post-war promise.

I walked into the centre. The hallway smelled of gym shoes and disinfectant, as it always had. Not five years ago I was picking the lad up from five-a-side footy here. It seemed like yesterday. A row was going on in the room marked Samaritans.

I went to the door that led through to the church. It wasn't locked and I stole down the narrow hall. I expected to find Corey or Brenda or both praying by the Virgin Mary. I stopped and looked up at her. She looked down at me with soft eyes, her alabaster skin glowing in the light of the candles. It'd had been decades since I'd been here, but the smell of the place, the incense, the candles, the old wood all came instantly back.

I went through to O' Connell's quarters. I climbed the stairs and arrived at a room that was vast. The ceilings were high with cornicing and the promise of luxurious furnishings; but there was nothing like that. His furniture was dwarfed by the huge space, and nothing seemed to match. It looked like it'd been bought ad hoc over the years. A leather high backed chair sat near a simple hearth. The grandeur of the fireplace had long been converted into a nasty fifties tiled affair. A few radiating bars hummed out a bit of heat, along with a sad glow. Next to the chair was a Victorian side table that was taped at the bottom. On top of that was a wildly oversized lampshade, probably from the Co-Operative Home Store, circa 1965. Next to these was a pile of newspapers and books. Newspapers were in piles everywhere. Each pile was topped with a full ashtray and half-full teacups. A football field away was the settee, an early seventies effort with thin brown cushions and a walnut stick frame. This too was loaded with piles of magazines and newspapers. In front of this settee was a round, glass-topped coffee table, which held another overflowing ashtray, more newspapers, and an almost empty whisky bottle.

'It's a disaster, I know. Years of bachelor living, I'm afraid.'

I turned and there was O' Connell. He gave me a closed-mouth grin. I'd barely seen him since Neil's baptism, once for Patrick Blaine's funeral. He looked the same as he always had; small, thin and old. His thick hair had gone white, but the heavy woolen jumper was still thrown over his Roman collar. As he got closer there was the smell, cigs and whisky.

'I get busy with things,' he said. 'I don't notice the mess. I've driven half a dozen cleaners screaming from the premises, so I have.' He extended his hand. 'How are you, son?'

I ignored it. 'Where is he?'

'Corey?' He got his cigs out and offered me one.

I rummaged for my own and realized I'd left them in the car. I took one of his Woodbines and he lit us up.

'Can I offer you a drink?' he said.

'Where is he?'

'He left about five minutes ago.'

I went to the door.

'He was getting a taxi. He'll be long gone.'

'To where?'

'I've no idea, son. Besides, wasn't it me you wanted to speak to?'

'Has Brenda been here as well?' I stayed at the door looking at this dwarf of a man, even tinier against the large room.

'I can't stop your wife coming to me,' he said, blowing out smoke. 'She's just doing what she thinks is right - that'll help. You can't blame the woman for wanting to keep her family. You, the boy - you're her life.'

I came in a bit and paced along the wall like a deranged tiger in a zoo.

'Sit down, son,' he said. 'You look shocking, man.'

I went and got myself a drink. I could feel him looking at me.

'I've long since gotten over it, your absence. Most of the others did similar, spending more time in the Legion. Not unusual. But there's something, Jackie that troubles you... and has troubled you a long time, since.'

'I'm just dandy. Don't believe all you hear from the missus or Corey Blaine.'

He eyes narrowed. 'I'm worried for you, son.'

I gulped down a drink. 'You don't know me.'

'I beg to differ.' He moved casually with his hand in his pocket, cig held at his belly. 'Since you were a child, I knew you.'

'Oh, here we go,' I said, getting another drink. The heat in the room was suffocating. I was starting to feel lightheaded.

'I knew your mother, a devout girl from the Old Country, she was.'

'And my dad's the devil was he?'

'I'd never call a lapsed Catholic that. He had his views, I suppose.'

'He didn't beat the Pope out of me if that's what you mean. He talked to me, wanted me to fit in - us all to fit in - to be English.'

'A Dubliner wanting to be an Englishman, that's a rarity.'

I took a drink, hating him. He went on.

'Will you get me a drink, man? I can respectfully have a drink at this time.'

I grabbed a glass and dribbled him out a drink. I left it for him and walked away.

'The Protestants have their superstitions as well,' he said, lifting the glass to his lips.

'It's not the same. It's about the *country*. It's not all about the bloody church. Country – Patriotism - Nation - that's the Holy Trinity. We're nothing without it.'

'We're more than that, surely.'

'Are we bollocks. Community. I live in Salford, not Dublin or Rome. I know the price if you don't keep hold of it.'

'The war.'

'Yeah the war.'

I went over to an open window and pulled aside the floating lace curtain. The room was stifling and sweat was pouring down the back of my neck. My shirt was stuck to me.

'You see, this is what irks me,' he said. 'Your last confession was before you left in, what was it – September of '44? You were barely nineteen. So, you weren't sold fully on your father's ideas then, were you? It was something that happened there, over in Europe that altered your views.'

'I've just told you, man. A country has to be strong,

committed to itself, the idea of itself. Otherwise you're – you're just *swept* away. There's no room for weakness, not in this world.'

'These are all abstractions to me.'

'Then what's religion? Except bloody abstractions.'

The curtains billowed gently from the window. I breathed in the cold air.

'Will you sit down, man. You look like you're about to collapse.'

I didn't want to but I did. I sat in one of the armchairs, low and enveloping.

He moved towards me. 'But besides this love, this thing for country you have, there's something else, isn't there… something that's tormenting you?'

His eyebrows were long and flicked up like horns. And his eyes glinted from the glow of the side lamp.

I almost laughed. 'You have no clue. None of you have a clue.' I drank the whisky. 'It's quite simple, Father. I need you to keep your nose out, end of. It's not complicated.'

He nodded and veered off. He dabbed his cigarette in the general direction of the ashtray as he wandered by it. I noticed his scoliosis was looking chronic.

'And what did Corey have to say, Eh?' I said. 'I'll bet he's been here running his mouth off as well, hasn't he?'

He walked over to the settee. 'I had hoped you'd tell me yourself. But I don't think you will.' He moved some magazines aside and picked up photocopies. 'He was here, yes.'

He put his specs on and leafed through them. I imagined they were the photos of afterwards. After we'd done it; all there in black and white. I wrestled myself up from the chair. He turned to me.

'He doesn't want to use these for anything sinister, Jackie. He brought them to me because, well, he wants to help you.'

I nearly laughed at that one. O' Connell leveled on me and did his over-the-specs look.

'Do you know what these are?' he said.

I sat in another chair. 'Yeah, I do.'

He seemed surprised at this. 'Have you seen them?'

I said nothing.

'Do you *want* to see them?'

I said nothing.

'It's this business that's making you suffer, isn't it?'

'He said that?' I smiled. 'He wants something from me, Father. That's what those are in aid of.'

'He did tell me about the soldier's ID, all that palaver. And you won't give it.'

'No, I bloody well won't.'

'Why?'

'If he didn't tell you then I damn well won't.'

'Pride comes before a fall, Jackie, you know that.' He leafed through them, shaking his head. 'These are hard to look at. And standing there, all of yous with the dead bodies... like hunters with a Wildebeest. It's heartbreaking, man.'

'That was him, that. That was his idea.'

'He said he was delirious with grief. He wanted to show that it didn't matter to him, he didn't want to look weak.'

'No, he was planning to do *this*.' I launched myself out of the chair and pointed at the photocopies. '*This* is revenge this is.'

'Well, he certainly doesn't understand, see, why you did this; changed the orders, then shot that man, then got him to...'

'I don't have to tell anyone why I did it, it was a war.'

'There's the rules of war, and there's wanton murder. And then there's Corey. Dragging him into this - this sordid act. Don't you recognize your responsibility to him, after what you made him do, and him suffering so much because of it? It's no wonder your soul's in torment, man.'

I snatched the photocopies from him. My lighter was out and I lit them. I took the burning paper to the hearth and let it smolder into black, flaky bits. I dropped what was left. It crinkled into nothing before our eyes.

'That doesn't alter anything, son.'

'You want a confession, Father? Dole out a few Hail Mary's? You see this?' I said pointing to the scar on my forehead and cheek. 'He did this, that kraut I shot. Seven months earlier. We'd barely been in Belgium a week. He did this.'

His eyebrows rose. 'Seven months earlier?'

'September. First day in the line, it was. He fell into my trench. We were being shelled to buggery and he falls in. We have a fight and he does this, before I see him off.' I threw my cig into the fireplace.

'The same man?'

'The very same. And I run into him seven months later in Germany, what are the chances. So I got him back.'

'You killed him over that?'

'He'd killed a lot of our feller's, that's as good a reason as any.'

'My God, the glibness of the man.'

'I've shot men who were surrendering for *no* fucking reason. And I know plenty that did. And enjoyed it.'

He paused and pondered this. 'Yes, I've had men confess to that. But it was in the heat of the moment, the blood was up and they were out of control. But *this*… this is calculated, cold blooded.'

'You had to be there, Father, you had to be there.'

His head inclined to me. 'What has happened to you, Jackie?'

I finished my drink. 'Come on then, Father. How many Hail Mary's, Our Father's and Glory Be's for that one, eh?'

He paused a moment. 'I don't believe you, Jackie Dunne. There's something else, another reason why you did this.'

'Don't over complicate it, Father. I've done a lot of stuff you wouldn't believe.'

I went down the stairs and back through the church, not looking at anything - the altar, the Virgin, anything. The smell of incense crept up my nose like a spider.

I was sweating like a pig and lurched back to the baptismal font. It was the kind that runs constantly, fed by a spring. I splashed my face, baptizing myself with it. I breathed. I heard a door go upstairs. I went back through to the community centre hall, with that smell of gym shoes and disinfectant, the yelling from the Samaritans room. I went outside and leant by the doorway. A young feller was coming up the path.

'Have you got a cig, mate?' I asked, like a tramp on a Salford croft. He gave me a Silk Cut and lit me up, moving on like I had the moggers. I stayed there until I was through with the cig.

Going down the path I saw Corey deeper in the graveyard. He was staring at a gravestone. I made my way over to him, passing a cluster of old headstones that were tilted in different directions, as if the ground was forcing the dead up through the topsoil. I could hear him speaking above the wind and distant traffic, but it was muffled. I struggled to listen. It was a prayer.

I went up to him. 'You've been a busy boy, haven't you? That Agfa Karat camera… Who'd have thought it, the state it was in. Jerry technology, eh?'

'Found it upstairs in the loft,' he said, without turning. He sipped from a flask. 'I was clearing things. The film was still in it. So, I looked up how to do it, the chemicals, the lot. It was a right performance, but it worked. All but a few turned out.' He turned to me. 'Did you see them? Up in the Father's rooms? He couldn't believe it.'

The wind sighed through the stones. I could hear the weathercock turning and squeaking on the church spire.

'Do you know how I felt,' he said, 'when I first saw them, those photos? After all these years, to see that lad's face again, a boy who could've lived a full life… who was that close to going home.' He held up his thumb and forefinger with a tiny space between them. 'Then family, kids, a life… do you know what that was like?'

'And you're doing this for what reason, Corey?'

'The camera was just there in mam's loft. And it was the anniversary of my Patrick's death.'

'And what are you going to do with them?'

He let out a deep breath. 'I want that ID tag, Jackie. That's all.'

'And what if Bill won't give the pay book?'

'That's between him and me.'

I stepped in close to him. 'I will kill you if you even *think* of going anywhere else with those photos. I will kill you. You understand me, Corey?'

He looked down at the stone. It read:

Patrick James Blaine. 1957 to 1972.
Beloved son of Corey and Finola Blaine.
He now rests with the Angels. Taken too soon but
forever loved and missed.

'I did this,' he said. 'And you're responsible as well, Jackie.'

The stone was a dark granite block. It stood out from the old, grey headstones that were covered with moss. A plane went over.

'You want to get me back for this, don't you?'

'I just want the dog tag, Jackie.'

'Sure you do.'

'But I am puzzled.' He turned and looked at me. 'You've always said it was revenge for the warden's family, but we'd killed enough by then. So, you've never really told me why. I know what you've told *some*... that they'd shot our lads who were prisoners, and this was pay back. But that's a lie, isn't it, Jackie? They never killed anyone that way, that battle group. So, you've never told me why... until Canada. *Then* I had clues, but that only answers some of it. There's more isn't there, Jackie... more than you're telling...'

He stared at me, his glazed eyes not moving.

I heard the scuffing of a heel on pavement and turned to see Brenda. She'd been standing by the church wall watching. She'd heard everything. Even in the dark recess I could see the expression on her face. Then she left. I watched her go down the path into a waiting taxi. She got in and it drove away.

I turned to Corey. 'Put that mother of yours in hospital, you.'

'The dog tag, Jackie...'

'Go to hell, Corey.'

As I was walking down to the car he called over the wind and the screeching weathercock, 'You think that my mam, suffering like that, has nowt to do with what we did? May God forgive you, Jackie Dunne. May God forgive us all.'

✻

I got to the car and the rain started. The church spire had pricked the clouds and they were leaking down on us.

I sat there steaming, thinking of absurdity of it all. Every time some bugger dies in your family, Corey, we to go through this? I opened the glove box and pulled out the diazepam. I necked a couple, swilling them down with whisky.

While driving I started to rally myself. Forget Corey and concentrate on now. Face the lads over this article; carry yourself well or you're finished, Jackie.

In the pub everyone clocked me then turned away. Was it anger or what? I couldn't tell, but no one said anything. They just shifted and avoided any eye contact. The air was thick with fag smoke as if folk had been overdoing the habit. Danny sat over in the corner mesmerized by his pint. His breathing was laboured.

'Is the fan on?' I ask Old Timer.

He nodded. The jukebox was silent, dead. There was always music on; without it the place seemed thin, empty and desolate. Folk were scattered all over like small pieces of wood blown there by a huge wind.

Old Timer put a whisky on the bar. I could see Danny in the mirror stroking his pint pot. Old Timer got a Mackeson and poured it into a glass. We drank. Still nobody said anything. Finally, I turned and said:

'Well, you lot have faces like a smacked arse. Buck up, it's not the end of bloody the world.' I turned to Old Timer. 'So. What do you think?'

'Eh, you didn't mention any names, that's all that matters to me.' He sparked up one of his Capstan Full Strength. 'But bringing those buggers in? Giving her power… a black woman having a say in our doings.'

The lads never understood Mary and me. I'd told them endlessly about meeting blacks in Europe. How we'd get blathered with the non-coms, kick the shit out of one another then spend the night telling stories. They'd play their Boogie-Woogie and we'd sing dirty songs. So, I was never funny with them, even back in Blighty. But the lads had never got me.

'She covers South Manchester from Moss Side to Hulme and Trafford and bleeding Withington,' I said. 'That means I do too.'

'It's cost you, it has…'

The diazepam was working on me. In the light from the bar Old Timer's ancient tattoos looked like a medieval skin disease. He saw me eyeing him.

'Get your shooter out, have it handy,' he said, funneling smoke through his nostrils. 'I'm serious. I'm not apologizing for exercising some common. There's too many in this town want you harmed.'

I said nothing.

'Fine,' he went on. 'You think you can trust that lot, fine. You'll come a cropper one of these days.'

I drank. I couldn't believe Mary would have a go at me, especially in my own gaff; but then again what better place. I sipped my drink, remembering the first time I'd met her, Saturday night about 1956. The Palace Theatre and Fats Domino. There was a good Mancunian drizzle on; the kind that has you soaked before you've finished mucking with your umbrella. There was a queue, all right, but it didn't matter. I was well known by then and walking into any venue, gratis. But an almighty barney at the kiosk was holding everyone up. A young black woman, a girl really, was creating because the doorman wouldn't let her in. I couldn't be doing with the agro or missing the concert, so I said, 'She's with me!' and hauled her in on my arm.

Once inside I couldn't get rid. She was just off the boat from Jamaica and looking for work. I thought what the heck. The black GI's in my coffee shop would feel comfy with her. And they did. So she stayed. Then she went out on her own but always included me in her doings. She was loyal, no nonsense - even if she was a pain in the arse. No, I'm not bringing down the shooter.

I went over to the jukebox. Danny had once tried to pepper the selection with Reggae. The lads had gone berserk. It was only his size and authority that saved him from a battering. We could've done with some King Tubby right now to soften up Mary a bit. I threw on some Sam Cooke instead, just for Theo.

Suddenly Danny had a coughing fit. He got up and went out to the back. I followed him, finding him outside by the water barrel. Breathing deeply, he took a blast of his inhaler.

'Are you all right?' I asked.

'It's putting years on me, all this.'

I looked about the yard. The old doghouse there was rotten and full of moss. I looked up at the back of my place and a drainpipe had come out. An annoying dribble of rainwater was dripping down, completely missing the rain barrel.

'Look,' I said. 'I'm not sorry for what I did. It had to happen.'

Danny just leaned against the wall and shook his head. 'Jesus, Jackie…'

'So, what then? I've landed us all in it, is that it?'

He looked at me then looked away.

'What?' I said. 'What?'

He continued taking deep breaths. It was cold and damp, but it was air without smoke. I heard the gate go and Brenda was standing there.

'What are you doing here? You're going home, right now.' I grabbed her arm. 'I'll get one of the fellers to drive -'

'I'm not leaving,' she said, throwing me off. 'I will talk to Mary come hell or high water.' She nailed me with her eyes. 'I am not leaving this pub until you let me talk to her.' She turned to Danny. 'You can't do anything to this man, Danny. Not when he's like this.'

'Don't make me look an idiot, Brenda.'

'You've already done that yourself.' She went back to Danny. 'He's not himself, Danny. I need you to promise me.'

'It's alright, Brenda,' Danny said, holding up his hand.

'You promise? Swear on your mother's grave?'

'I swear. He'll get no agro from me.'

I hovered in embarrassment by the gate. The security light made Brenda and Danny look as pale as ghosts. Why does it get worse? As we get older? Why?

Brenda went through into the pub. I followed, avoiding Danny's critical eye. I heard him behind me, sucking in the last of the outdoor air.

✳

When we got back in Mary was already coming through the

foyer. Theo and Adolphus followed her. A few of Adolphus's mates, tough mixed-race boys from Moss Side, followed. A few white Wythenshawe boys were with them. They seemed to drift in as if they didn't want to be here. They were soon all standing, hovering like lost kids at their first cub-scout meeting.

'Get them what they want,' I said to Old Timer.

'Not for me,' said Mary. She looked at Theo. 'We're not here to hoist drinks.'

'Let the lads have a drink, Mary,' I said. 'Let's not start in like this.'

She gave me a withering look then turned to her lads. 'Do what you want.' She noticed Brenda. 'I'm sorry about all this Brenda, but don't shove in. This is bad, this - very bad.'

'I'm sorry, but I do need a word. For all the years I've known you, Mary - just one minute.'

Mary nodded in the direction of the foyer. Brenda and her disappeared, while her lads meandered to the bar. Lippy and his younger mate helped with drinks; a peace offering that was promising. Sam Cooke was crooning away. One of the mixed-race lads went over to the jukebox.

'None of that,' snapped Theo. The lad backtracked and sat sullenly with his mates. Not a good start.

After ten minutes of shuffling and awkward silence, everyone was sorted. The two women had returned. Mary sat with Theo, while Brenda came and stood at the end of the bar. I got windy. I'd never talked to this many lads in one place before. I was getting stage fright and there was a lot at stake. I glanced around. It was like looking at a brick wall. I took a drink.

'Thanks for coming,' I said. 'You all know what's been going on these past two years. How things have changed, how bad things are getting.'

'None of is thrilled with Bill Shaw,' said Mary. 'But going to third parties to solve problems is a no-go. No one knows that better than you, Jackie'

'Has he mentioned any names? Has he?'

We turned to see Old Timer standing all Bolshie-like, his arms splayed wide on the bar.

Mary said to him: 'You know as well as I do what he's done, names or no names.'

I held up my hand. The silence was a dead weight. I started up again.

'You know how I struggled with this, Mary. I tried everything with Bill but got nothing, and short of sending the lot to the Costa del Sol.'

'That's not a bad idea.'

All looked to Adolphus. Even Mary and Theo were surprised. We all understood what sending someone to the Costa del Sol meant. Having them go missing, killing them.

'I'm just saying,' he said, shrugging.

It was a mad idea with no bearing in reality. Everyone kept looking at him.

'All right then, send Macker,' he said. 'If *he* goes the trade goes. Bill don't know the Scousers, right? So, Macker goes, problem solved.'

There were some mutters. He knew my mind on this. It was a deliberate challenge that I hadn't expected, especially from Adolphus. I tried to stare him down but he went on.

'Jackie man, we can sort this in two days.'

'Then we've got Bill coming down on us, plus all and sundry,' I said. 'And as sure as God made little green apples, if you want real agro, humiliate Bill by clipping his main feller.' I let that sink in. 'The trick with Bill is making him realize Macker's more trouble than he's worth. *That's* why I talked to the paper, *that's* why.'

'Are things really that bad?' It was a south Manc lad I vaguely knew.

'They're getting there,' I said. 'And if you call a half-dozen heroin deaths bad, then yeah, it's bad. The Peelers don't mind us making a bit o' graft on the side - there'll leave us be. But with kids dying left, right and centre it's only a matter of time. Then they close us down and folk start get nicked.'

Theo coughed. 'The problem is, Jackie, some think this is about your lad. So, explain here your real reason, 'cause they just don't know.'

Mary grabbed his arm. 'None of us signed on to clean this town up. We're barely surviving as it is.'

'You're barely surviving?' I said. 'Then what happens when this drug gets hold?' I moved to the centre of the room. 'This isn't just my lad; it's more than that. Where will it go, this drug? Eh? Will it ruin Wilmslow, Bramhall, Cheshire? Will it buggery. No, it'll be here where we live. Moss Side, Salford, Cheetham Hill - all our places. It will happen. Is Iran far? Is it fuck, it's round the bleeding corner. Cheap profits are through the roof - fuck off. Then there's turf wars and then there's *guns*.' I turned to Danny. 'What did we find last month, Danny?' He fumbled so I carried on. 'Some kid at the back of the club flogging smack. What did we find on him, Danny?'

'A semi-automatic pistol.'

'He couldn't have been more than sixteen.' I turned to Theo. 'You went home to Detroit four years ago, looking after your

220

mam. What was that like, Theo? A bleeding war zone, that's what you told me. And *I* know that 'cause I've seen it too. And what did it? What did it, Theo?'

Everyone looked at him. He sighed and said nothing, miffed at being put on the spot. I kept on him.

'Theo, tell them what you told me. Just tell the truth, mate.'

'Heroin,' he said.

Mary threw up her arms and there was murmuring all round.

'Well, it's true, hon. I gotta give him that. I said it.'

He looked at me resentful, but I knew he was on board. Of his eight cousins three were dead, three doing jail time, one for murder and two for trafficking. I didn't point this out since most of us knew it.

'Heroin,' I said. 'It's completely, utterly destroyed that city. Villains shoot one another all the time. It's a bloody catastrophe, and *that's what we can expect* if this vermin drug takes hold. That's our future.'

'That's all well and good,' said Mary, 'but none of us are looking to be heroes, Jackie. All these grand ideas... we just want to make some graft and have a quiet life, live to see the end of the bloody year.'

'No one will touch you, Mary.' I said. I looked round. 'Any of you.'

'Oh, come on man. They'll have a go at us as sure as Easter. It's easier than getting at you.'

'I won't let it happen.'

'You and who's army? Who will listen to you after this? You've broken the cardinal rule, man -'

'It's not the same as going to the Peelers -'

'It's worse.' She stood up. 'If you went to the coppers no one would know it was you. But you've said right there in print it's you. Everyone knows it's you.' She smoked aggressively. 'There's none of us protected now. Our Jez is still inside, three months to go. Will Alan Boyle protect him after what you've done? Will he hell as like. And if someone has a go at our Jez I'll never forgive you, Jackie, I won't.'

'Let him talk,' said Theo.

'He's talked plenty. I begged him…' She turned to me. 'I begged you not to do this and you did it anyway.' A whisper flitted round the pub. 'Brenda's just talked to me, not that she needed to. As if I'd do anything to you, man. How could I do that? So, I'll say right now to these lads here, that if there's trouble, they'll be sorted. There'll be no agro on Jackie Dunne, not while I'm standing. And you've all just witnessed that. But I have to separate myself from you. I have to - for me own sake. You've given me no choice, man.'

She shifted and made to go. Some stirred halfheartedly, not wanting to commit either way. The murmur grew. It grew and grew. Suddenly there was a bellow that topped it.

'Have any of you… any of you lot been listening to a blind word he's said?'

We turned to look at Old Timer.

'Did you hear what he's talking about?' He singled out the black lads and the mixed-race kids. 'He's talking about bloody community, this city. Are you in it or are you not? 'Cause if you're not - then piss off back to where you came from.'

The room erupted and everyone started shouting. I glared at him and he threw his arms up in frustration. But he'd lit a powder keg. Individual grievances flared, fingers pointed and gestures flew. Just when it threatened to blow out of control, all stopped.

There was Bill, Ray and Didds and a large crew behind them. Bill held The Evening News.

※

'Am I interrupting something?' He looked about the room. 'Well, the gang's all here. Roll out the fucking barrel and the rest of it.' He tapped his thigh with the paper. 'Quite the gathering, isn't it.' He looked to Brenda. 'Wives as well… Brenda, you've aged, love.'

'Because my life is in tatters and it's all because of you.'

'And it's not because of him?' He pointed to me with the paper. 'Have you gone mad, Jackie Dunne?' He turned to the pub. 'How do you all feel about this? Eh? Not too clever, I see - and you'd be bloody right.'

'We don't want any agro,' said Danny, moving in.

'There'll be none. But after his little performance, I'm well within my rights to be here. I will deliver a message whether you lot like it or not.'

'Say what you have to say and get lost,' barked Old Timer.

'Are you still flogging yourself to death behind that bar?' Bill turned to me. 'I will say it, I will and then be gone.' He stepped in, pointed at me again with the paper. 'You flush eight grand of mine down the crapper, you scrag one of my fellers, you cancel a meeting that could've smoothed everything and got us back to normal - *that's* bad enough. But then you do *this?*' He held the paper high. 'I'm nearly speechless, I am.'

'How much money do you need, you?' said Brenda. 'You've got the club, the pitches, half a dozen spielers and shebeens. How much money do you need, you bloody pig?'

223

'I've no argument with you, Brenda.'

'I do with you, though. You're a disgrace, man. You used to be a proper bloke, now look at you. You're nowt but a bloody pimp and a drug dealer. Your mother would be disgusted if she were alive today.'

'Don't waste your breath, Brenda.' Mary moved to her.

'And what about you?' Bill said, turning to Mary. 'What was your part in all this?'

'What?'

'Well, the whole bleeding lot of you is pots for rags mental.'

'All right, Bill,' said Theo, moving. 'She had nothing to do with Jackie's mind on this.'

'So, you say. But I wouldn't trust any of you as far as I could throw you. You'd *all* be tickled to see me go down as much as he would.' Bill nodded in my direction.

'They had nowt to do with this and you know it,' I said. 'You're just looking for excuses to have a go. You might want to take a gander at your own crew. I'm talking Mac Collier. And not here, surprise, surprise. He's the reason for all this palaver and you're still coddling the bastard.'

'The bottom line, mate, is that you've opened your grid. At least the lad's not a grass - a *rat, a snitch.*' He began to read from the article. "If police would concentrate their efforts on the triangle of Old Mill, Great Ancoats and Pollard Street area, Manchester's heroin problem will be over by Christmas." He's drawn them a bleeding diagram.'

'You broke all the rules when you started this filth. You know it'll kill this city and you're doing it anyway. You've lost all of your honour, so the rules of engagement do not apply, they just do not.'

'Mr. bloody High and Mighty.' He turned to the group. 'And you're all believing this shit? Not all, I see. It's a bit scant in here, Jackie. Have some of your lads done a runner on you? Don't blame them. Sensible. As for the rest of you still sitting on the fence, I'm opening up the books, and any of you - barring a few…' he looked to Mary and her crew, '… can come over to my side. All past grievances will be forgotten.'

'Whoever wants to go then go; there'll be no ill will,' I said, turning to my lot. 'I'll say nowt. But get ready to do hard time, 'cause he'll get nicked as sure as the rain.'

Bill scowled at me. Some of my lot were defiant, some dithering. No one would make a move now even if they wanted to, but the tension was back breaking.

'We've no time for your rubbish, Shaw so piss off.' Old Timer was coming round the bar.

'How old are you, mate?' asked Bill. 'You should be sitting in the sun retired, not mithered with any of this.'

'I'll be the judge of that.'

'You heard him - piss off.' Lippy stood up, throwing his oar in.

There was a rumble of agreement and a couple of the others stepped up. Bill raised his voice.

'Think about it. A couple of days and the drawbridge is up.'

One of my lads started a low chant.

'Who the fuck are Man United?
Who the fuck are Man United.'

'Eh, this article's no big deal for me,' Bill said. 'We'll just change locations. But *you lot* - the fun's just starting for you.'

'Don't you dare threaten my family,' Brenda said, stepping in. 'You'll have to answer me, Liam Shaw, and I will not rest -'

I moved to stop her. Mary was right by me yelling at Bill.

'Sort your women out, you lot,' Bill said, with disgust. 'I'm not here for a bloody cat fight.'

The chant from my lot grew louder, drowning out any argument.

'Who the fuck are Man United –'

The wives were pointing at Bill, shouting him down. Danny, Theo, Adolphus and me were in between them, blocking their path. Bill's crew postured, chins and chests out, and the pub erupted into shouts and jeers.

Then it was total war. All out brawling erupted and chairs flew; pint pots sailed and scraps exploded all over. I grabbed Brenda and hauled her through it all. The pub was on the brink of total disaster.

Then two gunshots rang out.

Folk flinched and dropped to ground. Stillness.

✳

A trickle of plaster dribbled from the ceiling. There standing by the door, with his Walther pistol pointing up, was Corey Blaine. The smell of a discharged weapon filled the air. I said:

'Corey… put the gun down, mate.'

'I need… I need to talk to Jackie. And, since he's here, Bill.'

Corey leveled the gun and swept it across the whole group. 'I'm serious.'

Nobody said a word. There was the faint laughter of kids from somewhere down the road.

'It's all right. I know what he wants.' I turned to Corey. 'Can we clear them out?'

He nodded. People slowly stood up. A few crept delicately to the door, while others were rooted to the spot. Brenda stepped forward.

'Corey, love -'

'I tried, Brenda, I tried. Maybe now they'll listen.' Corey turned to Bill. 'Get one of your lot to fetch it, that pay book.'

It was now clear that Corey was drunk, very drunk. But the booze had focused him. He looked calm, steely. We all knew how unstable he was in this state. Bill trod carefully.

'You hear that, Ray? Bring that display case that's in me office. Pronto.'

Ray backed off gently, turned and left. I addressed the gathering.

'Just give us a minute. Danny get them outside. Woe betide anyone who starts some 'at. Make sure.'

'You hear what the man said,' said Danny. 'Outside. And everyone stay in sight. Move it.'

Everyone filed out in silence. Brenda looked back at me then at Corey before disappearing into the foyer. The frosted glass saw the crews peeling off in different directions.

Bill slowly broke out his cigs.

'Are you going to hang onto that thing, Blaine?'

'For now... since neither of you've seen fit to help me and give me what was mine anyway. I'll get what I need then leave. But don't muck me about. I'm in no mood.' He swung the gun to me. 'I hear you've got the dog tag here. Where is it?'

'Upstairs in the safe.'

'Go get it.'

I went upstairs into the office and opened the safe. I took out the dog tag. Looking to the drawer where the Luger lived, I had a brief moment of madness. I ignored it and went downstairs.

When I saw Corey again I regretted not hiding the gun on me.

Bill was behind the bar getting whiskies. Corey watched with murder in his eyes. I held up the dog tag.

'Put it on the table,' said Corey.

I did and he snatched it up. He studied me.

'How difficult was that, Jackie? Eh? Is the pub going to collapse? Are floods and tides coming? I think not.'

'Can you put the gun down, man?' I said.

'The gun stays until I have what I want.' He turned to Bill and barked. 'Hurry up with that drink, man.'

Bill put the three whiskies on the bar. Corey went and got one, knocking it back in one. Bill did the same. I ignored mine.

'Come back round where I can see you,' Corey said.

Bill came round the bar. There was a silence. Bill poured another nip. Corey watched him. Then:

'How long will he be with that pay book?'

'Ten minutes tops,' said Bill.

Church bells in the distance cut through the silence. There was the laughter of kids again. Bill spoke:

'Can I just ask you something, Blaine?'

'Maybe.'

'Why all this palaver over these things now; after all this time? Why?'

'I told you. I'm handing them to the German War Graves thing.'

'So you said. But this commission's been there for bloody years. Why hand it in now?'

'That's my business.'

'It's mine now.'

'Ask Jackie.' Corey turned to me. 'He knows.'

'Can we just get on with this and leave it at that?' I moved to the bar, feeling Bill's eyes on me.

'What's he on about, ask you?'

I ignored Bill and got my drink.

'I asked you a question, Dunne. What does he mean, ask you?'

I breathed out and drank, feeling the whisky burn the back of my throat. I turned to him. 'Remember the photos he took... the POWs and us?'

'Aye.'

'We thought the camera was knackered, didn't we. Well, it turned out it wasn't. He's just developed the film.'

'What?' Bills eyes widened. 'There's photos?'

'All there in black and white, eh Corey?'

'Did you see them?'

'I saw enough to know it'd worked.'

'That camera was ruined,' Bill turned to Corey. 'You found it in that burned-out half-track.'

'German engineering, pal,' I said, pouring another drink. 'He'd saved it all these years.'

'Is it any worse than hoarding medals of dead men?' said Corey. 'That you killed in cold blood? Like murderers, psychos, keeping trophies of victims?'

Bill's eyes searched Corey, the cogs turning. 'Are you black-mailing him?' He turned to me. 'Is he -?'

'Trust you to think that,' said Corey.

'We blamed the resistance,' said Bill. 'And it worked... brilliant to blame the Werewolves. They attacked us - prisoners escaped and were killed in the fight. And the Colonel believed us. If you've got photos -'

'This is not about blackmail, Bill,' Corey said, through teeth.

'*I* don't give a shit, but Mr. British Legion here might. Is that what this is, 'cause he's got a lot on his plate right now.'

Corey spelled it out like Bill and me were infants. 'All I want is the ID of a boy I killed, so he can be buried properly and his family know where he is. What's so difficult with that?'

'In exchange for the negatives?' asked Bill.

'No one will see the photos.' Corey was getting impatient. 'This is personal, nothing more.'

'He doesn't want money,' I said.

Corey stared at the floor. Then: 'I never thought I'd develop it… the film. As far as I knew it was duff. A smashed-up camera found in a kraut kit bag.'

'It's Patrick, isn't it?' said Bill, it dawning on him. 'Isn't it?'

Corey snapped the gun up to Bill's head.

'Whoa, whoa, whoa.' Bill's hands were up, eyes closed.

'Corey, calm down,'

Corey pulled back; the gun was still trained on us. He settled. 'It *was* my Pat… the anniversary of his death. Last week cleaning out mam's loft, I just found it. So I did it myself. Got the chemicals, read up on how to develop film. And there he was… a fifteen-year-old cadet, shitting himself, forcing a smile while you gave him a fag, Jackie.'

'Did you get our lads?' asked Bill, 'My SS man and Jackie's officer?'

'All of them… before and after.'

Silence.

'Jesus Christ,' whispered Bill.

'And it all seems like yesterday, seeing them like that.' Corey was elsewhere for a few seconds. Then he came back. 'Let me lay that lad to rest. Give his family peace, then I can pray to his soul, *his soul*... and ask its forgiveness.'

'Soul? Forgiveness?' I shook my head and moved away.

Corey turned to me. 'I watched that boy of mine waste away. Fifteen years old, the exact age of the boy I killed.'

'For God's sake.'

'He begged me as he lay there, begged me for six more months of life and all I could see was that German boy begging me not to shoot him before I put a bullet through his neck! And I will be haunted – haunted by that boy's soul until *I beg* – beg for forgiveness and make amends to my God.' He swallowed back tears and looked up at us. 'And I can start with these fucking trinkets you both hold so dear.'

'Ray will be here in a minute,' said Bill calming him. We heard a car pulling up. 'I think that's him now. So everyone stay calm.'

*

The car door slammed. In a few seconds Ray was entering the pub where he stood all nerves and dither with the display case.

'Get it out,' said Corey.

Ray looked to Bill for help.

'Do it. Smash it.'

Ray swung the case against the bar and let it drop. It flopped over in shattered bits.

'That one there,' said Corey, pointing. 'The pay book.'

Ray picked up the document and warily handed it over. Corey flipped to the photograph page and checked. He flinched slightly at seeing the picture. He put it into his inside pocket.

'Are we done here?' Bill said, with a tinge of impatience.

'I'll leave you be now.'

Corey gathered himself and made it to the door. Ray and Bill relaxed as he opened it to go. But I couldn't help myself.

'But you won't let us be, will you, Corey?'

Corey stopped but kept his back to me.

'You're going to hand *everything* over to this Graves thing, aren't you - the photos, the scenario, the whole bleeding lot.'

Bill looked at me as if I was mad. Seething, I took no notice.

Praying to the *soul of an enemy* who was killed in a war? I couldn't stop myself. All the stuff he'd told Brenda, all that was boiling in my head.

'You want to drag me down, I know.' I turned to Bill. 'He blames me for this we know he does, fair enough, but he wants to see the *whole bloody English Army* go down with me. Don't you?'

Corey turned now. 'I've told you I've no interest in doing that.'

'You've just done it! You've *always* done it!' I leaned towards him, the bile mounting. 'The only war we haven't apologised for and you want to shit all over it! *Everyone* shot prisoners, mate - the yanks, the French, Dutch and the *krauts* - are you fucking kidding? But you want to bend it all and put us as the villains.'

'We were no better than them.'

'And we were no worse. But you'll always dump on England 'cause it's who you are - what you were brought up with. IRA this, Catholic that, the pair of you as bad as one another.'

'Just let him go, man.'

I turned to Bill, my heart thumping. 'I'm sick of it! Your hate for this country! Passed down like the clap! Your Fenian

Da - your Catholic shite! You're poison! My dad came over in 1923 - a bloody refugee 'cause he knew Ireland was finished. He grafted and slogged, did what he could to become an Englishman, but your lot cribbed and moaned for five generations 'cause you had to pick up a shovel and work for it.'

'And do the dirty work,' Corey snapped back. 'For His Majesty.'

'See? See? It's all coming out now. You'd rather we were speaking German would you?'

'Those people were beaten and we still pounded them with bombs. Then we robbed them, raped them, starved them; and why did we do that, Jackie?'

'You tell me, you're the bloody expert.'

'Revenge,' he said, his eyes full of hate.

'Revenge? Dear God.'

He let the door close and stepped in. 'For Dunkirk, Dieppe, Norway, Greece! Every time we were nose-to-nose with the krauts they gave us a kicking. We couldn't beat them fairly, could we – no - so we got back at them by killing their kids, their mothers, wives – from the air - in their cities.'

'Have you forgotten the warden, all our mates? Have you?'

'No comparison.'

I stuttered, trying to get out the right words. Corey stepped closer. 'Moral of the story – don't make the English look bad! 'Cause they'll make you pay. And we did, didn't we Jackie?'

'I'm done with this,' I said, waving him away. I moved to the stairs. I was going to bring the whole lot down, all the other kraut booty and choke him with it.

'What are you afraid of, Jackie?'

I spun around. 'Afraid? Me? Watch it, kiddo, I'm not afraid

of owt. You want to apologise to the Germans do it on your tod. It's a pity we didn't liberate Bergen-Belsen. You wouldn't be cribbing then, would you.'

'And I'm not the one slagging the British Army, you are! *You're* the one telling folk it was the NCO told us to do it, execute those fellers. *But it was you*. You changed the orders - carted us into the field to kill those men. And I bear that burden and so did my boy!'

My head pounding, I got another whisky. Corey was right behind me. He dropped his voice, low, sharp.

'And he'd seen that officer before, Bill, that lad he shot. That first day we were in the lines - he'd fallen in Jackie's trench, during that artillery attack.'

'Eh, what?' said Bill.

'They had a stand off, that's how he got the scar. It wasn't from shrapnel as he told us - it was a fight - him and the officer. Right, Jackie?'

I drank the whisky and gripped the bar rail in frustration.

'Is this true?' asked Bill.

I didn't answer but Corey filled the gap.

'And whatever happened in that trench you never said. But it was the reason you shot him months later, and it wasn't your face, was it? Or revenge for the warden, no. So, what happened, Jackie, to make you kill him – 'cause you feel lousy enough to visit me in Canada and pour your heart out to me!'

I slammed my glass down and spun on him. 'And what do you get out of this, Corey, when you've got your revenge? Absolution, is that it? You working on a red carpet to heaven, man?'

'It's better than doing this!' Corey grabbed the paper from

234

his back pocket and shook it in my face. 'If this article isn't your conscience speaking I don't know what is!'

'Oh, go away with you, man – go to hell!' I waved him off, moving to the door.

'Hold on, hold on.' Bill grabbed my arm. 'What does he mean?'

'I'm done here.' I sloughed him off and got entangled in some chairs. Bill was all over me.

'What does he mean about this article? What do you mean?'

'Trying to save that lad of yours won't bring that soldier back!' shouted Corey.

I whirled on Corey, grabbed the gun and flung it away where it skidded on the tiles. I snatched his lapels and pulled him to me.

'One more word, one more and I'll -'

'Whoa, whoa, whoa,' Ray was in.

'Let him finish.' Bill was inches from my face 'What does he mean about this fucking article?'

I tried to get free but Corey and Bill held tight.

'Guilt. He came to see me in Canada, told me he was feeling bad. Why Jackie – 'cause he let you live? So he scarred you but he spared your life, didn't he? That's why you feel guilty, that's why!'

I tried to pull back but they all came with me. We stumbled into the bar, rolled along then into more chairs. We were stuck there all three of us, not able to get away from one another.

'When you came to me you wanted to hear something -!'

'Shut it, shut it!'

'Let him talk!'

'- That what was happening -'

'Calm down – all of you!'

'– To Neil had nowt to do with that man, what you did. But I told you straight what it was! The Sins of the Father - The Sins of the Father are visited on the Child! And you couldn't handle it so you left. But you can't run, Jackie, 'cause here were are - here were are!'

I pulled from the clump and all of us, including Ray, fell about on the floor, tangled in chairs and overturned tables. We lay there like rubble. I got up and made for the back door. I went outside, through the gate and out across the road to the croft. The warden watched me go by him, as I walked and walked over the uneven ground.

FOUR

That snow bound meadow, bushes on the left lining the area. There's the farmhouse in the distance. The frozen river thrusts to the house then turns sharply. Shallow banks line the river with weeping willows and birch trees; the willows drooping, aching towards the solid river; some... some with their branches encased in the ice.

So quiet... complete silence. Strange that but for the crunching of boots; boots on the frosted earth and the deep breathing of men in motion. The German soldier, there he is, in front of me. I know that insignia... on his collar and his uniform. Next to him is the boy soldier stumbling with exhaustion. Behind him Corey holds his Lee Enfield rifle and that stupid camera. Click, click, click. Then the other prisoner, the Waffen SS geezer tromps along his eyes down. Behind him Bill smiles in victory, his helmet sitting at a jaunty angle, exposing a white-wall haircut, the chinstrap straining under the tension of his wide grin. He looks very happy indeed. The crunch of the boots and the sound of breathing is everywhere, all round me. Puffs of breath billow out of mouths, before disappearing. Then another cloud just as brief as the one before. A raven caws in the distance, its call cutting the air. A reconnaissance plane hums a million miles away.

The ceiling was unfamiliar. I was on a settee. Then I recognized the stink of the damp and the musty carpet. Neil's flat in Didsbury.

I sat up, feeling a sharp stab. My ribs. I looked down to find my clothes still on. I creaked vertical and wandered through into the bathroom. The mirror was a picture; fat lip, bruised cheek and a shiner looming. Knuckles scuffed and bloody.

I stumbled through a brew up, trying to figure out the mystery of last night. I remember ending up in a boozer over Moston way. I'd done a pub crawl, guzzled pints and pints, hopping from one hostile pub to the next, defiantly sitting at bars I'd never go into, inviting the challenges, the criticisms, the ridicule. And I'd done some leathering, and taken some, too.

I made a phone call to Brenda. No answer. She'd be with O' Connell and they'd be talking about me. I didn't care.

Then I remembered the contract signing with Brian. I checked the time and looking outside, I saw the car wasn't there. I'd had the sense to get a taxi at least. I phoned Brian and told him I was on my way. A taxi was summoned and ten minutes later I was heading over to the real estate office.

I thought of the run-in with Corey. He'd cost me. I knew Bill would use what he'd heard to ruin my street credibility.

My mind was flashing with all this.

Corey. Bill. Despite the resentment and anger my heart ached. What happened? I knew when we got back in '47 they'd both have my back; and me theirs, just like in Europe. After what we'd gone through this bond kept us sane, because you can't trust civvies. But your army mates, who at some point, saved your life while risking theirs – that's different. Trust holds you all together. It makes the chaos and indifference of civvy life bearable. Now that was gone, I felt everything shifting underneath me. All the foundations were crumbling. I felt completely and utterly isolated.

I tried not to think about it. Keep moving, keep moving - don't get pinned down.

✳

With no time to sort myself out Brian's reaction was classic.

'Rough night, Jackie?'

'You should see the other feller.'

He made light but you could tell he was shocked. I gave him a song and dance story, impossible to believe if he'd been anywhere near a newspaper. So, he wasn't convinced. My suit was a disgrace and my tie had gone walkabout. My waistcoat was trashed, and my fob watch, passed down to me from my dad, had also done a runner.

I signed the contract and he put it away. The deposit cheque would have to wait. He knew I was good for it. We shook hands and I made to go. He spoke:

'Do you want a lift? I see you came in a taxi.'

We got in his car, a nice Rover, and headed over to my pub. We drove for a minute or so in silence. I could hear him thinking or winding up to say something.

'If you need anything, Jackie,' he said, 'just ask. I mean it.'

I was surprised at the offer and didn't reply right away. Then I was touched. He thought I'd taken umbrage so he went on:

'I'm sorry but… You do know, without you getting to me when you did, things would've been very different for me. I'd be in jail now, or dead. So, I'm there. You get me, Jackie?'

'Ta…ta… appreciate it.' I did. I had to look out of the damn window. 'Just a few glitches to iron out and I'll be back in clover.'

We drove into Salford. Things just dribbled out of me as we glided along.

'You have an idea of yourself, not the same as what others see. I don't think of myself as a villain. But getting out is harder than staying in. That's why I want Neil to… well, be like you. Have a proper job. I knew you wouldn't have lasted two minutes in this game, same as our Neil. You're both not built for it. And there's no shame in that. But I did it all wrong with Neil. Giving him the club, even though it's all above board, it's still part of it. It was going to happen, him being dragged into it.' Then half to myself: 'Maybe I *should* send him away.'

He looked at me.

'It's a long story,' I said. 'Bad idea.' Stick with the plan, Jackie. Don't bottle out now.

'It'll work out,' Brian said. 'The record shop is a grand idea, a day job. And it can float itself, without any help or interference from… you know.'

We pulled up to my pub. Sure enough my car was still there. I turned to Brian.

'I'd better get over to the warehouse, eh? Check on the

bloody records. Make sure they're not all warped and scrunched to buggery.'

'Aye.'

Brian's confab had rallied me a bit. Keep busy, keep the ball up in the air, for Neil, for the shop, for all of it. Keep moving forward. You stay still and you're overrun. Counterattack; just as important, if not more so, than initial engagement. Keep moving forward, don't stay still and end up a sitting duck.

I started up the Cortina. I was heading over to the warehouse in Ancoats.

A bunch of cargo trucks were parked outside, serving a warehouse opposite; so I pulled the car round the back. I walked back to the main entrance, up the steps and unlocked the large industrial door.

The familiar waft of damp plaster met me as I walked through the high-ceilinged offices. I was soon in the glass-roofed warehouse where the records lay in boxes on trestle tables in three neat rows. The late morning sun poured into the drafty space making it warmer than the rest of the building.

I'd not been here since the Detroit balls up six months ago. Everything was just as I'd left it. The tarpaulin was still strewn over the tables and underneath it were thousands of 45s. I lifted the canvas and examined the clear plastic underneath. I raised it to check for any mold or water damage. It was unlikely, since most had survived a Detroit warehouse for years. I put the plastic and tarpaulin back and walked the length of the room, estimating what we had. One hundred and fifty records a box; fifty boxes per row and three rows. That was a lot of records.

Not bad to start. I figured a mid-sized van would hold it all.

I took in the rest of the room, wondering what it was like in the once busy warehouse. Bits of raw cotton were still dotted about; a reminder of the city's massive wealth; a city that had once been the centre of the world. My city.

As I looked at the outlines of where the machinery had been, I noticed footprints in the dust. There was a clump of them at the end of the row. I walked to the corner and looked down, noticing boot prints. The tarpaulin looked like it'd been tampered with so I hoisted it, then the plastic, and looked into one of the boxes.

It took a moment to take in what I was seeing. There, tightly wrapped in cellophane, were eight-kilogram bricks of heroin. The hairs on the back of my head prickled. I pulled the tarpaulin off all the boxes and laid the records bare. I inspected them all but found no more of the drug.

I stood back and lit up. My mind reeling, I started to unpick this puzzle. This wasn't Neil, this, it couldn't be. Why would he be looking for a hit if he had this lot on hand? Then it dawned. Macker. The tricky, little get. He must've gotten hold of a key, copied it, and stashed his wares right under my nose. What better hiding place? Jesus, I had to admire the swine for his cunning.

This was a golden opportunity. I could take the gear and plant it on one of Bill's gaffs. I'd then have a choice; use it as leverage to get Macker out of the city, or just shop the lot of them; tell the Peelers where it was and have the lot banged up. Eight kilos were enough for lengthy sentences, if they were convicted.

Panicked, I looked to the door. Macker or any of Bill's crew could show up any minute. I looked around and found an old piece of sacking on the floor. I picked the kilos up, wrapped them, and headed for the door. As I moved to the front, I looked through the office window. The trucks had moved on, but parked in their place and with the doors already opening, was the Vauxhall Viva.

The Scousers and Macker got out and started walking up the steps. I doubled back and hid in a small pantry-like room. I just made it as the front door creaked open. I heard the three come in and the door close.

'The door… it's open,' I heard Macker say. 'Jesus, no…'

'What? What?'

'Quiet.' Macker's voice went low. 'Eddie, you stay here. Frank, check the rooms downstairs.'

I was fucked. I had no weapon. But they did, guaranteed. I railed at myself for not locking the door behind me. Then I had to accept my position and act accordingly. I had to drop the load and rush them, make a break for it. Attack – there was no other way. I was about to do just that when one of the Scousers piped up:

'What about the back? Isn't there an exit?'

'Yeah, yeah,' said Macker. 'Right, check the back, down the side corridor.'

'What about outside, round the back?'

'This way's quicker. Keep to the right. I'll check the records. Frank, nip downstairs.'

I heard them pull out weapons. Then they were off. I waited until their footsteps had receded then slid out of the room, tiptoeing round the crumbling plaster. A nerve-wracking minute followed, handling the door with the awkward load.

My car was a good schlepp and they'd be on me in no time if they heard me.

I was down the steps in seconds and off at a clip, the bundle cradled in my arms. I rounded the corner, checking behind me. Nothing. I dumped the bag on the bonnet and rifled for the keys. I pulled them out and they fell right on a grid. They lay there splayed, teetering, about to fall into the hole. I breathed, bent slowly down and pinched one of the key rings, pulling the bunch clear. I cradled them around the door lock and opened it. I jumped in and realized that the load was still on the bonnet. I swore, got out and retrieved it, throwing it on the passenger floor. I got in, did a three-point turn and sped off. I checked my rear-view mirror. Nothing.

✣

I ended up over Smedley way. After parking the car in an alley, I sat for a few moments. I was getting too old for this shit. I rummaged in the glove box for my stash; barbs, chalkies, Ephedrine, Dexedrine, the usual. There it was, the Valium. I necked a couple and sat smoking.

I had to get rid of the gear, dump it in one of Bill's gaffs, and sharpish; I couldn't relax until then. I sat and thought. It didn't take me long to choose which one. I headed over to Harpurhey.

Bill's scrap yard was fenced off but I knew there was no guard dog. I drove by the office. It seemed empty, so I continued and ended up round the back. The area was deserted but for a few row houses across a desolate croft. All around was waste ground where neighbourhoods had once been, and in the distance, obscured by hanging mist, were abandoned houses and mounds of rubble.

I could see a group of youngsters kicking a ball against a battered wall about half a mile away, their voices mingling with the yap of a small dog. Fortunately a crumbling wall hid me.

I looked at the piles of metal, mostly cars, behind the fence. I saw an old Anglia, scrunched and sad, poking out from the chaos. There was a gash in the fence, probably made by the kids. It'd been lazily repaired with a couple of twists of wire. Using pliers from the boot of the Cortina, I set about untwisting the makeshift mend. It took a few minutes and hangover sweat poured down my face and neck. Finally, I took up my haul, pulled the fence to and slid in. In a couple of minutes I'd hidden the drugs in the Anglia's twisted boot and was back outside the fence.

I heard the base-like bark of a large dog getting louder. I got back in the car and trundled off on the cobbles, avoiding old prams, mattresses and the usual clutter that bedeviled the area.

I headed home. The place was empty, the missus nowhere in sight. Though I was glad she wasn't there, the silence was deafening. I wandered around a bit. The place smelled of furniture polish and clean laundry. I showered and changed then sat at the kitchen island smoking.

I thought of the morning's doings. Macker would have told Bill by now. They obviously knew nothing of me restarting the record shop. I got some pleasure from that. I chuckled over that one. I relished Macker's humbled face, Bill's slack-jawed expression, and the following rage. Then the quiet; the realizations as it all filtered down; the consequences, potential disasters and the cold facts. I wanted him to sit with that reality. I wanted him to sweat.

I went through a pot of tea and a few fags. I thought of my

crew. I put out my cig and left the house.

✳

'Look at the bleeding state of you, Jackie.'

I shrugged and looked about the room. The brick walls were painted a shiny, pale green. The place smelled of carbolic and cannabis. The visiting room of Strangeways Prison was full. I looked back at Alan sitting opposite, smoking a hand-rolled cig.

Alan Boyle was a Manchester hard man I'd known for years. He was bald, squat and solid as a Bull Terrier. A Cheetham Hill lad, he was once targeted by an Ardwick mob. He was to be killed. I knew of the contract and because Alan and me were fast I talked to the geezer over there. He owed me favours and I got him to call it off. Alan never forgot it.

He studied me, his own face a road map of scars. 'You're too bloody old, you are, for all this malarkey.'

The place was full of women and young kids. Over to our side was an inmate whose wife had sidled up to him. They had a blanket over their laps, and underneath it she was pulling him off. You could see the thing bobbing up and down. Their kid was close by running a toy truck along the floor, his driving noises matching the evermore-progressive contortions on his dad's mush.

Alan and me talked of Mary's kid, Jez.

'Those Trinidadians want his balls on a spit,' Alan said. 'And all this stuff with you hasn't helped.'

'Are you still on board? Can I still rely on you?'

'That's a daft question.' He looked at me and shook his head. 'You're a cunt, you really are, but that's a daft question.'

I nodded and bunged him some fags. He stuck them in his

prison overalls. The word would already be out that Alan was still with me.

'You're not doing yourself any favours, though,' he said. 'Neither am I. I hope it's all worth it, I do.'

Alan carried so much respect that the Trinidadians would continue to leave him and Jez Brown alone; for now. We gassed about family and the latest ructions then I got up to leave. As we shook hands I could feel his strength.

'It's funny, isn't it?' he said. 'They all look the bloody same, the Trinidadians, Jamaicans. Seems mad that they're at one another's throats, eh? But then again, they probably say the same about the Proddies and the Papist's. Mad world.' He sniffed and adjusted his prison overalls. 'Look after yourself, man,' he said. 'It's worse out there than it is in here.'

As I left I saw that the man being yanked off was now lounging and smoking in afterglow. His wife was chatting away about the latest family news, and the kid was still pushing around his dinky toy, not a care in the world.

I pulled up outside Danny's and immediately knew something was wrong. His downstairs curtains were closed. I pulled around the corner and got out. Bringing the German dagger with me, I went straight to the window. I listened. Music, loud music, was blaring out from a cranked radio on a Hi-Fi system. Trouble was, it wasn't reggae. It was The Sweet. 'Ballroom Blitz' was blasting away. There was nothing like Glitter Rock to drown out screams of one who was being tortured.

I wasted no time. I nipped down the ginnel to the back door. I tried it and it was open, so I snuck in. The music had finished and I could now hear muttering. Danny was breathing heavily. Then I heard him taking blasts from his inhaler. More muttering. I slowly opened the kitchen door and stole into the hall. Tiddles the cat came padding up to me, and I sweated like buggery expecting her to make a row and give me away. The front room door was open and I could hear Macker's voice. Luckily, the music was low but still audible, so it drowned out my fumbling and the cat's purring's. But I couldn't make out what they were talking about.

I peered through the crack of the door hinge. Macker held his Stanley knife and faced Danny. The big feller was in his underwear, sitting in a kitchen chair unbound, but gaffer tape was on the floor; bits still sticking to the chair and Danny's arm. His chest was full of bloody tea towels. The Scousers surrounded him. One had his back to me; the other was behind Danny, holding his inhaler.

The shotgun was on the settee. I cursed myself for not carrying the Luger.

'I've got to hand it to you, Danny,' said Macker, 'you're a wily bastard, you really are.'

'Very creative, Danny.'

'You're not telling fibs, big boy?'

'No, no, I'm not honest.'

I rammed into the door, knocking the first Scouser into the fireplace. Macker went for the gun but I threw the knife at him, and he flinched as it bounced off his forearm. The other Scouser went for the shotgun, same as me. He got there first but didn't have time to swing it round, so I rammed him into the wall. I could hear Danny up and grappling with the feller by the fireplace. I kicked mine a few times, nutted him, then shoved the gun under the bastards chin. Then I was hit in the side of the head. That sent me down, where another blow had me seeing stars.

'Get out!' screamed Macker. 'Move it – now!'

'Let's do him, Macker, let's do him!'

'No, no – let's go - GO!'

I heard Danny get a final smack and they were gone. I looked up to see Macker backing out with the shotgun. Crack. A round went into the ceiling lamp shattering it, sending glass everywhere. Then he was gone. I went through the hall and watched them go, leg it to the next row of houses. Then they were through the ginnel and out of sight.

Blood was trickling from my head. I put the kettle on. I took up a roll of paper towels and returned to the front room. Smoke from the blast hovered, and Danny was slumped on the settee having a cig. Blood was pouring from the cuts on his chest. I picked up the bloodied tea towels and threw him the paper ones. Then I went to the phone.

✴

Sammy the Surgeon was finishing up. Danny's wounds looked decidedly better. The rock station had been turned off, and Jimmy Cliff was giving his reggae sounds on the Hi-Fi. Danny was halfway down another Ultra Light.

Sammy was a retired Jewish doctor who'd do this kind of work for us. It avoided infirmaries and nosey NHS nurses. He tied his last stitch and wrapped up. He put away his tetanus needle, his surgical spirits and his paraphernalia.

'Well, I don't have to tell you the less movement you do the better.' He got to the door. 'There'll be no bouncing for a while.' He looked at me. 'And you, Jackie, that was a crack and a bit, that was. You'll need a follow up at hospital, a scan or something.' He knew he was wasting his breath. He looked at us both and shook his head. 'I don't how you do it, I really don't.' He got no response. 'Right,' he said. 'Look after yourselves, fellers.'

I paid him and he left by the back door. I put the kettle on again and watched him go. I touched my throbbing ear and the taped gauze that was hiding it.

In the twenty minutes it'd taken Sam to come I'd gotten the story from Danny. As I'd guessed they'd been looking for the dope I'd lifted. This was no surprise. There'd been revenge too, by Macker, for the hiding he'd taken from Danny on Saturday night; as well as the dumping of Macker's load into the Irwell. This all made sense. What *didn't* make sense was the conversation I overheard.

I hadn't mentioned this to Danny. Men will say a lot under torture and not mean any of it. Besides, I felt lousy that he'd been put in this position.

We sat drinking tea while his sixty stitches stung and my ear throbbed like a bastard. Sammy had given him a dose of morphine, so Danny was happily stoned.

'Eight bleeding kilos,' said Danny. 'You going to bend him, Bill?'

'If Macker's not sent packing, I'll shop him. In fact, after this… I'm just going to shop the bloody lot of them. I'm done.'

'Jesus, guv. What a song and dance. This could've all been avoided … sorted that little get out for good. Saved us all a pile of grief.'

There was silence for a bit while we smoked. He looked at

me through bleary eyes.

'How are you, anyway, the rest of it?' This was his shorthand for how we were handling our war experiences.

I shrugged. 'Why does it get worse as we get older?'

He exhaled and stared at the wall. 'I've never had a sleepless night, me. And I have a tally, mind. Well, you know. Lost count.' He smoked. 'But this *one*... It was bad. I remember it like it was yesterday. Little Malaysian cunt, he was. Couldn't have been more than sixteen. But he was trying to cut us to ribbons with an AK47. Killed about three of me mates. What do you do?' The cat jumped up on his belly. 'We kept him alive for two days... The shit we did to him. You could hear him all over the base... the brass weren't mithered.' He smoked. 'He'd be in his late thirties now. And there's not a day goes by...' He paused and shook his head. 'It's the days see, the daydreaming. I've created a whole life for the bastard - a job, a family, a whole life. I could tell you what he had for breakfast.' He turned to me. 'Does that make me soft?'

'I shouldn't think so.'

'And I saw someone. On the NHS, like.'

'You mean like a counselor? A psychiatrist?'

'Me doctor referred me. I told him about the daydreaming, see. Not being able to concentrate. So, anyways, I go to this bugger. But really... it was very helpful, explained a lot.'

'Oh, aye? What did he say?'

'He said this fantasy, that's what he called it; this fantasy... was a way of bringing the kid back. I was keeping him alive in me own head because deep down... deep down I was sorry I'd killed him. Nutty or what.'

He shook his head. I looked at the cat. She was purring on

his belly and dozing.

'I think that's why me chest is bad,' he said. 'I'm buggered if it's that defoliant. It's that kid. It's the bleeding stress.' He smoked and winced as he inhaled. 'I mean, all through me twenties I can't remember giving the little get a second thought. Even ten years ago I wasn't mithered – that much anyway. But since me chest has got worse… you start thinking about, what is it… your own…'

'Mortality… dying.'

He nodded. 'Then you're snookered. So, yeah, it does get worse as we get older, I'd have to agree with that.'

We sat for a bit. Then I called Bill. He was calm and resolved with the threats. He was going to kill me, kill me and carve me into bits and dump me into the Irwell. I stood and took it then I gave him my ultimatum. I gave him a day to send Macker packing otherwise I'd call the Peelers. They'd find the gear and he'd be nicked. I put the phone down as he was still yelling.

✳

I went home in the dark, the rain spitting and cold. I thought of Danny's war memoir. He was the other one I could rely on and I could feel him pulling away. I now felt like someone on an island, surrounded, cut off. The feeling of isolation got worse when I got home.

Brenda was finally in and she had tea ready. I don't know what I was expecting but it was the quietist tea we'd ever had. We sat at opposite sides of the dining table, me fiddling with my food; her focused on her peas. She didn't even comment on the state of my face; just shook her head. She'd made up her mind about something, that much was clear. She was distant, resolved about things. While storms were raging inside me, she was quietly solid. It was terrifying. Whoever said women were the weaker sex had never married or had a kid with one.

'I'm going over to the church,' she said, after clearing the table.

'All right,' I said.

I wanted her to go. Being around her was just too difficult. After she'd gone I drank a lot of Brandy. It was now about nine o' clock and I hadn't checked in with Neil. I was about to do that when the phone rang. It was the Detox Centre.

I whipped down Great Ancoats Street, hitting some decent lights, then onto Chancellor Lane and then Devonshire Street. I took a rolling left onto Stockport Road. I was heading to Longsight. Neil had gone missing.

On the phone I'd railed on the Beach Boy. Had he been taken? Had he disappeared of his own choice?

'I really can't say,' he'd said.

'How long's he been gone?'

'He was supposed to have a class - fifteen minutes ago. We looked for him immediately but it's anyone's guess -'

'Did he make any phone calls?'

'Yes, he did.'

'How do you know?'

'A client saw him do that.'

'When?'

'About two hours ago,' he'd said. 'He'd seen The Evening News. We tried, we tried to keep it away from him but he got hold of a copy...'

I'd called Mary, told her what was what.

'Mary, whatever differences we have please - call out the troops. I'm begging you.' That's what I'd said.

'I'll get on it,' she'd said.

I'd called Danny and told him to call the community centre, the church, tell Brenda. Maybe she'd have ideas where he could be. But fearing the worst, and fighting images of him strapped to a chair, I rocked at the wheel as I drove.

I got closer to Macker's and it started to rain. A Mini came careening out of a side street, narrowly missing me. I lay on the brake, the horn and swore blue murder. The bastard was dawdling, so I cranked it down into a lower gear, was about to pull around him, when a car crossed the centre line, pulling wide of a parked truck. I pulled back screaming like a maniac. I saw traffic lights ahead still on green, so I laid on the horn some more. We were getting closer, closer - we might just make it. But not five yards from the lights they turned to amber. He slammed on his brakes and I ploughed right into him. Crunch. I lurched forward over the wheel, my forehead touching the window screen before being yanked back by the seat belt.

I sat there for a few seconds, paralyzed with rage. Then I rammed the car into reverse and pulled away. There was grinding of metal, a bump and I was free. Then I saw a gangly hippy emerge from the Mini. Sensing a confrontation, I pulled the wheel to get round him but he blocked me. I pulled up sharp and the bastard leaned onto the bonnet, where he vented like a madman. That was it; I threw it into neutral and got out. He saw the look on my face and stepped back.

'Hey dude, you just wrecked my fucking ride, man.'

His accent was pure Wilmslow toff. I grabbed him round

the throat and hoisted him onto the bonnet of the Mini. The whiff of Patchouli oil peeled off him.

'You dozy bastard,' I screamed. 'Learn to drive, you shit.'

I held him down wanting to bash his brains in. Instead I shoved him across the bonnet where he rolled and scrambled to the other side.

'I'm calling the cops, you bloody maniac.'

I saw white. I looked down to see the Mini's bumper lying there. I picked it up and hurled it at his side window, completely obliterating it. The metal piece peeped out like a frosted leg. The stunned man, his long hair plastered to his head, put up his hands. He'd pissed himself. I got into the Cortina and sped off.

I pulled up outside Macker's house to see no cars, nothing, not even lights. I was at the window in seconds, lifting my elbow and smashing the thing. I reached in, unlatched it and hoisted myself in, cutting my hands. The dog was cringing in the corner. I pulled out the dagger and was through the ground floor in seconds, clicking on all lights then I was up the stairs.

The place was empty. I leaned against the wall, arms splayed out above me. I tried to think of where he would go if he were depressed. Would it be drugs he wanted? No, doing this twelve-step program thing, I couldn't believe that. But he was depressed about the article, so where would he go if he had a mood on? I looked down at the mangy carpet. There was a pile of records at my feet, Northern Soul 45s. The club. He could've gone to the club.

✳

Theo's Escort was already there. I got out of the car and ran to the door and it was open. I took the stairs two at a time, almost tripping and falling full length. I could hear music, a familiar song - a very familiar song.

I hit the club floor and my knees buckled. I righted myself but stopped dead when I saw the scene in front of me. On the floor unconscious was Neil, a needle by his arm. His mother was kneeling next to him with her hands to her mouth and rocking. Theo was pumping his chest and then blowing into his mouth. The soul song was playing, booming out, the song that was so special to Brenda and Neil, the song from the hospital that had given Brenda such comfort. It reverberated round the room like a sick joke.

Brenda looked at me with wild eyes then went back to Neil. There was a change in air as someone arrived from outside, but I couldn't take my eyes from what was in front of me. I couldn't move. Adolphus brushed by me and two ambulance attendants followed. They brushed aside Theo and started to work on Neil. One rooted through his mouth with his fingers, the other took his pulse. They huddled, all of them, stooped over him. His leg started to shake.

I backed off and stumbled up the stairs. I got outside and thought I was going to be sick. I wandered along the wall, legs buckling - tongue going thick like I had the flu.

I heard the commotion behind me. I heard them load him into the ambulance. I heard Theo calling me but I pawed at the wall and rounded the corner, the sky spinning. The sirens of the ambulance had faded into the distance when I went back to the car.

The bouncers made no moves to stop me. I stumbled down

into the basement club, entering a world of mad lights and thumping music. Down there, I was disorientated. A disco ball was spinning on the ceiling and the lights from it flecked round the room. A loud and violent beat, now, 'Purple Haze' by Johnny Jones and the King Casuals was blaring out. Jesus - Macker's favourite song. Dear God, what is going on? I made my way around the dance floor, the knife digging into the small of my back.

I heaved through into the back lounge and looked around; virtually empty. Everyone was on the dance floor. I got to the office – locked. I kicked at it and crash - it flew open but it was dark and empty. No Bill. I doubled back to the exit but I got caught up in the dance mayhem. Folk seemed to be blocking my way, dancers leered up to me, sweating, spinning - the song was blasted away, drowning me.

I saw the back of a blond lad. It was Neil! I grabbed and spun him around. His face was mad, wild, in another place. Folk moved back and gave him room for his dance delirium. He dipped, spun, shuffled and kicked, the way Neil used to when he could still do all that - but this was him times ten; extreme, fretted with sharp turns and mad thrusts. He was more like a deranged spirit than a human. Others started to spin, flip and jerk, doing wild routines. Barb and speed freaks lurched up to me and stared. The lights blinded me - sweat ran down my face… I was in a mad house, a jungle of souls, the world between life and death, no, no between death and heaven; a purgatory. My boy… my poor boy was in purgatory.

I was in the car - I was out of the car. I was at Bill's taxi firm on a side street in Rusholme. The light from the office threw itself onto the pavement and across the road. A small Pakistani man was hunched over a radio dispatching to the fleet of taxis. I peered in to the common area where Bill would sit reading the paper, drinking coffee or chairing meetings. He wasn't there. I leaned into a doorway and it started to rain.

I saw my son lying there; the blue veins bulging in his temples, the mouth drooling open to the side, the limpness of his body; then the shaking, the shaking of the legs. I glanced around trying to fill my eyes with other images, looking up into the corner of the doorway. It was a derelict house and an old cobweb flapped in the wind.

I heard footsteps and turned to see Bill hunched over with a bag of take-away. He passed by me, oblivious. It was now chucking it down. I stepped out. He stopped and turned and I went at him. He dropped the take-away and I hit him full running, sending us flying over a couple of rubbish bins where we rolled around, trying to get a handle on one another. It was a mess of arms and fists. He bit my ear and I went for his eyes. He thumped me in the temple, shoved me off and I rolled and he nearly managed to get up. Then someone slammed into him, knocking him into the wall.

It was Adolphus and he was going at him. Then Danny was in trying to separate them. Theo was in, trying to get a slam at Bill with the machete, but Danny yanked him away, then Adolphus was trying to pull Danny from Theo. Bill moved off a bit, but I rammed into him again and we slipped and rolled, a clumsy, aching clump of missed shots and frantic grappling. We reeled along the wall colliding into the rubbish bins and dropping to the floor again. I grabbed him by the scruff of the neck and punched and punched and punched. I stopped when he was no longer fighting back.

I was above him when he came to. We were soaked to the skin by now.

'He was twenty years old -!' I screamed.

'What you talking about, man -?'

'You killed him.'

Theo handed me the machete. I took it and raised it.

'Jackie – Jackie.'

'You murdering bastard!'

I went to strike him and he flinched. I pulled up and stayed there, the knife shaking in my hand.

'Do it,' shouted Theo. 'You don't do it now, you're a dead man - we're all dead!'

'Jackie, don't -'

'He'll never forgive you for this - do it.'

'Don't listen to him –'

'Do it.'

'He was my boy!'

Bill grabbed me by my collar. 'You did it!' He shook me. 'You killed that lad! You! You hear me?'

I said nothing. I went to say something but I choked.

'Jackie! Kill him!'

'He did it!' shouted Bill, drilling me with his eyes. 'He knows he did, so stop this fucking nonsense right now! You did it, you know what I mean, Jackie… you know exactly what I mean.'

I released him. Danny was leaning on the wall, his shirt bloody from the burst stitches. He started to have an asthma attack, gasping like a fish out of water, fumbling for his inhaler. Adolphus was scrambling on the floor, looking for the puffer. Theo snatched back the machete, shoved me out of the way, and made to strike at Bill.

A can of Fanta hit the wall above him. Then another cracked into his head making him drop the knife. I turned to see Ray and Didds dashing to Bill's side, pulling out weapons. Adolphus found the inhaler and Danny chewed at it like a drowning man.

I watched Ray and Didds drag Bill off. Then I left. Theo was calling after me then Adolphus, their voices lost in the rain.

FIVE

I remember the first time I saw it in him... in Neil. He was about seventeen. After his first do with the barbiturates, his first overdose. He'd had his spell in the hospital and the detox place. We'd finally got him home and he'd just had a bath. He was sat on the settee watching the telly. His thick blond hair was pulled back from his forehead. Then he turned and looked at me. And there he was, Walter Holl. There was the Oberleutnant. The pale blue eyes, the thick, blond hair. Just the glance was enough to show me he was still around; was still around and would probably never go... until he was ready.

Then he would take him. I knew the ghost would keep Neil alive until he was of the age that Walter Holl himself was killed - by me - just before his twenty-first birthday.

I emptied the last drop of the bottle.

I heard the buzzer. It went again. I went to the window and looked through the curtains. Outside Neil's flat was Theo. He saw me and signaled for me to open the door. I sat down.

Theo was now tapping on the window so I looked up. The amber from the streetlights made his skin glow. He hovered there but I ignored him. He knocked again. I could hear him now.

'Jackie… Jackie. He's alive… Neil's alive.'

I refocused my eyes on him. What? What did you say? I said this to myself.

'You need to go, Jackie. He's at the Royal Infirmary.'

He stayed there for a bit then he left. I heard him go to his car. I heard the door go. He drove off.

The winds whipped down the roads and alleys of the city. The rain, riding the blasts of the wind, came down in burst and spits, lashing the faces of those I passed. Hedgerows shook like creatures were inside rattling them.

Mary was sat outside Intensive Care.

'Where the hell have you been?' she said.

I went inside. Neil was intubated and rigged up to a drip. Wires lead from him to a machine of switches and gadgets. Brenda sat at the side of the bed with her prayer beads. A doctor was shining a light into the eyes of my son. I could only stand… look. The doctor turned then came over to me.

'You must be…?'

I nodded. He guided me to a chair and sat next to me.

'He's in an induced coma. We need to take the pressure off

the brain, the body… the organs. It helps with recovery.'

'Will he…?'

'It's impossible to know if there's brain damage. He was showing very poor vital signs when he came in. But he was alive, you have your wife and her friends to thank for that. They used CPR until the ambulance arrived and they took over… So now it's a waiting game.' He looked toward the door. 'The nurse will be in with some tea.'

He left. Brenda stayed glued to Neil. Then slowly, without looking up from her beads, she spoke.

'We took turns each pumping that boy's chest blowing into his mouth and where were you? Making someone else pay? He could have died… and you were out there blaming someone else.'

She got up and came to me.

'That song… that song that gave me such faith was playing as he was dying… as if that wasn't a sign, as if it wasn't.' She handed me the prayer beads. 'Talk to him, pray - whatever. But do something. In this room.'

I took them and she left. A few seconds later I heard the door go. I turned and there was O' Connell.

'She wants me to pray for him, Jackie. It can't do any harm, son, can it? It can only do good - you know in your heart it can only do -'

I got up, ushered him out, closed the door. 'You won't go in there,' I said. 'You won't. Wait here. Do not. Do not.' I walked down the corridor and found the common room. Seeing Brenda and Mary sitting there, I went in. 'What's O' Connell doing here?'

Mary stood up. 'She needs some support, Jackie.'

'I am not having it - itching to give him Last Rights – I'm not.'

'Give it a rest for two minutes, man,' said Mary. 'Can't you see the state she's in?'

'It's all my fault, Mary. Didn't you know that?'

'It's all right, Mary,' said Brenda. 'Let him go off. But he will pray.'

'Not with him in there,' I said.

'You will pray to that German lad. You hear, Jackie? Pray for forgiveness… from his *soul*.'

I turned to Mary who had no clue. 'This… this Mary, is what I'm dealing with.'

'What are you both talking about?'

I turned to Brenda. 'Go on tell her. Or shall I?'

'What? What?' said Mary.

I went and got O' Connell. I yanked him to the door then hauled him into the common room.

'You'll want to hear this again, Father.' I shoved him towards Brenda. 'Are all you sorted?'

O' Connell straightened himself. A woman who was waiting in the room got up and left. Mary turned to me.

'Don't make a scene - not here, man.'

'You need to hear this, Mary. This is what all the palaver's about. We killed three POWs, me Corey and Bill. And I, and my boy apparently, are being punished for it – by God - for that. That!'

'God's got nowt to do with it,' said Brenda. 'It's you.'

'Oh, sorry, my guilt, I beg your pardon. A fucking kraut, Mary who'd killed dozens of our men - and this - *this* is supposed to be doing my head in? Am I missing something here? Are folk mad?' I paced about the room. 'And if I beg this man's *soul* for forgiveness then our boy - our boy will get well. He'll get well and we'll all live happily ever after, right?'

'Yes, we all know who the bad men were, don't we,' said Brenda. 'We don't need a bloody compass to know what was going on in the war, man.'

'Well, thank you for that much, Brenda.'

'But you'd seen him - you'd see him before, hadn't you. He killed a man in cold blood who'd spared his life.'

Spared his life. I gritted my teeth. Corey, Corey, Corey...

'Go on.' she said. 'Tell them. Tell them what happened, what you did.'

'Alright,' I said, 'all right, you want hear the story then here it is. Are you all comfy? Not a week in Belgium and we're in the front line. Corey's over there, Bill over there and shells falling all over - our shells, mind. And I'm on me tod, 'cause the bloke I shared with had legged it, buggered off, 'cause he wasn't having this. Anyway, I'm there being shelled to buggery and in falls this bloke, almost on top of me. And it's a German, isn't it. I thought he was one of ours at first until he pulls a knife and does this.' I pointed to my scar. 'Nice. First day of action and I'm a dead man.'

'And what did he do?'

'What did he do, Brenda? He left after the bombardment was finished.'

'He could've killed you.'

'That would've been a waste of energy, wouldn't it. My screams drawing attention, they're not daft, you know. Seasoned soldiers, love - tactical decisions.'

'Maybe he was just being human.'

I turned to Mary and O' Connell. 'You see, *this* is why we don't talk about the war, 'cause folk expect a fairy tale.' I went back to her. 'Being human?'

'He could've killed you, but he let you live.'

'Like I said, Brenda, tactical decisions. So, off he went. Nicked me fags outta me top pocket and was gone.'

'And then you killed him.'

'Later on, months later, yeah, I did. We had a job to do, Brenda.'

'Job? You were told to take them to hospital and you disobeyed orders – you took them into the fields and you killed them.'

'You had to be there, love.'

'Stop pretending you don't care! You told Corey you were struggling with it, when our boy had nearly died and might die in the future. In Canada, you talked, didn't you? And he told you what you needed to do - and you didn't take heed, did you?'

'Take heed of his rubbish; his fucking Irish clatter? I'm an Englishman in case you hadn't noticed.'

'This has nothing to do with religion, son,' said O' Connell. 'You do something that makes you feel lousy, it makes a hole in your heart and you try to fill it. You dig a brick up off the floor and it leaves a hole. Unless you fill it in you just keep tripping up over it, and that's what you keep doing, son - tripping up and soon you'll bring the whole bloody house down around you.'

'Then let it come down! So he spared me, let me live? More fool him; he should've had more sense. You don't win a war by playing fair, you don't. How do you think we've held onto all this? Got all this?'

'Got what?'

'Everything we've got, woman - in this town, in England, all of it! You don't hold this lot together by whining and moaning, by being *weak*. I feel lousy, millions feel lousy - it comes with the territory. You move on.'

'I don't understand you.'

'Yeah, you do. You know damn well if I admit I did some 'at wrong I go all the way - all or nothing, that's who I am. The Legion, the papers, they all get an earful and I am not doing that. 'Cos that's being a traitor and I am not bringing the whole thing down, I am not, 'cause I am proud – *proud!* I share this burden with millions who've held these islands together for a thousand years. Why? Because the alternative is ten times worse, love, ten times worse.'

'You'd chose all that over our boy?' said Brenda. Her face was glass. 'You'd choose that?'

'There is no choice, don't you see? I am an Englishman and without that we are nothing, do you understand? We are nothing!'

She ran to me and slapped me about the face then pounded on my chest, she collapsed at my feet, still holding onto me. Mary and O' Connell tried to pull her away but she was clinging to me to, sobbing.

I came out of the hospital. I walked through the car park to the houses behind. There was a dark alley and I couldn't see the end. I started to run, the sound of the bombardment got louder and louder. I ran. I couldn't see where I was going but I ran faster and faster, thinking that any minute I'd reach the end and the wall that just had to be there. But it didn't come.

So I just kept running deeper and deeper… into the darkness.

✳

'Those drumbeats…'

That bloody drumbeat thumping out round the whole room - jukebox cranked up as loud as it'll go… take another swig.

'Sing, Sing, Sing,'

Benny Goodman… Benny fucking Goodman - another swig…

'That bloody drum beat… gets you right down in the middle of your stomach… Benny, Benny, give it some stick, mate…'

Another swig… what now?

Press that button…. 'Hell's a Poppin'… crank it louder… crank that bloody jukebox as loud as it will go. Drums, trumpet, piano… wander about… drink, swig from that bastard bottle. Empty… grab another… stagger… bump into that… what was it…?

Press that button…. 'Hooked on Swing'…. Larry…

'Give it some stick, mate…. give it some horns, those bloody horns and the drums…'

Stagger, bump… mind that bastard chair…

Button on jukebox – press…. 'Aint Nobody Here But Us Chickens'…

'Benny, Benny, Benny…'

Stagger, fall…. up… swig that whisky… down, down, down it goes… press that button… what's this? Yes. 'Caldonia'… give it all you've got Louis…

'Louis fucking Jordan…'

Fall… get up… fall… press that button… 'Rum and Coca Cola'… the girls… give it to me baby… drink, stagger… fall… crawl… reach jukebox… press button …

I pull the trigger and bang, he falls forward. Everyone stops. The SS man looks to me then Bill. He starts to run but Bill cuts him down. He struggles a bit and Bill shoots again. The cadet looks at us and starts to cry. He can't even beg he's so terrified. Then he starts.

'Do him, Corey,' shouts Bill.

'No, no, let him go,' shouts Corey.

'We can't let him go,' I say.

'He's only a kid.'

'Shoot the bastard.'

'Shoot him, Blaine, you gutless swine. Or we're all in it.'

'I can't!'

'You can! You've killed dozens before him, man!'

'Not like this!'

'I saved your life, Corey Blaine,' I scream. 'You fucking owe me! Finish it, put him out of his misery!'

Corey raises his rifle. The boy moves towards him, falling to his knees.

Corey backs off.

'Shoot him!'

'Shoot him!'

Corey shoots. The boy's head jerks back as the bullet hits his neck. He falls grotesquely and his body shakes. I finish him. Bill goes to the SS man, shoots him in the head with the Walther. Then I look to the Oberleutnant. He is crawling, still alive. I go up to him and he finds the strength to turn to me.

'Nein, kamarad… we are friends… bitte… please, I beg you.'

What's playing now? 'Candy'… The Pied Pipers… where… where you taking my boy? Pied bastard Pipers… knock chair over… fall.

SIX

I opened my eyes. The warden was looking down at me. I was lying on the wall couch of my pub; I could smell the worn leather. The warden stepped back, pushing a mug of tea towards me. How did he get in? … Yeah… I'd brought him in, I remembered now, and he'd been here all night.

I sat up and looked around. There were smashed glasses everywhere. Bottles, crisps and peanut packets lay all over the floor. The scrim on the stage had been torn down and tinsel was everywhere. The jukebox window was cracked.

We sat there for a bit, me drinking my tea and the warden sipping a Mackeson. Light shone through the frosted windows and bathed the room in a cold light. I checked my watch. Eleven o' clock. The phone on the bar rang. We let it ring and it stopped. It rang again. I got up and answered it. I was still drunk.

'What?'

'Guv? ...Guv.' It was Danny. 'You alright?'

'I'll get them all, the whole lot. They don't know what's coming... You still there? You hear what I said, Danny Simms? I hope you're dug in deep, mate, 'cause I'm bringing them out - the big guns.'

'I've just been raided. Customs and Excise... Turned the house upside down, they did.'

'For dope?'

'What else?'

'Makes no sense.'

'You think we wouldn't be targeted? We're all up for grabs now, all up for grabs. It's just a matter of time before they pull up outside your gaff.'

'They've nowt on me...'

I could hear his chest wheezing.

'I have to tell you something, guv....'

'What?'

'I didn't flush it... the two kilos of smack from Macker the other night. I hid it... behind the cistern in the men's toilet. I hid it.'

I didn't know what I was listening to at first. It banged around my head like an echo. Then I thought he was having me on.

'Not the time, Danny, not the time.'

'Jackie, I'm telling you straight up. I didn't flush it. I hid it, up behind the cistern in the men's lav.'

I didn't know what to say. There were so many questions that all came at me in a jumble.

'Don't ask me why, guv. I just thought it was mad to flush it, you know. If I was honest, I was thinking of the money. Eight grand down the crapper. Are any of us getting any younger? I'm sure as hell not and I've still got fuck all to me name, Jackie. Fuck all and I can hardly breath.'

I thought of Neil finding it down there. I put the phone down. The phone went again. It rang until I picked it up.

'Guv, don't hang up.'

'Did Neil… did he know it was there?'

'No, he didn't. Nobody knew. Maybe it fell from behind the cistern. And when he was down there, maybe he found it. I don't know.' He was quiet for a bit. 'I'm so sorry, mate. I meant to tell you. But things just…'

'Why?'

'It was daft, I know. I knew it would cause ructions. So I kept it secret, thinking we could hand it back. But then I got greedy and thought I could make some money… If the coppers do a sweep and find it - bang go the plans to get Bill. That's all I'm saying. We should do it today. Get rid of it, sharpish.'

'I'm not mithered.'

'Chief. If the Peelers find that gear you'll be nicked. Do you want to take the blame for Bill Shaw? Do you?'

'You do it.'

'You've got the keys to the place.'

'You know where I am.'

'Guv, I am trying here. I've been loyal to you for years, years. I've never asked for owt. I fucked up this once badly, and it's had consequences, dire consequences and I can't say how sorry I am. But now I'm telling you that you need to shift that smack, 'cause if you're caught with it, it's not just jail, it's the

Legion - it's all of it. All this agro we've been through will be for nowt.' He took a blast from his inhaler. 'I'll be down there in an hour. If you need to punish me, do it then. I'll take it, whatever it is, then shift that gear where it won't be found. Or flush it – just get rid.'

He hung up.

❋

In shirtsleeves at the upstairs sink; head under the cold-water tap. I drenched myself, grabbed a towel and dried off. I combed my hair back. I took up the black coffee and carried it into the office. I took another gulp, put down the mug and picked up the Luger; the oil, the smell. I dropped the clip and slid it back in. I went down to the pub.

The old warden watched from his seat by the wall.

'What?' I said 'What?'

I slipped the Luger down the back of my trousers. I walked by him and looked in the pram. The ragged doll lay there. He picked it up and offered it to me. I left. Before shutting the door, I turned and looked. The old man was stroking the doll's head. I pulled the door to and locked it.

I drove, trying to control my drunkenness. Tony Bennet was singing 'Life is a Song'.

❋

I pulled up to the club and got out. I lit up and looked around. The street was completely empty. The traffic noise from the city seemed unusually distant; as if the small, cobbled alleys of Gaythorn belonged to another time and place.

Water ran from the gutters down into a drain, gurgling as it went. A flock of starlings suddenly erupted from a building. I looked up to see a raven, perched on the warehouse opposite. It eyed me, shifting its head. I watched it for a few seconds. I hadn't seen a creature like that in years and it seemed, even from this distance, to be aware of me. Then it lost interest, let out a shriek that echoed through the alley, and took off after the starlings.

I was starting to feel really rough. I thought of making myself sick to get it over with; but I was loathed to create such a spectacle, even alone like this. I pulled out the keys and went to the door and let myself in. I'd see for myself if the kilos were there. If they were, I'd flush them into the canal.

The door creaked open. I went into the kiosk and clicked on the lights. Then I locked the door behind me. I dithered at the top of the stairs as the image of Neil, unconscious on that floor, hit me. But nausea soon sent me down into the dark of the club.

The smell of dead mice made me feel sicker. The basement was pitch black, but there was enough light from the exit signs to get me to the Gents. I burst in, hit the cubicle and was sick. Arms spread-eagle against the wall, I pulled the chain and watched the water gurgle away. I stared at the bowl until the final hiss of the cistern dribbled to a stop.

I looked up at the cistern and checked behind. I stood on the toilet bowl and checked the top. Nothing. I got down. Then I saw something. Little heaps of powder, spillage, lay on the floor. Danny was not lying. The drugs had been here. But now they were gone.

I heard the click of a light switch in the club.

I'd locked the front door and Danny didn't have a key. So,

who was this? I pulled the Luger from the small of my back and clicked off the safety. Then I crept forward, straining to see who might be there waiting for me. I was brought up short when I saw Macker sitting at one of the alcove tables. On the table was a mickey of Jameson's and a large envelope. I moved further in. Then I felt a pistol barrel on the back of my neck.

'Don't make a move, mate.' It was Bill. 'Put it down… slowly.'

I put the Luger down and Macker grabbed it. He backed off and Bill came round from behind me. His lip was stitched and his eye was swollen and going yellow.

'Give it me and grab him a chair.'

Macker handed the Luger to Bill, then got a chair and placed it behind me. Bill sat in the alcove.

'Sit down.'

I did. Bill put the Luger on the table. With his Walther still trained on me, he took out his cigs and lit two.

'You'll be needing this, man.'

He indicated to Macker who took the cig and brought it to me. I took it and the kid retired to a pillar beside Bill. The fridge hummed.

'Before we go any further,' said Bill, 'I'll say this. I'm sorry about Neil. I had nowt to do with it. Sounds like he came down here, all moody like, found the smack Simms had left and then…' He shook his head, inhaled the Park Drive. 'Did you hear what I said, Dunne?'

'When did you find out about the drugs? Behind the cistern?'

'Don't blame Danny Simms for squawking. He's a tough bastard, the cuttings he took, but he can't last long without his precious inhaler. That's when he told Macker he'd stashed it.

Besides, when we told him why we wanted to talk, he was okay with this, setting this little meeting up. So, it's no double cross, Jackie. He's a fucking marine that man, even if he is a bit thick.'

Macker shifted from the gloom. 'I came down and got the gear after Neil had been here. None of us could've known he would find it and…'

'Get to whatever you've got to say,' I said. 'Or are you just going to shoot me?'

Bill shook his head. 'You don't believe me, fine. You should know me better, Dunne. There's still some things sacred.'

He waited for that to land. I said nothing.

'I just wanted you to know. It's important to me.'

'He's still here.' I indicated Macker. 'And whether you had nowt to do with Neil or not, I hold you responsible.'

'We're *all* fucking responsible, all of us!' He stood up and smoked aggressively. 'Look at the state of you, man. And me.' He pointed to his face. 'You've not just buggered it up for me but for yourself.' He picked up the mickey and drank. 'Nowt for you, Jackie, I can smell you from here, you hardly need anymore.' He placed the mickey back on the table. 'By rights you should be long dead, the bleeding agro you've given me. And I've swallowed some ribbing, I have, for not acting when I could've. But my patience, my patience is now at an end. And even though we go back to playing marbles, even with all the history, I was ready to kill you. And it was in the works, especially after your little threat yesterday. But then who should call me… but Corey Blaine.'

'What did he want?'

'I'll tell you in a minute.' Bill smoked and took another drink. 'This is what's going to happen. You stop it, whatever it is you're planning. You'll tell us where it is, the gear. And if I *am* nicked, you will not be a witness and you will not testify if it goes to trial. You understand?'

'He'll say anything with that pointed at him,' said Macker.

'Be quiet,' Bill said.

I looked at both of them. Then I nodded. 'All right. We have a deal...' I put my hands on my knees to stand. 'Is there anything else?'

'Stay put.' Bill turned to Macker. 'Show him.'

Macker took up the envelope, opened it and came over. He pulled out the photocopies and put them on the floor in front of me, fanning them out like a hand of poker. He stepped back.

'That bloody Agfa Karat camera.' Bill continued. 'Jerry technology. No wonder they're still running Europe.'

I looked down at the photographs. I looked back up.

'Corey,' Bill said. 'He knew you'd kick off and try to get even for your boy, and he knew you'd be dead within a week. So, this, *this* is how you live, Jackie. This is my guarantee that you stay tight lipped.' He paused, waiting for a reaction from me. 'Look at them. Pick them up.'

I did nothing. He signaled to Macker who took a few up and placed them in my hands. A distant police siren drifted in from outside, causing us to pause. It faded into the distance. Bill continued:

'Take a good and proper gander. Gave me the willies when I saw them and I'm not even mithered.'

I looked at the photos.

'Powerful images, those,' he said. 'Takes you right back, doesn't it. I can see it does. So, you will keep schtum. Right? If you don't, if you don't, they go to your Legion and anywhere else where they think you're it. But they won't just go there. They'll go to the Manchester Guardian, and that lot, who hate this country to start with... Can you imagine the field day they'll have with those pictures?'

I look at the photocopies.

There's a picture of me going through his clothes, that Oberleutnant. Taking his Iron Cross and his pay book, his wound badge, his identity tag. I take them all. There's Bill doing the same to the SS man. It's all there. Corey's recorded it all.

'It'll make national news, that,' says Bill. 'And then they'll be sent to this German War Graves effort, where they'll create a stink-and-a-half and an international scandal, no less.'

He waits for a reaction from me. But I just take in the images.

'I'll wipe the planet with those photos 'til folk get wise to what it was really like. And that's not me being a Mick, that's the truth, that is. Undeniable. You think folk will look at that war the same way again? Will they hell as like... Now, do we have a deal?'

Bill waits for me to say something.

I'm in the slit trench, what's left of it, shivering in the corner. The noise, din, the sheer horror paralyses me. I think I'll die, I know I will die, right here in this hole. I pray:

'*The Lord is my Shepherd I shall not want...*'

A shell burst and he falls in. He falls on top of me, and rolls off. He's still for a minute. Stunned. Then he comes round. I see the knife. The blood blinds me, is warm, sticky, but I feel nothing. He makes to lunge to finish me off and I close my eyes and wait to die. Nothing happens. I open my eyes, squinting with my one good eye and the soldier is just looking at me.

I see him looking down. I know he can see it, that I've crapped myself... shat myself with fear. But he looks up and gestures with his hands. He's telling me to calm down, that the bombardment will be over and then he'll leave. He knows I'm no threat so he'll call a truce. I can see it in his hands and face. He could kill me... but he chooses not to.

'Dunne! Dunne.'

I look up at Bill.

'Answer me. Do we have a deal here?' He's leaning in, Bill, waiting for my reply.

'I was ashamed, see.'

'What? What Jackie?'

'He'd seen me at me worst. That's why he had to go.'

'Eh? Can you make sense, man?'

'He'd seen me crying for me mam; sitting in a pile of me own shit. Useless, afraid...'

'What are you talking about, Jackie?'

'So when I recognized him months later... then he recognized *me*... he had to go, you understand? He wasn't living to tell that story, what he'd seen - the kind of cowardice he'd seen - in an English soldier. He just wasn't. So that's why I did it. He showed mercy and I paid him back like that. The war was over for him. He would've had plans to start a new life and I snuffed it all out... He was someone's son...'

'Don't, Jackie, don't.'

I look up at Bill. 'He never cried for his mam like they usually do. Not natural, is it? And I think... I think I heard

280

him say 'Papa' just before. I think I did. Or did I just dream it?'

The photos fall from my hands and onto the floor. I buckle, trying to save them. My hands arrange them and they shake, but I need to put him back together. The record shop, the club, none of it's too late. We can start all over again, see. Start from scratch.

'Don't you do this, Dunne. Don't go all mental on me, man.'

'I killed my boy, that's what I did. Look.'

A convulsion and I think I'm crying. Bill moves and raises the gun - racks a bullet into the chamber.

'I will shoot you, Jackie Dunne. This is your last chance. You take those photos and you leave here right now. Alive!' He holds the gun to my head. 'Are you listening to me?'

'I want him to wake up, Bill… just wake up.' I look down at the pictures and they are wet. My tears are making them wet.

I hear a click. Bill stiffens. I look up to see Macker holding the Luger to the back of Bill's head.

'Give it to me or I'll shoot,' the lad says.

'What?'

'Give me the fucking gun.'

Bill holds up the Walther and Macker snatches it, putting it into his pocket. He stands back, training the gun on us.

'What the hell are you doing?' I hear Bill say.

'Are you going to let him do this?' says Macker. 'He leaves here and you're done, we're both done.'

'Put that fucking thing -'

'Shut it! You said if he didn't go for it, he wouldn't leave this room, that's what you said.' He turns to me. 'That's what he said.'

'Put it down, Mac,' says Bill.

'Why would I listen to you?' The boy waits for an answer. 'Eh?'

Bill says nothing.

'You're weak.' The boy spits at Bill. Now he's turning to me. 'The pair of you, fucking weak!'

Bill takes a step in. 'Macker!' he screams.

Macker fires to the side. It zips and pings into the back hall. The sound is deafening in the small space.

Bill tries another tack. 'What are you doing, lad?'

The boy's eyes are wild, his breathing heavy. He looks back and forth between us. 'One of you... one of you isn't leaving this room.'

'Have you lost your mind, lad?' Bill's voice is high with nerves. 'Have you?'

Macker ignores him. He turns to me and takes his time. He wipes a sweating forehead. Then: 'Say the word, Jackie, and I'll do him right now. It can be just like it was. I worked hard for you and I can do it again, go straight, whatever you want, just say it.'

Bill is quiet but now says: 'Son -'

'Don't son me, you!'

He's squaring off, spreading his feet, ready to fire. Bill's hands creep up in surrender. The boy speaks to me now.

'He did it. Planned the whole thing. Get Neil away, steal him away so he can hurt him. Revenge - that's him, Jackie.'

'You treacherous lying, little get.' Bill is trying to stay calm. He turns to me, his voice shrill. 'He's lying, man!'

I get up. I've regained my composure. I wipe the back of my hand across my nose.

'Where did you get the key, Bill?' I ask, half whispering.

'What?'

'The key for here, this place.'

'Danny. We got them from Danny, why?'

'Danny didn't give it you though, did he?' I turn to the kid. 'No, *you* did, Macker, 'cause Danny never had a key for here. And there was no key on Neil. So *somebody* got it from him; after they cranked him with heroin.'

Bill turns to Macker expecting him to deny it. The boy looks to me.

'I didn't mean to do it. He came to me at first. He read the article, wanted to make things right with me. Said it was his fault and he was … "making amends." Some twelve-step thing he talked about... I wanted the gear from the cistern, that's all. I knew Neil had a key, so I lured him down here, telling him I'd left a record, a collectible.' He wipes hair from his forehead. 'Once we were down here he played a record. I went to the bog and put the gear into a record case I had. As we was leaving, I dropped it and the gear fell out and he saw it. We had a row, a fight - I knocked him out. I was leaving, I didn't want to hurt him anymore but then I tripped over that Tesco bag... with the needles from the alley.' He looks at Bill then me. He becomes defiant. 'You have to let the dying die, don't you?' He murmurs this, his face softening. 'He's a dead weight, Jackie. But he's gone now and he'll never wake up. So, life goes on.'

'I knew nothing, Jackie,' says Bill.

'Say the word, Jackie, and I'll shoot him. Right now. Then he'll be gone, dead… and things can be just they way they were.'

'Just the way they were?' I whisper.

'Be my dad...' he gulps, holding down tears. 'I want you to

be my dad.'

I look at him. He thinks I might say yes and all will be forgiven. I walk to him, put my hands on his shoulder. His matted hair falls over dead eyes. Through the greasy clump I see the flicker of tears. One rolls down his cheek, catching the light from the bar.

I bring my hands to his throat and I start to squeeze, my thumbs on his windpipe. His eyes widen and he coughs, gasping for air. The gun goes off. I feel burning - my stomach. He shoots three more times. I fall onto him. He steps back, I collapse on the bar struggling to hold myself up. I hear the gun drop to the floor.

'He made me... He made me do it,' the boy wails.

'Get out! Get out!' Bill shouts.

'Jackie, Jackie!'

I hear him sobbing as he leaves. Bill grabs me as I crumple to the floor.

'Get up,' he says. 'You can hack this, you bastard.'

I can only look back at him as he lowers me.

'I'll call someone.'

'Don't go.'

'You'll die if I don't.' He looks at the wound and back up at me shaking his head. 'What has happened here?'

'I've made a pig's ear... is what...'

My hands start to shake. I cough and taste blood. I feel it on my chin.

'Look at the state of yous. Say a prayer, man. Do what you have to do.'

'We saved the world... from Hitler... didn't we?'

'Go away with you. Say your prayers, man. There's no bloody

priest here, so say them.'

'We saved the world…'

I hear men's voices. Is that Danny?

'My wife, my poor wife. Neil… he's all she's got left. He has to live, Bill… he has to.'

'You're not dead yet, you bastard.'

'Please…'

'I'll do what I can.'

'Dear God…'

I feel a change in the air as men come down the steps. They loosen my waistcoat. I see a uniform above me. Where's Danny? My throat is filling with blood. I don't have a lot of time.

'Say your prayers…'

I'm being lifted. I try to cross myself but my arms wave about clumsily. Pray, man, pray….

'Help me… I resolve with the help of… of thy grace… to confess my sins… In the name of the Father… the Son… and the Holy Ghost… Dear Lord… I am sorry if I have offended thee. I fear my loss to the entry of heaven… I detest all my sins…

I am sorry, so sorry… Oh, my boy… my boy…'

About the author

Born and raised in Salford, Manchester, Simon emigrated to Canada when he was twenty. He has lived and worked all over North America and come full circle. Apparently, you can take the boy out of Salford but you can't take Salford out of the boy.